A Light in the Dark

Kelly Bedford

ISBN-13: 978-0-9958313-0-8

To my husband and best friend, Jayson Bedford, for your unfaltering support and love. My journey into writing started with your simple phrase:
'There's no reason why not.'

Chapter One

The Voices were always with me, before, asking for help to find the ones they had loved. Their pleas have risen to a deafening clamor since the city went dark.

I was about four years old when my parents realized there was something different about me. They assumed I was talking to imaginary friends, playing make-believe. Until I would unnerve them with messages from the ones they had lost. Stories from their childhoods. Secrets, long since forgotten.

My dad tried to ignore it, tried to pretend I was a normal kid. My mom did her best, and was always there when I needed her. We moved a lot, in hopes that a fresh start in a new place was all I needed.

But you can't outrun the dead.

My early years at school were tough, and now that I'm older I really feel for my parents, and what they must have gone through. How do you explain to a five-year-old that they shouldn't tell their kindergarten teacher, whose fiancé had tragically died two years earlier, that he wouldn't be sad if she stopped wearing her engagement ring? All I remember is the Voice telling me that giving my teacher that message would make her happy. It hadn't. That was the first time I had had to switch schools to escape the judgmental stares and disapproving whispers.

That same teacher had contacted me several years later, though, and my mom had invited her over to our house so that we could talk. I remember that she had gripped my hands like I was a life-preserver in a vast open ocean, desperate for something to hold on to, to keep herself from sinking into the depths. By the time I had relayed all of the messages from her long lost love, however, there was a lightness about her that suggested the removal of a great weight. After my teacher had

1

left our home, my mom had hugged me and told me that she had never felt more proud.

My mom had some discreet little cards made up for me, so that I could try to help others who were struggling. It was tricky to approach people out of the blue, and give them just enough information that they could decide for themselves if they wanted to hear more or not. Some people contacted me the same day that they received my card. Some people waited years to get in touch. Everyone reached out, eventually. That's the power of love, I guess. The heart continues to feel for the ones the eyes can no longer see.

High school was a lot more difficult than elementary school, and social media didn't help. I only had a few more weeks of senior year to survive, though, and then me and my mom were going to make a fresh start in a new city. We hadn't decided where yet, but we were both looking forward to it.

My mom has always been my best friend. We don't look much alike – she is blonde and tall and has big green eyes. I look more like my dad, who has blue eyes and dark hair – I even inherited his dimpled cheeks.

It had been years since my dad left us. They tried to tell me it wasn't my fault, but I knew it was. Dad just couldn't handle how different I was. Right after he walked out, my mom had tried to find me some friends who were different too. Other kids who were being followed by those who had lost their way. I don't know how she did it, but eventually she discovered a summer camp especially for kids like me. We were all from different cities, so we'd meet up every year and spend a few weeks feeling like we finally belonged somewhere.

I remember the very first time I arrived at camp like it was yesterday. I was nine years old, I was so nervous, and I was totally convinced that no one would understand me here, either. I was self-conscious about everything, from the blue t-shirt I was wearing, to my hair, which was pulled back in its ponytail like always. My mom and I walked into the big log cabin holding hands, both of us unsure of what we would find. The front of the cabin was almost all glass – it had huge windows that reached just about floor to ceiling. The main area was a little kitchen and a sort of den with wood stoves and a lot of comfy-looking couches and chairs. I could see several doorways leading off from the den, and I figured that must be where we would all sleep.

The first person I met was one of the leaders, her name was Audrey, she had long brown hair like mine, a kind, open face, and I think she was about thirty years old. As soon as she saw me, she smiled and walked over to where my mom and I were standing. She shook my mom's hand, and then mine, and told us that she knew we were anxious about the camp, and about being apart for a few weeks – we'd never been separated longer than a school day – but that she knew I was going to fit right in. Talking to her, my mom and I both felt our worries lift. I later learned that Audrey is an Empath. She feels other people's emotions and is able to absorb some of those feelings.

Before she learned how to deal with her ability, she spent most of her life hiding from the world because it was so overwhelming to be constantly bombarded with other people's emotions. It wasn't until she met her husband, Eric, that she started to fully understand her gift.

Eric is the other leader of our camp, and his ability is very similar to mine. He hears the Voices of the dead like I do, but he also has what he calls his Guide – a Voice that is louder than all the rest. Some would call him a psychic, but he says that the flow of information he hears comes from his Guide. He hasn't always had these gifts – he says they started just after his seventeenth birthday when he had barely survived a motorcycle accident. Feeling invincible and exhilarated, he'd flown along the highway at speeds way over the limit. He hit a curve in the road too fast and wasn't able to make the turn. His motorcycle crushed his body when it bounced over him, and he was declared dead at the scene. In the ambulance they discovered that his heart had started beating again. He says that during the time that his heart had stopped beating, he saw a white light and felt a profound peace that drew him toward that light. But something pulled at him in the opposite direction, too. His time wasn't finished yet – he had things he needed to do.

Audrey says he fought his way back to life because he hadn't met her yet, but knew she was out there, waiting for him.

Eric says that as he left the peace and light to return to the world of pain and suffering, he felt a deeper consciousness attach itself to him – he had found his Guide. He says the

Voices were an added bonus. He also says that if it hadn't been for his helmet, he would just be another Voice in *my* head these days.

At camp we were a group of kids of all ages. That first year, there was one boy who was two years younger than me, and I think the oldest one of our group was a girl who was eighteen. Age didn't seem to matter to us though, that wasn't what defined our group.

It was incredible to me that I had met other people who were also haunted by the dead. Eric and Audrey told us not to call ourselves haunted – 'gifted' they called us. It took a long time for me to feel like what I was hearing everyday was anything remotely like a gift.

During the days at camp we'd get to know each other, and each other's gifts, better. We'd swim and canoe and fish and do all the usual summer camp activities. Eric, who had light brown hair and a constant tan from spending so much time outside, was really passionate about teaching us outdoor survival skills too, so we'd spend a few hours every day learning about different edible plants, building simple shelters out of available resources, and how to make fire without matches. It was really easy to talk to each other during the light of day. As soon as night started to fall, though, we'd all gather around the fire and the real classes would begin. Eric used his Guide to be *our* guide. He'd start up the difficult conversations to get us talking, and he'd help us face any fears we had. He always seemed to know which questions would get us talking. We'd tell stories about encounters or apparitions or visions, and Audrey would hover around the circle, giving silent support to those who needed it most at that moment. Some of the kids at camp, like my friend Josh, have pretty horrifying visions, and they are the ones who need the most help, and a lot of the time Audrey sticks to them like glue.

I met Josh in the afternoon on my first day at camp. When I first saw him he was laughing and joking with Eric and some of the other kids, and when he saw me he beamed at me, too. I never would have guessed that ten minutes before, he had been visited by three victims of a horrifying car accident. Josh's visions don't last very long, but they are usually intense and terrifying for him. They don't give him much information, more like flashes of someone's last moments.

4

Josh, who has short blond hair and brown eyes, is two years older than me and has been going to our camp since he was five. He was the first kid to attend it. Eric's Guide had led him to Josh, knowing somehow that he needed help. At five years old Josh was seeing full apparitions of the dead, as they had looked when they had died. Victims of accidents, murders, suicides, and other sudden, violent deaths appeared to him, making their final requests of him, in highly-colored, shocking clarity. Josh was terrified, and his parents were terrified, and they didn't know what to do.

Eric had knocked on their door one day, and offered to help, in any way he could. He started having sessions with Josh, every day, several times a day if Josh needed it. Josh slowly started to come out of the nightmare world he'd been imprisoned in – he even started sleeping through the night instead of waking up screaming every few hours. When he saw the improvement in Josh, Eric knew what he needed to do, because surely Josh wasn't the only child who needed help. And so our camp was born.

In the past, whenever I would start to feel sorry for myself because of the Voices, I would just imagine growing up with Josh's ability, and the whispering in my head didn't seem quite so unbearable.

Later that first night, after we had gathered around the campfire, Eric asked Josh to describe his vision and told all of us to really focus on what he was saying. I had felt a little embarrassed staring at Josh like that, but as soon as he started talking he happened to look into my eyes and suddenly three Voices rang out in my head, pleading for help. After Josh had finished speaking, Eric asked us if we'd experienced anything related to his story. There was total silence, until finally I put up my hand, feeling scared but somehow brave, too. Suddenly all eyes were on me, and I remembered very clearly why I always tried not to draw attention to myself. I noticed Audrey make her way over to me, and once she was standing behind me, I found my voice again.

'They are scared for their friend - there were four people in the car, but one was thrown farther than the rest and wasn't found by the emergency response team. He's badly hurt, but alive.'

At my words, Eric jumped up and whipped out his phone, dialing 911. He paced as he described the accident, saying that he knew for a fact that four people had been involved. He gave his name and number and hung up.

'The operator knew exactly which accident I was talking about, it only happened a few hours ago. They're going to organize a search team to try to find the fourth person.'

Eric turned and looked at me. 'You probably saved a life tonight, Grace. Hopefully we'll hear back from the operator soon, and we'll know for sure.'

We all sat in silence for a moment, each of us lost in thought, all of us, I'm sure, hoping for a good outcome for the fourth person.

Then Eric asked us each to tell a little bit about ourselves, and a little bit about our gifts. Josh went first, telling us that he was eleven years old, that he had been having the visions since he could remember, and that camp was his favorite place to be. He said that he missed his parents while he was away, but he was glad to meet people who were like him. He grinned at me again, this time a little more shyly. I smiled back, feeling a few butterflies, and, for the first time ever, that I belonged.

***

As each of the other kids around the campfire told us what their gifts were – there were six of us that first year I attended – I was astonished to discover that I was actually lucky to just hear voices. Josh had his visions of people right after they had died; a girl named Katie, who was sixteen, would have the same scene play over and over in her head until it finally actually happened, and unfortunately the scenes always ended in someone passing away. She had tried for years to prevent anyone's death, but, with Eric's help, had realized that it wasn't her responsibility to try to save the world. That when it is someone's time to go, it is just their time, no matter how hard she tried to help.

Another girl named Jane had a similar gift to Katie's, but it was always Jane herself who featured in the scenarios instead of strangers, and her visions only happened while she was asleep. She had spent most of her eighteen years believing that she was about to die, not knowing that she was actually seeing someone else's last minutes played over and over. Eric had helped her realize that it wasn't her own life that was in constant danger, and then he helped her come to terms with the difficulty of knowing that others were actually going through what she was seeing.

Katie and Jane had been coming to camp since it had started six years earlier, and I've never met two people who were better friends than they were, they just understood each other so completely.

When it came time for me to talk about myself, I almost felt embarrassed to say that my gift wasn't as traumatic as everyone else's. Just hearing the Voices of those who had already died seemed like nothing compared to watching someone's final moments over and over. But the group understood how much something like that could affect your life, and maybe I had earned their respect by giving Eric the information that might help the fourth victim of the car accident.

There was another boy that year, with a similar gift to mine. His name was Michael, he was short and small with red hair, and he was twelve years old. He would get flashes of insight into a person's thoughts or memories if he came into contact with them, and sometimes even if he just touched an object, he would be given information about the person to whom it belonged. Michael liked to wear gloves, and I couldn't blame him. I'd go around in a top hat if it would give me a break from the Voices... No, I wouldn't... but it would be really nice to just have silence once in a while.

The last person to talk about their gift that night was a seven year old boy named Kevin, who looked pale and sick. His dark hair accentuated his pallor, and his eyes looked sunken in his face, as though he hadn't slept in weeks. He looked as scared as I had felt, and I decided then to try to make him feel as comfortable as I could. Audrey hovered behind him until finally, staring unblinkingly into the fire, he told us about his gift.

'Sometimes I lose track of things. I end up places and I can't remember how I got there. My mom and dad say that when it happens, sometimes I'll tell weird stories, sometimes even in different languages, and it scares them. I asked if I could come to this camp to try to get help, but if it doesn't stop I know they're going to put me into a hospital for crazy people, I heard them talking about it. I'm not crazy! I don't want to go!' Tears filled his tired eyes, and he started to cry.

I got up and went to sit beside him, and put my arm around him. Eric sat on his other side, and Audrey stayed behind him.

'We are going to help you, Kevin, we really are,' said Eric. 'We can teach you to control your gift and we can tell your parents that you aren't crazy, and we will help your whole family in any way that we can. We'll get to work right away; I have a few theories about what is happening during your blackouts, and I know we can help you.'

Kevin finally looked up from the fire, wiping his eyes on his sleeve. 'Thank you,' he whispered, with a quiet sniffle.

I couldn't imagine how awful it would be, knowing that my parents wanted to hide me away, and I made a mental note to give my mom an extra big hug when she picked me up from camp.

By the time we finished up around the campfire that night, Kevin actually looked cheerful, and it wasn't only me who was working extra hard to make sure he felt safe and supported. I was so happy to see everyone making an effort to talk to him about being scared at first, and about how much camp had helped them. They all offered their own theories on his blackouts, and we all planned to help him stay out of hospital.

It was as we were getting ready to put out the fire that the three Voices rang out again.

'They found him... He'll survive... Thank you...'

I stopped in my tracks, causing Josh to bump into me.

'What is it? Are you alright?' he asked.

'They found him! The fourth person in the car accident! He's going to survive! They found him!'

At that moment Eric's phone rang, and as he listened to the person speaking, he stared at me, his smile growing wider and wider.

'Gracie's right,' he said when he lowered his phone, 'they found him unconscious, hidden in a patch of bushes, but they've got him, he's stable, and he's going to survive.'

Suddenly everyone was cheering and high-fiving and hugging, and I felt an elation that I didn't even know I was capable of.

'We make a good team,' Josh said to me, smiling shyly again, causing my butterflies to flutter some more.

'Great work everybody!' said Eric, and then he said to Kevin, 'this is what we can do if we stick together, help each other. We can do great things!'

Kevin beamed.

As we all started the short walk back to the cabin for some hot chocolate before bed, Eric suggested that we put marshmallows in our hot chocolate to celebrate. The cabin, with its huge wall of windows, had just come into view when Kevin suggested that we have a contest to see who could fit the most marshmallows in their mouth. We were all arguing about how many we could each fit, when suddenly the lights in the cabin flashed on and off. Eric took the lead and told us all to stay behind. We watched him go inside the cabin, and turn the lights back on. He came back out to tell us he was going to do a sweep of the cabin to make sure it was safe.

As our eyes got accustomed to the sudden brightness, we could see that the huge windows on the front of the cabin had all frosted over with a thin layer of ice. As we stood there trying to figure out how there could be frost on such a warm summer's night, the lights flashed off again. Before Eric could even turn around to go back inside, the lights blazed back on. Several of us gasped.

The frost on the windows was no longer a perfect white. Hundreds of handprints now dotted every inch of the glass from top to bottom.

The lights flashed off and on again. In the brightness that glared from inside the cabin, we could see that the windows were clear again. The ice and the handprints had vanished.

We all looked to Eric for guidance, who, for a moment, looked too shocked to speak. He cleared his throat. 'Don't worry,' he said finally, 'it's nothing to be afraid of... a gathering of this many gifted people is sure to draw the attention of the departed.' Not altogether reassured, we made our way inside the cabin.

In spite of all the weird stuff that would happen when we were all together, camp was the only time that I really felt comfortable with myself. We helped each other grow and learn and cope with our abilities, and the bond between us grew stronger every summer. When camp ended for the year, it was the hardest time for us – knowing we'd have to wait a whole year to see each other again, knowing we were going back to having to deal with everything on our own, but especially because it meant that we were headed back into a world where we didn't fit in.

I found out a few months later that Kevin, who had truly blossomed during his first stay at camp, and who had even learned to know when he was about to have a blackout episode, had been checked into a psychiatric hospital by his parents. I cried for hours when Eric told me, it was just so unfair that his family didn't even care about the progress he'd made. When I told my mom about him, she offered to call Kevin's parents to see if I could visit him, but his parents didn't want Kevin to have anything to do with our group, and even tried to give my mom the necessary information to have me locked up, too.

My mom had hung up on them, looking furious. She had grabbed me and hugged me tightly, and I could feel her shaking with rage.

I thought often of Kevin, and wondered how he was doing. Sometimes I'd daydream that our group from camp would plot a scheme to break him out of the hospital, and that my mom would adopt him, and that we'd all live happily ever after.

When I told Eric about the idea, he said he was all for it, except that the police probably wouldn't understand, and that we'd all end up in big trouble, especially Kevin.

I felt despair for Kevin, and anger toward his parents, but I also felt hugely grateful for my mother, who tried her best to understand me, and who, above all, supported me and loved me, especially when times got tough.

***

I'd made the mistake exactly once of trying to tell a close friend about what I was going through. I should have known better, really, but I just felt so alone, and I thought that maybe she'd understand, because we'd been inseparable for a quite a while.

I was twelve, it was Friday night, and we were having a sleepover at my house. We'd just finished watching a movie, and she suggested we play Truth or Dare. She dared me to jump in our neighbor's pool in my clothes. I knew they wouldn't care, so we snuck out of the house and I crept up to the fence that separated our backyards, and peeked though the space between the boards. No one was around, so I jumped the fence and then leapt into the pool. She jumped in too, and then we raced back into my house, giggling like crazy and dripping all over my mom's floor.

After we'd dried off and changed into our PJs, she chose truth. I asked her to tell the truth about something bad she had done. She thought about it for a moment, and then told me that she would steal stuff from stores for fun, and money from her stepmom's purse because she hated her. I was shocked, but didn't want to offend her, so I asked her for another dare. She dared me to take a drink out of the bottle of whiskey that my dad had left behind, and that my mom had never gotten rid of. I told her that I would, if she did too. We poured out two glasses, and at the same time, each took a great big gulp. It burned my throat and tasted horrible.

Coughing and laughing, we both dumped the rest of our glasses down the sink. The whiskey made us pretty sleepy, so we crawled into our sleeping bags soon after that. Then she asked if I wanted truth or dare. I said dare, but she got annoyed because I always chose dare. I said that it didn't matter to me, and I chose truth.

She asked me to tell her a secret that no one else knows.

And I did. I told her all about the Voices, about growing up feeling so disconnected from everyone else, and I told her about summer camp. It must have been the alcohol that broke the dam of silence I'd so carefully maintained until then. And it must have been the alcohol that made me believe I could trust her.

After I finished talking, she thanked me for telling her and said that she felt tired and wanted to go to sleep. I fell asleep thinking how glad I felt that I finally had a normal person to confide in, who I could trust so much. Maybe other people would feel the same, and I could have sort of a normal life.

In the morning, my mom woke me up to tell me that my friend had felt sick in the night and had asked to go home. I assumed it was because of the whiskey, because I felt absolutely terrible.

On Monday morning I arrived at school, thinking about the math test I'd write later that day, and not much else. I was looking forward to seeing my friend, and maybe talking to her a little more about camp. As I walked down the hall to my locker, I seemed to draw the stare of every person I passed by. They whispered behind their hands, and followed me to my locker, snickering as they came. I raised my hand to open my locker, and all of a sudden someone leapt out of it, screamed 'BOO!' and pushed me to the ground. They were wearing a white sheet with eyeholes cut out.

Everyone was laughing as I sat there fighting tears of humiliation and betrayal. The person wearing the sheet whipped it off, and threw it at me. It was my friend. She crouched down in front of me and said, staring me right in the eyes, 'Instead of just talking to them, maybe *you* should become a ghost, too!'

She walked away from me, laughing as she went.

It took a move to a new city and a complete cut-off from social media to escape having trusted an average person with my secret. My mom had called Eric immediately and he was able to grasp enough of the story from my broken, gasping sentences to know how to help me. He'd been treated badly after his accident by those he'd trusted, too.

Over the next few weeks, I spent a lot of time on the phone with him. I don't know what I would have done without him. My friend's betrayal brought an end to the confidence it had taken to give people the business cards my mom had made up for me. A lot of Voices went unanswered. A lot of people never received the messages their loved ones longed to give them. The ripples caused by my friend's bullying had spread farther than she could ever have imagined, though I'm sure I never crossed her mind after I left.

After the whiskey incident, I was very careful about who I allowed myself to become close to. In fact, I didn't allow anyone in. I kept my head down and my mouth shut. I would email with my friends from camp, but kept myself completely closed off from anyone at school. My mom was amazing, as always, and always seemed to know when it was time to get in touch with Eric. She surprised me on my sixteenth birthday with a cell phone of my own, and it was pre-programmed with the phone numbers of everyone from camp.

The very last text I got before the city went dark was from my best friend from camp. I barely had time to read the message before my phone died.

Something bad coming. Meet at lake.

I was at school, waiting for last period to end, and all of a sudden the hairs on the back of my neck stood up. There was a second where I just looked around, trying to see if anyone else had noticed anything, and then all the lights went out. I mean everything just shut down. At the time the teachers assumed it was a power outage, and since it was the end of the day we were dismissed early.

Perfect. Friday afternoon and out of school early. I planned to stop and get food on my way home, maybe stop at some drive-thru and grab a burger, and then enjoy having the house to myself until mom's shift ended. I rushed out of school with everyone else, and jumped in my car. But it wouldn't start. I pulled my phone out to call my mom because I was supposed to pick her up from work today, and that's when I remembered Emily's text.

Something bad.

Of course my phone was dead when I really needed it. I decided to walk the couple of blocks home and call my mom from there. I'd contact Emily from home too, and see what other details she had about what was coming. At camp Emily was the only one who knew things were going to happen, right before they happened.

I'd met her at my third summer of camp. She showed up for her first day with her dad, and we hit it off right away. We're the same age, we like the same books and movies and music, and we even look a little alike. We both have long brown hair and we're about the same height – but her eyes are brown and mine are blue. She's really funny and sarcastic and outgoing, and in that way we're total opposites – I'm pretty quiet and a little shy and I always think of funny things to say hours after the moment has passed.

Emily and her dad have the same gift of knowing what is coming in the future, but her dad's ability isn't as precise as Emily's – he can see random details of major events on the horizon, but can't tell exactly when they'll occur. Emily knows exactly what is going to happen, and when. She can be a little spooky sometimes, with her predictions. But then I guess we're all a little spooky.

The walk home from school only took about fifteen minutes, and when I got home I went straight for the phone. I picked it up and put it to my ear. There was nothing – no dial tone, no sound when I pressed the buttons.

Perplexed, I went to the desk in the kitchen and tried booting up the computer. Again, nothing. The lights in the house didn't work either. I stuck my head out the front door to see if our neighbors were around. I thought maybe one of them would have a cell I could borrow to call my mom. That's when I realized how quiet it was. Walking home I'd been too preoccupied about the car and mom and Emily to notice the silence…

The silence pressed heavily against my eardrums like it had suddenly become solid. Not a leaf rustled, not a bird chirped. The world was holding its breath.

Suddenly an enormous shadow painted the whole street with darkness. It was gone as quickly as it had appeared. I looked up to locate the shadow's source and my heart dropped into my stomach.

A huge plane was gliding a few hundred feet up in complete silence. It soared across the patch of blue sky above my neighborhood and then out of sight. I couldn't believe what I'd just seen. The airport was miles away, there was nowhere nearby for that plane to land safely. People were going to die. Lots of them. I started running in the direction the plane had gone – toward the center of town. I had only taken a few steps when the ground shuddered beneath my feet. The sound of the massive explosion reached my ears, but was drowned out almost instantly by the Voices. Crying, moaning, screaming. Pleading.

I forced myself to keep moving, and was soon joined by several others who had heard the explosion and had come running. I could see a billowing cloud of black smoke rising against the blue sky, and I could hear the Voices, but nothing could have prepared me for the scene I was about to witness.

Twisted chunks of smoking metal. Burning pieces of wreckage I couldn't identify. And the bodies. All those people. Just gone. An hour ago there had been offices, restaurants, apartments and shops filled with people going about their days. Living. They had all been swallowed by the crater that belched black poison into the air.

As I stared helplessly at the smoking remains of a tricycle that had landed a few yards away, the ground began to shudder again. I looked up to see that several of the buildings surrounding the crater had started to crumble. Their collapse set off a series of smaller explosions which sent rubble flying in all directions. I was too close. The debris rained down and I tried to run, but something struck the back of my head. I hit the ground hard and felt a searing pain in my arm as it was crushed under the weight of my body. The shock, the pain, the despair all clouded my mind.

14

As I lost consciousness the last thing I heard was my mom. Her Voice.

***

'Mommy! Mommy!' I was six years old and had just fallen off my bike. My mom scooped me up like she had a thousand times, comforting me with kisses and wiping away my tears. 'It'll be alright my little sweetheart, don't worry Gracie, mommy's here…'

'MOM!' I snapped back to reality, and as my eyes tried to focus on my surroundings, the memory of what had happened crashed over me, threatening to drown me once again in a sea of darkness.

I sat up slowly and found that someone had splinted my arm. My head had bandages on it, too. There were a few other bandaged people sitting nearby, and one man who seemed to be tending to the injured. He saw that I was trying to stand and reached out to steady me. 'Take it easy, you've got a pretty bad bump on your head,' he said.

'I need to find my mom' I told him, 'she works at the hospital, she's a nurse there, I have to find her.' I remembered hearing her Voice as I had passed out. 'Please! I have to see her!'

'Easy, easy, just stay calm,' he said 'what's your mom's name?'

'Ava Charles,' I told him, and I heard his breath catch in his throat. His expression flickered from recognition to sadness as he looked at me, and then I could see it in his eyes – that he knew my mom, and knew who I was. Suddenly I didn't want to hear what else he knew. 'I'm so sorry to have to be the one to tell you this…' he began 'your mom-'

I turned and ran. I ignored the shooting pains in my arm and the throbbing in my skull. I ran as fast as I could, trying to escape the sorrow in the man's eyes, and what it meant. She couldn't be. She just couldn't. The hospital was miles away from where the plane had hit – she should be safe. I thought I'd heard her Voice because I was fainting, that's all, of course I'd hear her, she's the one who always gives me comfort when I'm hurt. Who else would my mind call up when I'm laying broken on the ground? She had to be alright, it wouldn't make any sense if she wasn't.

I skidded to a stop and dropped to my knees. One of the things I'd been taught at camp was how to close my mind, to control how much access the dead had. Terrified of what I might hear, I closed my eyes and allowed the gateway to open.

Expecting to be bombarded with hundreds of Voices, I was surprised to hear nothing. I let my mind open further, but was only met with a more profound silence. Just as I started to feel relieved that at least I wasn't hearing my mom, a gentle Voice whispered, *'She's not here.'*

I hesitated, wanting to ask for more, but afraid of the answer I might get. The gentle whisper continued before I was able to form the question. *'Once she saw that you were being cared for, she was able to go Beyond.'*

Emily's text suddenly came to mind. *Something bad.* I slipped back into the shadows of unconsciousness.

Chapter Two

I have hardly any memory of the days following the plane crash. I must have stumbled home. I must have slept and eaten. I must, at some point, have figured out that it was okay that I was still breathing.

I missed my mom so badly, I felt like all of my insides had turned to lead, and it weighed my body down so much that for days at a time all I could do was lay there in the dark. I would lie in my mom's bed because the pillow still smelled like her, and sometimes I would convince myself that she was going to come through the front door any minute, so I'd get up, rush to the door and throw it open, expecting her to be standing there, with her keys in her hand and a smile on her face. These moments of complete denial were the hardest to overcome.

Once in a while I would wonder what had happened – why there was no more power, and what had caused that plane to fall from the sky. One night a distant scream outside had broken through my cloud of sorrow, and I had felt a brief moment of fear before my grief had dragged me under again.

Since the day that everything had happened, I could no longer quiet the Voices. Lately I could even see a shadow shift in an unusual way, or a faint outline of a figure to go along with the Voice I was hearing. If it weren't for camp and knowing about Josh's ability to see figures that others couldn't, I would have just assumed that I was cracking up. I wished I could talk to him now.

I wondered if Josh had received the text from Emily too.

***

Weeks passed, but the day I'd lost my mom still felt like yesterday. It still didn't seem real. It was too much. Too much had happened. Too much horror, too much loss… The only concrete proof I had that any of it was real was the stiffness in my injured arm. So when I started to doubt that it all could possibly have happened, all I had to do was flex my wrist and I knew it was true. That day had happened. It was all real. The world had gone dark and I was alone.

It had taken a while for people to realize that the power was not coming back on. At first there was minor looting – people stealing TVs and other electronics, not aware that what they had put so much effort into taking was actually completely worthless. In the days and weeks following the blackout, the riots had started. With no running water and no trucks to bring food into the stores, people got desperate pretty quickly. I had tried only once to go out and get more supplies, but it had been too dangerous and I'd turned back for home before I got into trouble. I saw grocery stores being ransacked and stripped bare and fights to the death over blankets, matches and can openers.

The city burned.

Several times, a loud knock on the front door sent me flying in terror back to my mom's bed to hide under the covers. After a while I would go and peek out of a window to see if whoever had knocked was still hanging around.

I could see the smoke rising over the trees in my neighbor's yard, and there seemed to be more and more every day. With no way to fight them, the fires consumed everything within reach, and would continue to burn until nothing remained.

I wondered what had caused the power to all go out at once, and why it wasn't coming back on after so many weeks. Emily had told us once about how her dad was prepared for any outcome of any disaster situation. Since his gift of foresight wasn't specific enough to give him details about an upcoming event, and Emily's gift only showed her what was coming immediately before it hit, he'd decided to be totally prepared for anything. Emily had told us about how her dad had seen a post-apocalyptic future, where tens of thousands died in a couple of weeks and there was no way to return society to the state it had been in before the disaster. That was all he'd been able to see. Emily told us how he'd been researching possible causes of such devastation, and he'd come across electromagnetic pulses – something that could potentially shut down the power grid for years. Emily hadn't really gotten into it, but she'd said that nuclear missiles exploding in Earth's upper atmosphere could cause an electromagnetic pulse, and sometimes the sun would have explosions on its surface that had a similar effect. The huge burst of energy would just disable anything with electrical components.

I thought of my phone, my computer, my car, the lights in my house – everything had quit working at the same time. An electromagnetic pulse seemed like a plausible cause.

I thought of the plane that had crashed – had it suddenly just lost power and the only option for the pilots was to glide to earth and hope that the crash site was as clear of people as possible? Suddenly it hit me that there must have been thousands of planes in the sky at the time, and hundreds of people aboard each one. All those poor people, knowing what was coming and powerless to stop it. And then all of the crash sites. My city was small compared to some of the major centers, but the damage it had caused, and the number of lives that were lost was staggering. I couldn't even begin to imagine the devastation that thousands of planes could do to cities whose populations were in the millions.

There must have been a lot of car accidents too, if all of a sudden everyone had just lost control of their vehicles. And with no ambulances or fire department to come to their aid, thousands of people would have been trapped in their vehicles, waiting to starve, or bleed to death…

How many people had died that first day? Millions? And in the weeks following that first horrible day? I'd been so overwhelmed by my own pain that I hadn't really stopped to think about what the rest of the world might look like now. I'd hidden in my house for weeks, never considering the people who relied on electricity to survive each day. The sick, the elderly, all of the people who were in the hospital where my mom had worked.

No wonder I couldn't quiet the Voices anymore – how much of the world's population had joined the desperate chorus in my head?

***

As my food and water supplies had started to run out, I decided that I was going to see if I could get to the lake, like Emily had said. At camp the lake had always been our meeting place when we had snuck out after lights-out. Now that the lights seemed to be out forever, it seemed like the perfect place for us to meet.

It would take a while to get there – it was twelve hours by car if you only stopped for small breaks. In my head I had calculated that it would take about three months to get there on foot, but I hoped that by riding my bike I would decrease that time pretty significantly. Winter was approaching, but I knew I had a couple of solid months of decent weather ahead of me, and that I'd make it to the lake with enough time to really get ready for the cold, snowy months.

It was a huge decision to travel hundreds of miles, alone, with minimal supplies, and I had flip-flopped about whether I would do it for weeks. At first I couldn't even consider leaving this house because it represented life with my mom and I couldn't just walk away from that comfort. Plus the desperate hope that my mom would just suddenly walk through the front door had kept me anchored to the house as well. I wondered whether I would have thought of traveling to the lake if Emily hadn't texted me. I knew that I would have. Even if my mom had survived, and we had the option of staying in this house together forever, I know I would have suggested the lake, with or without the hope of meeting my friends there. It was just too perfect. The cabin was nestled in a dense pine forest and had wood stoves, which would keep us warm and allow us to easily boil water and cook our food. There was a big vegetable garden near the lake, and I knew the cabin's pantry was stocked with a good supply of veggies that Audrey had preserved, plus a large amount of store-bought provisions like pasta and rice. I know my mom would have wanted to make the trip to the lake – we could have built a new life there, hidden away from the dangers of the more densely populated areas. Our house was fine shelter for the warmer months, but it was never meant to be without a working furnace and plumbing. The cabin had everything I would need.

***

As the days passed I started to realize that there really wasn't anything left for me at my house, and now that my arm felt so much better, there wasn't much reason for me to delay leaving any longer. Plus I felt drawn to the only place I had ever belonged.

I gathered up some clothes, what was left of my food, a few water bottles and some toiletries. I grabbed the camping stuff and the little tent we had used when my dad was still around, and crammed most of it into the backpack I had used for school. The tent and sleeping bag I attached at the top and bottom of the bag, like my dad had shown me. Knowing that water was going to be a big problem before long, I tied a canteen and a small pot to the side of my backpack, so I would be able to boil any water I found, and then I double checked that I had lots of matches. I grabbed my dad's old hunting knife and some extra rope too.

On the last day before I set out to meet Emily, I walked around the house, hoping I hadn't forgotten anything I might need, and saying a silent goodbye to the house I'd spent so much time in. The last thing I packed was a photo of my family on my fifth birthday. I took it off the wall in the living room, and out of its frame, and I tucked it safely into the first aid kit my mom had put together years ago, when I would still come home with skinned knees. I stared at the other photos my mom had arranged on the wall, and wished I had enough room in my bag to bring them all. My entire life was displayed here, starting with a photo of my mom holding me when I was a few hours old. Mom hugging me on my first day of school; holding my hand for my first time at camp; mom smiling bravely as she taught me to drive – she had captured all of it, and had displayed it proudly. It broke my heart to leave the photos behind, but at least the memories were saved forever in my mind.

For dinner I ate the last of my garden tomatoes and strawberries. Wherever we moved, my mom had always insisted that we have a little patch of earth to grow our own food. The carrots and cucumbers were already packed carefully in my backpack with the tins of tuna and beans. I had also emptied the rain barrel in the garden, which had been my sole source of water since the plumbing no longer worked. I had been boiling the rain water over our fire pit as needed, and now had the rest of it stored in my bag.

I hoped to get a good sleep so I could start my journey feeling pretty rested. Just before dark I went and checked the air in my bike tires, and then locked it up beside the back door like always.

I snuggled down into my mom's bed for the last time, and lay awake, wondering what the future held for me. I wished I had a little of Emily's gift; it would be nice to feel a little more prepared.

It was as I was drifting to sleep that I heard the front doorknob rattle. And then the sound of a window being smashed. *Someone was breaking into my house.* I panicked, trying to think of what to do. I ran for my favorite hiding place – it was the one I'd always used as a kid when we'd played hide and seek. In my mom's room there is a bench built into the wall underneath the window. It's almost like a big chest with a lid that opens on hidden hinges. My mom liked to sit there with me on her lap and read me stories. When I would hide in there, she'd pretend to get tired of looking for me, and sit down to read. It always made me giggle and she'd act all surprised and jump up to find me.

With my heart pounding, I grabbed my backpack and climbed into the bench. Then I pulled the lid down over myself and waited.

I could hear several pairs of feet stomping though the house; it sounded like whoever had broken in was trashing the place, and looking for supplies.

'Find anything?' said one of the intruders, in a deep and gravelly voice.

'Got some pretty decent knives from the kitchen, and I found some duct tape and rope,' said a second man.

'All right, torch it and let's move on' said the first man.

I could hear them splashing something all over the place, and then I heard the match.

I sprung up out of my hiding place, grabbed the backpack and raced, in just my pjs and socks, for the front door. Flames were licking their way up the walls and the smoke burned my eyes and lungs. I made it outside and gulped gratefully at the fresh air. I looked around for the men, and saw, by the light of my burning home, that they were breaking down my neighbor's door. I knew my neighbors were already gone; they had asked me to come with them to a refugee camp outside of the city, but I hadn't been ready to leave my house yet. I wondered for a second if I'd be able to get to my bike before it burned with the house, but I knew it was a lost cause; there was no way I could get that close to my house again, there was just too much heat and smoke.

I started to run in the opposite direction, and suddenly found myself sprawled out on the ground. A whimper met my ears and I saw that I'd tripped over a girl about my age, whose blonde hair and terrified face were blackened with soot. A trickle of blood coming from the corner of her mouth caught the firelight as she struggled against bonds at her wrists and ankles. She whispered for help, so I undid the ropes and helped her to her feet. 'Who did this to you,' I asked her, 'what happened?'

'It was a group of men; some of them were beating up my dad and then three of them took me from my family. I don't know who they are, but they said they'd be back for me – we need to get out of here!' She grabbed my hand and we ran away from the light of the fire which now engulfed my entire house. I wondered what kind of creeps we'd both barely escaped from.

As we ran, a Voice started speaking urgently, telling me which direction we should take. I did what he asked, and soon we came upon a woman and a little boy, both covered in soot, huddled under a tree. 'Mom!' cried the girl, and she ran into her mother's arms. All three started crying, and after a moment, the girl asked about her father.

'They burned the house down, honey,' said the mother, 'we'll need to find a place to go... Daddy... Daddy isn't going to be able to come with us...' the mother didn't seem able to say any more.

I told them about the refugee camp that my neighbors had gone to, gave them one of my blankets and a can of beans, and then I turned to leave.

'*Thank you...*' said the Voice who had been our guide. '*Thank you for my daughter...*' and I felt his presence lift... He had found his way Beyond.

As I walked away from the girl and her family, I started to seriously doubt my decision to go and meet Emily at the lake. I'd acknowledged before I'd started packing that it would be dangerous to travel such a huge distance by myself, with barely any supplies for the journey. I knew that the world had gone a little crazy since the Darkness had descended, but to see it first-hand – the kidnapping of a young girl and the senseless murder of her father – made me realize how daunting a task I had set for myself. I didn't even know for sure that Emily, or anyone else for that matter, would have made it to the lake. Part of me wanted to turn back and join the girl's family as they made their way to the refugee camp. A huge part of me wanted to track down the despicable monsters I'd just escaped from, and burn *them* to the ground. Part of me wanted to just sink to my knees and weep for what the world once was, and for how quickly it had deteriorated.

The only option that really felt right was to stick to my original plan. I took a few deep breaths to calm my frazzled nerves and then began my journey. I would make my way out of the city and onto the highway headed west. Whether Emily was at the lake or not, I had to try.

For the first time, the Darkness felt like safety. I had always lived in one city or another, so I'd never really seen what true darkness looked like – there was always a light source from somewhere. Even at camp, in the middle of nowhere, there had been lanterns lit around the clock. Now, in a world without power, even in the center of town I knew I wouldn't be able to see my hand in front of my face. There was just enough light from the fires to see my path out of my neighborhood, but eventually I had to stop and wait for the light of morning.

The smoke from the fires had obscured the stars and moon, and I had become invisible. I didn't feel as afraid as I would have expected, completely alone, after being chased out of my home – I could hide from the monsters in the dark.

***

In the morning as I made my way out of the city, I passed by the destruction that had happened in the last few weeks. Abandoned vehicles lined the streets; some overturned or charred from the rioting. The smell of smoke was constant, stinging my nose and making my eyes water. Debris and ash seemed to cover every surface. Power lines criss-crossed overhead, now nothing more than pointless metal vines in a jungle of concrete.

I had hoped to come across a few more supplies on my way out of town, but any stores I saw that were untouched by fire were now just empty shells, gutted and cleared of anything useful. When the riots had happened people must have stripped everything clean before heading to the refugee camp.

What I really needed now was a pair of shoes. When I'd fled my house I was only wearing socks, and the soles of my feet were starting to feel sore. I couldn't help but roll my eyes. After everything I had done to prepare, with checking and re-checking my supplies, I had somehow managed to leave my house without shoes. They were only *slightly* essential for a three month trip which I would now be walking, since I had also lost my bike in the fire. *Why* hadn't I thought of packing a spare pair of shoes? It was such an obvious necessity!

My feet were really starting to hurt and I didn't want to end up with some kind of infection – I tried not to imagine the slow, agonizing death I would suffer if I needed antibiotics for something, but couldn't get them. Suddenly I realized that there were probably people going through that very thing right now. With no clean water, no sanitation and a major food shortage, people were probably starting to drop from all kinds of infections, from drinking tainted water or eating spoiled food out of complete desperation.

It astounded me, in that moment, just how dependent we had been as a society, on the government, on technology, and on the transportation of food – and even on simple things that we took for granted daily, like toilet paper, or, in my case, a pair of shoes. I had thought I was as well-prepared as I possibly could be for this journey I had assigned for myself, but I hadn't counted on being chased out of my house like that.

I decided to make finding shoes a priority. I had a good stock of supplies, and I refused to drop dead because of something as simple as shoes. I came across an empty cardboard box and figured if I cut it down and strapped it onto my feet, at least it would help cushion my skin and protect me a little from cutting my feet on broken glass and whatever else the streets were littered with these days.

I hid in the backseat of a car that had been abandoned on the side of the road to trim down the cardboard. It was too light out to stay on the street for too long – I felt too exposed.

As I started to take my dad's old knife out of its sheath, I happened to look up and for a moment I couldn't believe my eyes. Right across the street, hanging by knotted laces from one of the dead power lines, was a pair of running shoes! Excited, I reached out to grab the car's door handle and stopped myself. How on earth was I going to get up there to get them? Would those cables even hold my weight if I was able to climb up somehow?

Figuring that the better option might be to try to knock them down, I looked up and down the street, trying to locate something that could help me reach them. There was a school bus that had been abandoned fairly close to where the shoes were hanging. The power line ran parallel to the bus, so maybe if I could climb up there I'd be able to reach them and drag them toward me. I just needed to find something long enough to reach them with.

I spotted a long, jagged piece of broken plywood a few feet away from the bus. That might just do it! After checking that the coast was clear, I opened the car door, jumped out of the backseat and raced across the street to grab the piece of wood. I felt splinters pierce my hands as I ran the short distance to the bus, but I didn't care. I wanted those shoes – it felt like life and death to me in that moment.

When I'd reached the front end of the bus, I pushed the wood onto the hood. I hurried around to the front tire and used it as a step to hoist myself onto the hood. My backpack was so heavy that I wasn't sure I could make it onto the bus's roof while wearing it, so I tossed it up, along with the piece of wood, before hauling myself onto the roof, too.

Carefully I stood up, and picked up the piece of wood again. I crept my way toward the back end of the bus, which was closest to the shoes. When my feet were as close to the edge as possible, I slowly reached out for the shoes. The plywood just barely touched the toe of one of them, and it set them spinning a little, tightening the laces around the power line. If I could just snag the laces with the jagged splinters, maybe I would be able to pull them closer. I reached out, stretching my arms as far as I dared, and touched the wood to the laces. It caught! The jagged wood had attached itself to the shoelaces, and I was able, bit by agonizing bit, to inch them along the power line toward me.

They were hanging within reach when I saw that they were looped around the power line a couple of times. Feeling pretty delighted with myself, I put down the wonderful piece of wood, and was just about to swing one of the shoes over the line and undo the loop, when I heard footsteps. I dropped to my stomach, now cursing myself – I had become too focused on the shoes to keep a proper lookout, and could only hope that whoever was approaching wouldn't notice the shoes, which were still swinging too much to be natural.

'Bring the ladder over, and get up there!' barked a deep, gravelly voice.

That voice. It sent waves of dread coursing through my body and made me feel like I wanted to throw up. I'd know that voice anywhere. It belonged to one of the creeps who had burned down my house.

'Hurry up,' the voice snarled, 'I want this street stripped before nightfall.'

I could hear a clatter and then glass breaking – it sounded like someone had climbed up to one of the apartment buildings and smashed a window to get inside.

I held my breath, hoping with every cell in my body that they wouldn't find me. If they searched the whole apartment building, all they'd have to do is look out the window of one of the upper floors and they'd find me. If they planned to clean out every building on this street, they were going to find me. If they started lighting things on fire again, I would have no hope of escape. I needed to get out of here.

I raised my head up a couple of inches to try and see how many of them I was dealing with. The one giving orders was standing in the middle of the street and had his back to me, but he looked tall and very strong.

The lower windows of the apartment buildings had bars over them, and the main doors were all pretty secure-looking, so the monsters were using ladders to get into the upper floors, and then bringing their loot out of the main doors by unlocking them from inside. I looked around at the rest of the street and I could see four ladders leaned up against four different apartment buildings, but I had no way to know how many people were searching each one. My only option was to try to slide off the hood of the bus without being seen, and then try to sneak away.

If I made it onto the street without being seen, I could use all of the abandoned cars for cover, and sneak my way down one of the side streets. I wondered if I should create some sort of diversion to draw the attention of the leader away from me. He still had his back toward me, and there was still enough distance between us that I could maybe make it if I just went for it.

Looking regretfully up at the shoes, I started to inch my way back toward the hood of the bus. When I reached my backpack I looped one arm through one of its shoulder straps and dragged it along with me. I reached the front end of the bus feeling grateful that I was already feet-first, and that I wouldn't have to do any kind of maneuver to spin myself around. Still on my stomach, I slithered my body down onto the hood, also grateful, for the first time since being chased from my house, that I was not wearing shoes. My socks made no noise as I crept across the hood, swinging my backpack onto my back as I went. I used the tire to step down, and made it to the ground. I edged my way around to the front, and pressed myself against the bus, giving myself a second to try to calm my strained nerves and steady my racing heart.

I snuck one more look at where the leader was, but couldn't see him anymore. I was only about five feet away from the closest car, but I couldn't risk him seeing me. Suddenly his voice barked out, and my heart nearly leapt out of my chest. He was at the back of the bus already.

'Get a ladder over here, and cut those down.'

My shoes. He'd seen my shoes. I couldn't wait another second – I darted out from the front of the bus toward the abandoned car and skidded to a stop, listening intently for any indication that I'd been spotted. All eyes seemed to be on the bus now, so I crept along to the next abandoned vehicle, and then the next. I slunk down the closest side street, and hid behind the building on the corner to catch my breath. I chanced a peek back at the bus, and saw two men on top of it – one was untangling the laces of the shoes, and the other was tossing the piece of plywood off the roof.

***

After my second close-call with the monsters, I decided to avoid staying in one place for too long. I felt like our paths had crossed too many times already, and I wanted to do anything I could to avoid falling into their vile hands.

After I'd escaped from the top of the bus, I had run several blocks and hidden in a gutted coffee shop. I was still too worked up to eat, so while I waited for my appetite to return, I searched the shop for anything useful. I found a roll of sticky tape, a straw and a bunch of those cardboard sleeves that you put around a hot cup of coffee so you don't burn your hand. I put a few of the sleeves around my feet and taped them in place. Then I arranged some in two rows the length of my feet, and taped them together to make soles. I taped the soles to the sleeves already around my feet and then criss-crossed tape across the soles to make them stronger. I was running out of tape, and all I really had so far were a couple of paper slippers. I attached the heels of the soles to my socks with the last few inches of tape, and stood up to test them out.

They weren't too bad, I supposed – they would protect my feet better than socks at least, but they were not going to last long – they'd probably disintegrate if I got them wet, and would tear off instantly if I had to run at all. Which might be a good thing, considering they had very little grip and zero support. In a race I'd be better off without them, but for now, they were perfect for shuffling my way out of town.

I ate a small meal of crackers and cucumbers before heading out into the street again. Night had fallen while I'd assembled my makeshift shoes and eaten, and once again, I was grateful for the dark. I could see flames licking the sky in the distance and guessed that the apartment buildings, and probably the school bus I'd hidden on, were on fire. Did the monsters plan to pillage and burn every single building in the city? It seemed like it. The sooner I could get away, the better.

I slowly crept my way along the darkened streets, pausing now and then to listen for any sign of danger. The smell of smoke was more powerful in the air, causing my vision to become blurred as my eyes watered. My coffee-sleeve slippers were a lot noisier than my socks had been, and I worried that someone would hear me coming and ambush me.

It struck me how much my worries had changed since the Darkness had fallen. Homework and college applications seemed like a million years ago. I felt like I'd aged at least a decade since the world had gone dark, and it seemed astonishing to me that I had taken so much for granted. The loneliness I had felt before seemed like a vacation compared to the isolation I was dealing with now. At least then I hadn't been in constant physical danger. At least then I could count on three meals a day, and somewhere to rest my head. At least then I'd always had my mom…

I had to push aside thoughts of my mom so that I could keep moving. It would not do for me to crumple in a heap on the ground right now; I had to keep it together. The steady hum of Voices was enough of a distraction that I was able to cover a lot of ground, and keep my mind from wandering back to thoughts that would slow my progress.

One of the Voices suddenly increased in volume and urgency. Keeping most of my focus on my footing and the path ahead, I gave some of my attention to the Voice.

'*She is near…*' it whispered, '*please help her…*'

I saw a delicate glimmer in front of my eyes – I could have sworn it was a face, but before I could focus on it properly, it flitted away and into a doorway ahead. Cautiously I followed, and found myself in a small bookstore. One thing that I truly regretted leaving behind was my favorite book, but I just couldn't justify the room it took up in my backpack – not when I could fit a few extra pairs of socks and underwear in there instead. I decided that if I was still here when it got light out, I would see if I could find a copy and cram it into my bag. There was more room now anyway, because of the food and blanket I had given away.

From what I could see of the store, it looked mostly untouched. I guessed people didn't have a lot of use for books now that there were much more pressing concerns to focus on. I wondered how this bookstore had even managed to stay afloat before the Darkness, when everyone had their noses glued to their electronic devices. I shuddered to think of how quickly the bookstore would go up in flames if the monsters came looking.

I could see the shimmering light hovering at the foot of a narrow staircase. As I walked toward it, it floated up the stairs, and then dissipated. The Voice, however, continued to whisper.

'*...Please...*'

I followed it up to the top of the staircase, which opened onto a small office, which was lit by one flickering candle. I could barely make out a desk and a figure huddled under a blanket on the floor.

I approached warily, unsure of what I would find when I pulled back the blanket.

'Hello?' I said quietly, not wanting to startle the person, but also feeling a sense of urgency about not hanging around for too long.

The figure stirred, and then groaned. I moved closer to their head and saw that it was a woman lying on her side – she looked vaguely familiar, but I couldn't think where I'd seen her before. I took off my backpack and pulled out one of my water bottles. Sitting down beside her, I filled the bottle's cap with water and held it to her lips. Her eyes, slightly sunken into their sockets due to hunger and dehydration, looked up at me gratefully.

Little by little I gave her half of the bottle of water, and eventually she sat up.

'Do you have any food?' she asked me, her eyes raking over my backpack hopefully.

I gave her a couple of crackers, telling her to take it slow and not make herself sick by eating too quickly. She waved my advice off, reached out and grabbed the packet of crackers, tearing the plastic wrap open to get at them more easily. Suddenly I remembered where I had seen her – it was the day before the power went out, and my mom and I were finishing up our grocery shopping. We were pushing the cart toward the closest check-out line, when this crazy woman cut us off so she could beat us to the next spot in line. She hadn't even looked at us; she'd just bullied us out of her way so she could get there first. Mom and I hadn't cared; it had given us more time to giggle at the absurd tabloid headlines.

Looked like I was dealing with Crazy again.

I suddenly felt a little more possessive of my crackers, so I reached out and took them back, telling her I'd give her more in a few minutes, if she was able to keep the first ones down. She glared at me, but didn't argue. Instead, she asked how I'd found her.

I hesitated, not wanting to freak her out with the truth, but the Voice prompted me to tell her, so I did.

'A ghost. A *ghost* told you where I was,' she scoffed, 'you have *got* to be kidding me.'

I was glad she seemed to be feeling better, but Crazy was definitely starting to annoy me.

'Yes. Your sister Debbie told me where you were, and asked me to help you. She also says that no matter how long you look for it, you're never going to find the stack of cash – it never existed. So you may as well leave her bookstore and go to the refugee camp already.'

She spluttered, incapable of articulating her surprise. I felt a petty satisfaction – some people were just kind of fun to enlighten.

'Paper money won't be worth anything anymore, you know.' I told her. 'Unless you use it for kindling, I guess. Plus, I've seen a group of raiders who are slowly burning down what's left of the city. I'd listen to Debbie.'

Finally she found her voice, '*Fine*, I'll *go* to the stupid refugee camp. Where is it anyway... could you draw me a map?' She got up, rummaged around in one of the desk drawers for a moment, and then handed me a piece of paper and a pencil. As I started to draw the basic outline of the city, she suddenly lunged at me. No, not at me, at my backpack. *Crazy was trying to rob me!* I jumped up, ready to tackle her if I had to. She charged at the staircase, swinging my backpack onto her back as she went. Out of the corner of my eye I saw the glimmer of white again, and all of a sudden Crazy was sprawled out on the floor – she had tripped over a broom handle that Debbie had toppled into her path just as she went by.

I rushed to her side and pulled my bag off her back, and slung it onto mine, ready to run for it if I needed to. But I didn't need to worry – she must have bumped her head on the door frame as she'd fallen. She was breathing, but unconscious.

'... *She'll be fine... thank you for your help...*' whispered Debbie, '*...she was always a little...*'

'Crazy,' I muttered, and I was sure I just caught Debbie's quiet, sad laugh.

I finished the map to the refugee camp and left it on the stairs, where it couldn't possibly be overlooked, and made my way back down to the bookstore. When I got down there, I could see the misty white shimmer had come to a stop in front of one of the shelves. Curious, I took the few steps to the place which was most well-lit, and my eyes fell upon a very familiar book cover. Debbie had illuminated the path to finding my favorite book. Extremely touched, I whispered a heartfelt thank you, and then I felt her presence lift.

I zipped the book into my bag and left the little store, noting a lightening in the eastern sky. It would be daylight soon, and I hadn't traveled as far as I'd hoped.

I would have been willing to stay at the bookstore, but now it was just one more place I wanted to get away from. Society's moral code had been eradicated by the Darkness – people who, before, would steal your place in line, were now willing to steal everything you had. As far as Crazy had known, stealing my backpack was a death sentence for me, and she didn't even think twice about it.

I wondered what the leader of the monsters had been like before the world had gone dark – I guessed he'd committed worse acts than butting in line at the grocery store.

With that thought in mind, I quickened my pace, keeping my eyes peeled for a place to hide during the daylight hours. I spotted a sporting goods store and figured I may as well check it out for some proper shoes, thinking at the very least it might have a comfy little cubbyhole where I would be able to get a few hours of sleep.

I stepped through the broken front window, and as I'd suspected, it was stripped completely bare of all shoes. The racks which had once held clothes were equally empty – not even a hanger was left. The slight hope that I would find a faster way to travel, like a bike or a skateboard, was extinguished before I had even really had a chance to acknowledge it.

At the back of the store there was a doorway. I approached it cautiously and peered around the doorframe. It was a stockroom, which, not long ago, would have been full of hundreds of boxes of shoes. Sighing wearily, I ascertained that the area was deserted, and then I poked around a little bit. I found a spare set of shoelaces and some paperclips, and I tucked them away in my bag, thinking that you never know what might come in handy.

The stockroom was on two levels, so I climbed the metal stairs to try to find a place to rest. There were a bunch of collapsed shipping boxes laying around, so I stacked them on top of each other for some padding. I didn't want to take my sleeping bag out, just in case I had to make a fast getaway, so I curled up with one of the big boxes over me, which offered a little warmth and would also shield me from view if someone came into the stockroom.

I pulled out the sleeve of crackers and nibbled the last few while I tried to quiet my mind enough to sleep. I tried pretending I was back at camp, surrounded by people who truly cared about me. It was Josh's laughing face that swam into my mind just as I dozed off, his brown eyes smiling into mine… his blond hair shining in the sun…

***

The rest of my trek out of the city was pretty uneventful. It seemed like most people had fled in hopes of finding help at the refugee camp. Thankfully, I didn't come across the marauders again, but I could see that there were new columns of smoke rising over the city. Soon there would be nothing left but a smoldering pile of debris.

The day was hot; I guessed it was late August or early September – I'd kind of lost track in those first few weeks, while I was lost in my haze of grief and pain.

I had decided to follow the highway west. It was the route my mom and I had always taken to get to camp, and I didn't want to risk getting lost on some other path. I walked in the ditch along the highway, so I was less visible to anyone else on the road, and so I could give my feet a rest – the tall dead grass was much better for shock absorption than the paved road. My coffee-sleeve shoes were about to give out, and I hoped they might last a little longer if I walked on a softer surface.

The sun blazed down and I could feel my skin burning. I took a shirt out of my bag and draped it over my head to try to protect myself; it helped a little. The sound of crickets and grasshoppers almost drowned out the hum of the Voices. The sweet smell of hot vegetation filled the air; it was as though the plants themselves were gasping with thirst. I took a small sip from my water bottle – I was trying my best to conserve what I had but it was so hard not to gulp it all down, with the air being so hot and stifling. My hair stuck to the back of my neck and my shirt was damp from sweating so much. I added sun stroke and dehydration to the list of dangers I was facing these days. To keep myself moving, I daydreamed about diving into the cool water of the lake at camp, and sipping icy lemonade, and running through the sprinklers in the back yard at home while my mom tended our little garden.

I had decided to travel by daylight now that I was out of the city; I guessed I'd walked for several miles already, since leaving the city limits. I was exhausted, having navigated my way out of the city after only a couple of hours of sleep at the sporting goods store. Sleep. I don't know if you could really call that sleep. More like half-dozing and half-listening for danger. My mom once told me how, after I was born, she could sleep through a massive thunderstorm, but at the tiniest whimper from me, she would jolt instantly awake. I guess I kind of understood that now – she was half-listening for me.

As the day wore on, the dry grasses beside the highway were broken up by low shrubs, which in turn gave way to sparse groups of small trees. It wasn't much protection from the sun, but I was grateful for whatever I could get. I tried not to think about how little food I had left – just one can of tuna and a few wilted carrots; I would have to find something soon, or I was going to have to add starvation to the list of dangers. I munched on a carrot as I walked, and tried to remember everything my dad had taught me, years ago, about edible wild plants. Water lilies came to mind first, but I'd have to find water to find lilies. When he'd take me fishing I'd spend most of my time searching the lily pads for frogs, and the white flowers for fairies. It seemed like an eternity had passed since then. Dandelions tasted super gross and bitter if you didn't cook them for a long time, but they grew everywhere and it was a comfort to know if I could just swallow them, they would keep me going. Dad would boil them for us, which, with a bit of salt, made them taste a bit less awful, but right now I couldn't imagine wasting a drop of my precious water on boiling anything.

As evening began to approach, I could see some ominous dark clouds in the distance ahead, and every now and then hear a soft rumbling of thunder. I would pitch my tent tonight and hopefully it would keep me and my backpack dry if that storm rolled over.

As the sun dipped behind the storm clouds, the wind picked up suddenly, and goosebumps broke out all over my skin. I headed a little farther away from the highway, thinking I'd better get my tent pitched before it was too dark and too wet to manage it.

I struggled against the wind to get the poles figured out, and then threading them through the tent itself was no picnic with the fabric flapping all around me, but I got it done, and was glad the tent was a pretty simple one. I unzipped it, threw my backpack in, and climbed inside, just as the first few drops of rain splattered down.

Once inside, I pulled out my little pot and placed it just outside the tent. Then I zipped the door-flap shut again, and took a minute to just sit and feel grateful that I'd managed to hang onto all of my stuff so far. I decided to eat my can of tuna, knowing that dandelions would be on the menu sooner or later. I savored every bite, wondering if I'd ever taste it again, knowing deep-down that I probably wouldn't. When I was finished, I put the empty tin outside with the pot to catch a little extra water.

I unrolled my sleeping bag as the rain really started to hammer the tent. The noise was unbelievable, but the storm was a comfort too – it meant that hopefully no one would be on the road tonight, and that my bright blue tent wouldn't be seen from the highway; there was nowhere to hide it on the flat expanse of grassland. Snuggling down into my sleeping bag, and ignoring the throbbing in my feet, I took my book out of my bag. It was too dark to read, and I was too exhausted anyway, and I fell asleep clutching the book to my chest like a teddy bear.

I dreamed I was in the middle of a gunfight; shots rang out all around me and I could hear someone shrieking in the distance. I tried to run and take cover, but there was nowhere to hide; the world had been swallowed by flames. The person who was screaming was a woman; she ran at me and was wailing in my face. A man was chasing her; I couldn't see his face, but I knew somehow that it was the leader of the marauders. I took the woman's hand and tried to get her to run, but even the floor was aflame. I forced myself to look down, and saw with a shudder of horror that my feet were melting. As the fire licked up my legs, a particularly loud gunshot finally woke me up. The vision ended but the sounds of the storm that had invaded my dream continued. The high winds shrieked ceaselessly as the thunder crashed, and now that my eyes were open, I could see the flashes of lightning that filled my tent with fleeting bursts bright as daylight.

I can't have been asleep for very long, and now that I was awake, I knew I'd never be able to drift off again with what sounded like a hurricane happening outside of my tent. I felt around to see if there were any leaks but thankfully everything was still dry – how that thin layer of nylon was keeping out this typhoon was beyond me.

My feet were still throbbing pretty badly, and I decided that it might be time to lay my coffee sleeve shoes to rest, and finally look to see what condition my feet were in. I slipped off the makeshift shoes and gingerly peeled back my filthy socks. Just having them in the open air made my feet feel a lot better. I was tempted to unzip my tent and stick my feet out into the rain, but didn't want the tent to flood, so instead I rummaged in my backpack until I found the little first aid kit. I knew there were several alcohol swabs in there that I could use to treat any sores I had, and then I had a bunch of adhesive bandages to cover the damage with. I waited for a flash of lightening to try to get a good look at my feet, but the light was gone too quickly to see much. All I could tell was that my skin was covered in a layer of grime – the ash and dirt that had found its way through my socks had mixed with the sweat from my feet, and had created a disgusting paste of gunk that was now caked between my toes and ground into every crease of my skin.

Again, I contemplated sticking my feet out of the tent; this job was too big for a handful of alcohol swabs. I convinced myself that the rain had let up a little, rolled up my pant legs, and unzipped the bottom corner of the tent flap a couple of inches. I carefully stuck my right foot out of the tent and then snugged the zipper as close to my leg as possible. The rain beat against my foot, but I was grateful that it was coming down so hard; hopefully the downpour would be able to carve some of the gunk away without me having to rub it too much; my feet were so tender already.

I laid back and let the rain wash my right foot for several minutes before switching to the left. Once they'd both had a few minutes each in the rain, I stuck my socks out of the little gap in the flap and soaked them thoroughly before wringing them out. I did this several times, hoping to wash out most of the dirt, but feeling fairly certain that they'd never be clean again.

After I was finished trying to clean my socks, I pulled the pot and tin of water inside so I could rehydrate myself. Once I had quenched my thirst, I filled my canteen and bottles, and then placed the pot and tin back outside. Then I decided that I may as well try to sleep again – tending to my feet was going to have to wait until I had good light anyway.

I used my wet socks to mop up the puddle that had pooled due to the open flap, and then I curled up in my sleeping bag once more, shivering a little from the cold air of the storm. As I lay there wishing for sleep, the woman from my dream suddenly popped into my head again; the dream had been so vivid and she had been so scared, and completely cornered – I hoped with all my heart that she had just been an invention of my sleeping brain, and that her screams really had just been the whistling of the wind.

The storm continued to rage as the light of morning trickled into my tent. I'd spent another sleepless night worrying the hours away, and I was really starting to feel the effects of exhaustion and hunger. My brain felt foggy, yet I was somehow more jumpy than ever, and I just couldn't seem to warm up. When I had decided to leave my house, I had packed my backpack knowing I would be traveling during the cooler months of autumn, but even layered under all of my shirts, sweaters and my jacket I still couldn't shake off the chill that had seeped into my bones. The temperature had dropped dramatically due to the storm, and the damp air crept into my clothes, making me feel clammy and chilled, like a bad case of the flu.

Scared that I actually did have a fever due to infection, I took care of my feet as soon as I had enough light. As far as I could see, there were no open wounds, just a lot of extremely dirty blisters. I decided to take the day off from traveling since it was still pouring, and instead I spent the day reading my book with my feet propped up on my backpack. I nibbled my last carrots, trying to make them last as long as I could, and I actually started hoping that when the rain let up I would open my tent flap to find a field of dandelions waiting for me.

I guessed it was around three in the afternoon when the rain finally stopped, and I was way too hungry to face another night shivering and starving, so I decided to pack up my tent and continue my journey west. I put on all five pairs of my socks, with the dirty ones on the outside to give a little protection to the clean ones. I filled my bottles again from the pot of rainwater, and drank the rest so I could strap the pot to my backpack. As I rolled up my sleeping bag, one of the Voices suddenly rang out louder than the rest, making me jump so badly I dropped my sleeping bag.

'*Take them... please, take them... save your souls... take them...*'

Not knowing what I was agreeing to take, and whose soul it would save, I told the Voice that I would do my best. Heart still pounding from being startled, I gathered up my sleeping bag, feeling silly for not being used to the Voices after so many years.

I took my tent down, still wondering about what the Voice had said. My five layers of socks soaked through almost instantly, and I thought longingly of the hiking boots I had intended to wear on this journey.

I strapped the tent to my backpack and then slung the bag onto my back, looking around as I adjusted the straps on my shoulders. It really was breathtaking, with the gold of the fields against the darkness of the receding clouds; the sun peeked out for a moment and suddenly the gold looked molten against the charcoal sky. I turned toward the sun to feel its warmth on my face, and that's when I noticed the tire tracks. I hadn't seen them yesterday in the dusky light, and I had been too intent on getting under shelter to really look around, but I could see now that the tracks stretched from the highway into the grassy field ahead. I hadn't considered the cars racing along the highway, whose drivers would have suddenly found themselves helpless captives in several tons of speeding metal.

At least on the highway there was lots of space to try to come to a safe stop. I squinted at the horizon, trying to see if a vehicle was visible, but all I could see was more grassland.

I guessed that the car couldn't have traveled too far through the grass, and who knew, maybe at the end of those tracks I'd find a treasure trove of supplies. I took the first few steps toward the tracks with great care, worried that all of the blisters on my feet would burst under my weight, but the five pairs of wet socks actually had a nice cushioning effect. Soon though, the socks had absorbed so much water that I found myself struggling to walk with the heavy, floppy things at the end of my legs. I sat down and stripped off the four top layers, leaving one clean pair on, and then pulled the outer, filthy pair back on, hoping they could still protect the cleaner inner pair a little. I wrung the remaining socks out and stowed them back in my bag, making a mental note to hang them to dry the first chance I got. Standing up, I took a couple of tentative steps, wincing as the blisters throbbed angrily.

Removing a few layers of socks had made walking more manageable, but I could tell my feet weren't going to last long if I kept this up.

Wondering if I should just get back on the road toward the lake, I glanced toward the place where the tracks disappeared and received my second heart-stopping shock of the morning. A woman was standing there – no, not standing – floating. I couldn't make out her face, and her limbs were barely defined: they sort of faded away into nothingness. It looked like she had blond hair, and as I strained to make out any features of her face, she vanished.

'*Save your souls...*' whispered the Voice.

Feeling like I was being pulled forward, I started walking toward the end of the tire tracks again. As I walked, I wondered why I could suddenly see these wispy apparitions, when I'd only ever heard the Voices before. I had seen Debbie at the bookstore as a glimmer of light, and now this woman had been visible to me as well. Was my gift changing or getting stronger? I couldn't think of anyone from camp who had mentioned something similar happening to them. Eric's abilities had come on suddenly, but only after he'd been clinically dead – I hadn't heard of anyone's gift suddenly shifting like this.

My musings were cut short by my arrival at the edge of a dip in the field. At the bottom of the slope was a narrow pond full of water, in which I could see a small white car. It had come to rest half-submerged in the water, after what must have been a terrifying ride from the highway.

The Voice urged me forward again, so I carefully made my way toward the car. The passenger side of the car was completely under water. As I got a little closer, I could see that the driver's seat was not empty. A woman was still buckled into the seat, and had tipped sideways, so that the top third of her body was under water. Maybe she had bumped her head and before she'd had time to regain consciousness the car had filled with water and she had drowned?

I didn't want to look too closely at her body. She had been sitting there for so long, and I just didn't want to think about what state she might be in. The awful, quiet drone of flies was already telling me more than I wanted to know. There was nothing I could do for her; I just wanted to get out of there. As I turned to leave, the Voice rang out louder than ever, stopping me in my tracks.

'*TAKE THEM ... Save your souls... Please...*'

Take what, I wondered desperately. I didn't want to have anything else to do with this ghastly scene; I didn't want to have to go looking for some unknown object in a car that contained human remains and had been baking in the sun for several weeks. It was too much. For all the times I had heard the Voices, knowing that what I was hearing was some form of lingering energy of those who had died, I had never been faced with such an explicit and up-close view of physical death. Even at the site of the plane crash, where I had seen first-hand the horrors of such a catastrophe, I had not felt the true impact of physical death. Maybe the plane crash site was all too cinematic; the sort of thing I was used to seeing in movies. But here, this woman's life had ended without explosions or drama, and since then she had just been sitting quietly, while the body that had laughed, danced, and lived, slowly decayed away.

Suddenly it seemed unfair to me that she didn't have a proper burial surrounded by friends and family, and that her body might take decades to finally return to the earth, once the car finally rusted away. Could I bury her myself? It seemed a little crazy to expend energy that I didn't have on such a difficult task. And the thought of moving her... I just couldn't face it.

Maybe I could break one of the car's windows, and then she'd be more open to the elements... But I was already so weak from hunger and exhaustion, just the thought of trying to swing something heavy at the window made me weak at the knees.

Why it mattered so much in that moment that this woman have a little respect shown to her remains was a tough question to ponder. Maybe it had something to do with not knowing where my mom had ended up, and hoping that, wherever she was, she had been laid to rest with dignity.

Swallowing the lump in my throat, I turned back to the car. My plan was to at least try opening one of the doors, and then I'd run for it if I couldn't handle any more than that. I was reaching out for the driver's side door handle when I looked into the back seat. There, spilling out of a duffel bag with the rest of her workout clothes, was a pair of running shoes. They even looked like they were close to my size. Feeling excited, I grasped the handle and gave it a tug, with my mind focused entirely on the shoes.

The burst of air out of the car hit me like a brick wall, and suddenly I was on all fours, retching and gagging from the smell. I crawled away up the slope as fast as I could, trying to hold my breath as I continued to choke.

When I felt like I had put enough distance between myself and the car, I stopped crawling and lay on my stomach, pressing my face into the dry grasses and damp earth, hoping to cleanse my mouth and sinuses with the earthy smells, but knowing that the reek I had just encountered would follow me forever. As I lay with my face in the grass, trying to slow my racing heart and not throw up the water I had drunk, it crossed my mind how ridiculously difficult it had been to get my hands on something that, a few short months ago, had been so simple. Even water had been easier to obtain than shoes so far, and that had been my top worry on setting out on this journey in the first place. And once again, there they were – so incredibly close, and so impossibly far.

I raised my head off the ground and noticed several horseshoe prints in the earth nearby. I wondered who had ridden this way, and where they were now. I tried not to feel bitter that even the horse had shoes to wear.

I took off my backpack and rolled onto my back and lay staring up at the shifting clouds. I had to get those shoes. But I did not want to go near that tomb again. Maybe the worst was over, and the car would have aired out a bit, and if I was really fast about it I wouldn't have to see or smell too much…

I lay there for several minutes, trying to will myself to do what was necessary, but at the same time wishing I could just move on from this place. I reasoned that I had nothing to fear from being near the poor woman's body – it wasn't like she was going to suddenly grab me and try to eat my brains – this didn't seem to be that kind of apocalypse…

Finally, it was the moisture from the damp earth seeping through my jeans that forced me to my feet, and I was glad to have an excuse not to keep freaking myself out with the idea of running from living, as well as dead monsters.

I turned back to look at the car again. From this angle it looked perfectly normal, nothing to see, no horrors hidden in wait for an unsuspecting girl just trying to survive…

Survival. Those shoes meant survival. There was no question in my mind anymore. I took a deep breath, summoned as much courage as I could, and dashed back toward the car. I focused on the shoes, not allowing myself to look at the front seat or the nightmare that it held, and trying my best not to breathe too deeply. When I reached the car, I leaned into the backseat, grabbed the duffel bag and crammed the shoes and workout clothes back into it.

'Yes!' I hissed quietly, feeling elated. I clutched it to my chest and started to back out, when I noticed a little stuffed bear on the seat. My dad had given me one exactly like it just before he left my mom and me. I seized the bear and as I straightened up my vision went a little blurry and I could hear the blood rushing in my ears. Hunger and fatigue and bending over too far had almost caused me to faint. I steadied myself against the car's frame to avoid toppling over; just that little bit of pressure and the car sank another few feet into the water. The shoes would have been lost if I had leaned on the car before I'd grabbed them. At least the deeper water had obscured the woman's body – it was a better burial for her than I could have hoped for, since I was unable to do anything more.

Incredibly grateful for my success, and still feeling fairly woozy, I walked a few steps away from the car and plunked myself down on the ground.

I opened the bag and pulled out its contents. I found two pairs of clean socks, one pair of long black yoga pants and a red t-shirt. The extra clothes would be extremely useful as the weather became colder – I would layer them all on top of each other if I had to. I also found a deodorant, some soap and a small towel. And the shoes.

I stripped off my damp socks and pulled on one of my new pairs. Then I slipped on the shoes.

They were a little loose in the width, but miraculously the perfect length. The cushioning under my feet was really going to save my soles from any more blisters. Save my soles... I thought of the Voice that had led me to the car. The dead were making puns now? Really?

I giggled as I stuffed everything back into the duffel bag. Then I noticed a couple of pockets on the side of the bag, and unzipped them to see what they might hold. The smile on my face wilted and I felt a sob building in my throat. The dead woman's gym membership card photo smiled up at me. Her name was Olivia Riley and she looked like she was just a few years older than me. I carefully placed the card back into its pocket and zipped it up tightly. Now feeling a little disgusted with myself for actually laughing over this poor woman's belongings as I pillaged them, I opened the second pocket. Inside I found a sturdy lock with its key in the slot and – I almost couldn't believe what I was seeing – *a granola bar.*

I got over my self-disgust immediately, and unwrapped the glorious, sticky, sweet bar. The first bite was heaven, and the second I barely chewed before I swallowed. Then I slowed down and nibbled away at each ingredient... seeds, oats and almonds... and chocolate chips. I slowly chewed each morsel, savoring the flavors and the crunch. When I had about a third of the granola bar left, I wrapped it up and put it in my pocket, wondering how long I would actually wait to just finish it. I looked around for my water bottle and remembered that I'd left my backpack on the ground up the slope.

Hauling myself back to my feet, I took a few tentative steps in my new shoes. What a difference: I could feel my blisters protesting a bit, but I suddenly felt like I could walk a million miles. New shoes and an energy boost from Olivia's granola bar: today was turning out to be a great day.

I started to walk the short distance to where I had left my backpack, but before I'd taken more than a few careful steps, I heard what sounded like several people coming toward me through the grass. I dropped to my stomach again, my heart pounding frantically.

'Let's just make camp here,' said a female voice, 'it'll be dark soon and we've been walking for hours.'

'Fine,' said a male voice, 'I'm tired too. We'll rest here for the night and then keep going as soon as it's light tomorrow.'

I could see my backpack just laying there in the grass, and I knew if they came to the edge of the slope that they would see it, and me, immediately. They had given me no reason to fear them, but from what I'd seen of humanity lately, I didn't have much faith left in strangers.

I scuttled a little closer to my backpack, still on my stomach, hoping that the noise I was making would be covered up by the sound of them making camp. Bit by bit I made my way toward my backpack, my ears strained for any sign that someone was about to discover me.

When I reached it, I slipped my arms through the straps and flattened myself into the grass again, waiting...

The man's voice rang out, much closer than I would have expected, 'I'll check the area, to make sure we're... hey, there's a car down there! It looks like it's full of water, but there might be supplies we could use!'

That was my cue. I leapt up, and took off running.

'HEY!' The man's voice shouted, 'Hey you! Come back here!'

I ran faster than I'd ever run before, hoping with all my might that he wouldn't follow. There was no way I could keep this pace up for much longer. My lungs were already burning and I felt like my knees would buckle at any moment.

After a couple more seconds, I spun around, ready to fight – I could not run any farther. But the man was still standing at the edge of the slope, staring in my direction.

I collapsed to the ground, gasping and trying keep from throwing up. The man just stood there staring, then gave an exaggerated shrug, and finally he started toward the car.

As soon as I had caught my breath, I stood up and started walking again, feeling immeasurably grateful for Olivia's shoes. I would never have gotten away if I had still just been wearing socks.

Suddenly a powerful wave of nausea rolled through me and I had to stop and try to take some deep breaths. There was a stitch in my side and I just couldn't draw a proper breath. I willed myself not to throw up.

44

The smell from the car, which had coated my throat and sinuses, and the memory of what the car held were all it took. I found myself on all fours again, my body heaving as it expelled the granola bar's precious calories and protein. When it was over I crawled a short distance away from the mess, and I allowed myself, finally, to cry. For my mom, for the world, for Olivia, and for myself, too.

Sweating and shaking from being so violently ill, I wiped my face with my sleeve and tried to pull myself together. Keeping an eye on the man in the distance, I curled up on my side and thought about my mom. Whenever I had been sick in the past, my mom would gather every blanket in the house, lay them all on the couch and then we'd both snuggle under them and watch my favorite movies. We'd have snacks of ginger ale and crackers and I'd always fall asleep in her arms. When I'd wake up I would always find her gazing down at my face, and she'd tell me that I was *her* favorite movie.

Once in a while she would declare a normal day a 'sick day' and we would both start fake-coughing and talking with fake croaks in our voices, telling each other about all of our terrible fake symptoms, trying to make the other person crack up with more and more ridiculous ailments. Laughing and fake-coughing, we'd haul all of the blankets onto the couch, order pizza – because we were both too fake-sick to cook – and then eat cookie dough for dessert.

Those were some of my favorite days with my mom.

Now, curled up on the hard ground with the weight of this new and horrifying world on my shoulders, I felt like I would have given anything just to snuggle in her arms again. I closed my eyes and concentrated really hard on how it had felt to be held by her... The warmth of the sun could be her hand on my cheek... The gentle breeze could be her soft breath in my hair... The tears streaming down my face could be her tears too... I knew that she, wherever she was, was missing me just as much as I was missing her. I sank into in the comfort my imagination had created for me, and somehow, I fell asleep.

When I woke, it was night and I was stiff from being in such a tightly-curled position on the uneven ground. I listened hard to make sure the people from the camp nearby weren't creeping around, but they seemed to be leaving me alone.

I had difficulty sitting up because I was still wearing my backpack, so I eased the straps off my shoulders and placed it in front of me. I gulped a few mouthfuls from my water bottle, and then searched my bag for my toothbrush, thankful for the full moon and the light that it cast. I felt weak and shaky, from hunger and fatigue and being sick. I found my bag of toiletries and used a tiny amount of toothpaste to help freshen my mouth. Just the action of brushing my teeth perked me up a little, but the familiar, minty burst of flavor worked like a stimulant, comforting me, and making me feel a little more human again.

I finished brushing my teeth and then took out the comb I had packed. My hair was a tangled dirty mess, but eventually I was able to comb through it and pull it back again, securing it in its usual ponytail. I applied some of the deodorant out of Olivia's bag and then tucked it into my bag of toiletries, along with the soap I had found. The smell from the car still clung to the duffel bag and its contents, and the whiff I got when I zipped the bag closed made me gag again.

I took a few small sips of water and tried to decide how I could air out Olivia's bag until I could find clean water to try to wash the smell out.

I remembered that I had found some paper clips and shoelaces at the sporting goods store. Breathing through my mouth, and as little as possible, I emptied her bag again. I used one shoelace to tie the yoga pants to my backpack, and the other shoelace to tie the duffel bag itself to my backpack. Then I used the paper clips to attach the teddy bear, the red t-shirt and my damp socks to my backpack, hoping that at least if everything was exposed to the fresh air, it would help with the smell.

I tucked the lock and key into one of the smaller pockets on my backpack, and then I placed Olivia's gym membership card into the first aid kit, next to the photo of my family. I was glad there wasn't quite enough light to see the photos – I had done enough crying for tonight, and I just wanted to get moving again.

By morning I had covered a lot of ground, and the light of day made it so much easier to negotiate my way over the lumpy clumps of tall grass and low shrubs.

I finally felt like I could eat the rest of the granola bar, which surprised me – usually when I had thrown up a certain food, it took years before I could even consider eating it again. I hadn't eaten shrimp in about six years for that very reason. Times change, I guess.

As I walked, I unwrapped the granola bar and took a tentative nibble. It was as delicious as before, and it was gone so quickly that I wished I'd taken the time to sit and enjoy it. I took a few sips from my water bottle and kept walking, keeping an eye out for any dandelions – the granola bar had made me hungrier than I was before I had eaten it, and I wasn't feeling as repulsed as I had felt a few days ago by the thought of eating the bitter weeds.

I walked all day and part of the night, feeling more thirsty now than hungry. The hot weather I had experienced on my way out of the city had been broken by the thunderstorm, and now seemed to have given way to the fresh cool air of autumn. I took small sips from my water bottle as I walked, and wondered how much more distance I could cover before I started to feel too weak to continue. I had no food, a dwindling water supply, and was more exhausted than I'd ever felt in my life.

Something was pulling me forward though, keeping me going when I just wanted to stop. None of the Voices had risen above the usual din since Olivia's, and I wondered if it was merely hope that was pushing me onward, and not some silent, special guide.

When I finally felt like I would collapse if I walked any farther, I stopped, took off my backpack and unrolled my sleeping bag. I didn't have the energy to pitch my tent, and it was already so dark that I wouldn't be able to see what I was doing anyway.

Fully clothed, I snuggled down into my sleeping bag, one arm looped through the straps of my backpack. I swallowed the last of my water, laid my head down to rest, and waited for sleep to carry me away.

But it didn't. I lay there, staring up at the twinkling stars, making a different wish on every one. I wished that I would make it safely to the lake, I wished that I would find Emily there, and Josh, and Eric and Audrey. I wished for food and water. I wished that the world could go back to the way it was, even a little bit, so I could feel safe again. I wished for peace for everyone who had died, before and since the world had gone dark, and then wondered if there were more Voices or stars in the sky...

Chapter Three

Maybe I was too afraid to sleep out in the open, or maybe I was scared that if I fell asleep I wouldn't wake up, but either way I was on the move again as soon as the first light of morning appeared. I hadn't slept at all while it was dark, but resting my body seemed to have helped. I was glad to feel that my feet no longer throbbed when I walked – now if I could just find some food and water, I would be able to cover a lot of ground before the weather got really cold.

In the distance I could see a long row of tall pine trees that were a little too neatly aligned to have grown naturally. Maybe they marked the perimeter of someone's farm land, or maybe they gave a house relief from the sun – whichever, I found myself hurrying excitedly toward the trees, already imagining that there was a generous family living there, who would just be settling down to a delicious breakfast, and who would invite me to eat as much as I could... Suddenly I remembered the ruin my own house had suffered, and proceeded with more caution. I took off my backpack and detached all of Olivia's stuff from it, so I could tuck it all inside my bag instead. I didn't need to have extra things for someone to grab me by, if I needed to make a fast getaway.

I reached the tree line and peeked through a gap between two trunks. I could see a beautiful old three-storey house. It was white with red shutters and a red door. I could see stables in the back, but the horses were nowhere to be seen; maybe the people who owned the house had been the ones who had left tracks by Olivia's car? Maybe by now they had ridden to the refugee camp. I climbed the steps up to the porch and knocked on the red door. There was no answer, so I knocked again and waited. Still no answer, so I decided to try the doorknob. The door swung open and I called out to make sure the house was really empty, but no one answered.

I stepped through the doorway, and followed the entrance hall deeper into the house. On my right there was a door leading to a large sitting room with big windows and a fireplace. Farther along the hall were the dining room and kitchen. I entered the kitchen and started opening the cupboards. They were completely bare. Feeling disappointed, I opened what I thought was going to be just another empty cabinet. It turned out to be a pantry, stocked high with cans of food, bottles of water and bags of rice. It had been over forty-eight hours since I had eaten the last few bites of Olivia's granola bar, and I had been trying to ignore just how hungry I was, but now, in the face of all this food, my stomach growled loudly.

I heard someone giggle.

Great, were the Voices laughing at me too, now? 'Very funny,' I muttered, as I opened a can of soup, but my words were punctuated by another loud growl from my empty stomach, which actually made me grin. It also brought about another round of titters from the giggler.

I ignored the Voice and settled down on the floor to eat my soup. It was rice, beef and veggie chunks in a thick brown gravy. Maybe the best thing I'd ever tasted. I remembered Emily saying something about how you can last three minutes without air, three hours without heat, three days without water, and three weeks without food. She was full of survival tips and facts. Because Emily's dad only had glimpses of what was coming, he'd decided a long time ago to just be prepared for every possible catastrophe, and Emily always filled us in on what he taught her. She called it his obsession – it annoyed her most of the time, but if they had both survived the Darkness so far, I bet they were doing just fine.

After I had finished a can of peaches for dessert, I figured I'd explore the house a little, and see if there was somewhere that I could maybe get a little sleep. I was so tired; it had been weeks since I'd had more than a couple of hours of sleep at once. Before I did anything else though, I filled my bag with as much food as it could hold, just in case I needed to make a quick escape. I'd learned my lesson the night that my house had burned down. I went cold every time I thought about what could have happened if I hadn't grabbed my backpack before I'd hidden. The monsters might have found me. Thankfully, now only my dreams are tortured.

I found myself drawn to a door just off the kitchen, which led down a flight of rickety wooden stairs. As I descended, the smell of dust and mildew filled my nostrils. There was one warped and yellowed window that allowed me to see where I was going. The basement was just one big empty room, with a concrete floor and shelves that lined the walls. To my right I could just make out a slight bump in the floor. Squinting in the gloom, I approached the place where the floor seemed to swell higher than the rest of the area. It appeared that a hole had been dug, and then refilled with a patch of newer concrete. Wondering what could possibly be buried here, I felt a chill go up my spine. A frigid breeze disturbed the hairs on the back of my head, like someone was standing right behind me, blowing their icy cold breath on my neck.

I felt frozen in place, like I was being held there, against my will. I tried to move, but my muscles had all seized up. Suddenly I found myself on my back on the dank basement floor, and as I looked up into the dark ceiling, I heard a shovel scooping up earth, and then I felt the earth cascade down over my body. I struggled in vain against the invisible force that was holding me so tightly in place, and all the while, dirt rained over me, suffocating me. Just as the last shimmer of light was blocked out, I took one last gasp of air.

And I woke up.

Panting, I realized that I had fallen asleep before I'd even finished my soup. I looked over at the door which led to the basement and shuddered. I finished my soup and washed it down with a bottle of water. I packed my bag from the pantry, and got up, preparing to leave – I didn't want to stay here any longer than I had to. I made my way back out of the kitchen, and passed a staircase on my left which must lead upstairs to the first floor. I considered checking the house for any warm clothes that might come in handy as fall shifted into winter. The stables hinted at an outdoorsy lifestyle – maybe I would find something I could use upstairs. I turned back toward the staircase, thinking of woolen blankets and hiking boots.

'Did you know that you talk in your sleep?' said a Voice, and I saw a shadow shift at the top of the stairs.

The dead were really keeping me busy today. I changed my mind about searching the house – I had packed enough to keep me warm for my journey, I just wanted to get back on the road.

I moved toward the front door. I'd really been hoping that this would be a place to spend a few days, but it seemed that rest and peace were just not in the cards for me.

'Hey! Where are you going? You just got here – don't go!' pleaded the Voice from the top of the stairs. 'I won't laugh at your tummy rumbling again, and I won't bug you about sleep-talking, just please don't go!'

I paused, realizing it was a young child's Voice I was hearing. Sighing, I turned away from the door and made my way back toward the stairs. The light from the sitting room didn't reach the staircase, so I couldn't even see half way up the stairs. I started to climb, thinking that the sooner I helped this little one go Beyond, the sooner I could get out of here.

I reached the landing of the first floor, and as my eyes adjusted to the dimness, I could see a full-bodied apparition of a little boy. He looked like he was about seven years old, and he looked like he could have been my little brother with his short dark hair and big blue eyes. The grin that lit up his face made me smile in return.

'Thank you for staying – my name's Andy, what's yours?' he asked.

'You're welcome, Andy,' I said, 'my name is Gracie. Is this your house?'

'It's not my house,' answered Andy. 'I don't remember how I got here – the last thing I remember is that I was falling asleep in the backseat of my sister's car. When I woke up I was here. I haven't seen my sister in a long time. I've been hiding upstairs. I don't like to go outside because I don't feel safe out there. There are Bad Ones out there.'

Eric had told me that sometimes the dead I would encounter might seem confused or lost, or might not even know that they were dead. I was glad I'd stayed in the house a little longer – Andy really needed my help.

'I'm glad you came out to talk to me, Andy, I'm going to help you if I can,' I said.

'Thank you!' he cried, 'I knew you were a Good One!' and he threw his arms around my waist.

Wait.

I was being hugged by a ghost.

Wasn't I?

I looked down at the little boy and saw that his face was scrunched up, like he was hugging me with all his might. He looked very solid, and I reached down to pat his back – he felt very solid too. Maybe a he was a poltergeist?

At camp, sometimes things in the cabin would be rearranged while we were all outside. We'd come back in to find all of the plates and cups and cutlery stacked up in impossible towers. The knives, forks and spoons would be standing end to end, with plates and cups balanced on top; we would try to replicate the towers, but we never could. At least not without a lot of glue. Eric told us that it took a lot of energy for the dead to physically move objects. He had never mentioned whether they could make themselves physically solid, though...

Andy let go of my waist and took my hand. 'Come on,' he said, 'I'll show you where you can get some sleep. You won't even have to sleep on the floor this time!'

He pulled me up to the third floor, where there were two large rooms separated by a landing. He led me into the room on the left, which was painted a bright sky blue, and had a big comfy-looking bed in the corner. I sat down on the edge of the bed, and dropped my bag at my feet.

'Get some rest,' said Andy, 'you look like you've been awake for weeks!' And as he left, he closed the door behind him.

I laid my head down on the fluffy pillow and pulled a blanket from the foot of the bed over myself. Wishing I could talk to Eric about this new phenomenon named Andy, I fell asleep.

***

When I woke up, I was so warm and comfortable that for a moment I was convinced that I was back in my bed at home. The realization that I wasn't at home, and would never be at home again, descended over me like a veil. Sorrow took up its usual place in my chest, and I considered just laying here until I passed out from starvation, or dehydration.

And then I remembered Andy. He needed my help.

I sat up, and tried to clear the sleepy fog from my mind. I must have slept pretty hard, and judging by the silvery light now streaming in through the gap in the curtains, I'd slept the entire night. Without nightmares. Without any dreams at all. Even before the Darkness, I'd always had vivid dreams, but I couldn't remember a single one from last night.

I got out of bed and yawned, stretching the kinks out of my muscles. I opened the curtains and the early morning sunlight burst in, highlighting the dust motes that swirled around the room.

A soft knock on the door made me turn, and there stood Andy, completely solid, with a bottle of water in his hand. He held out the water to me, and I took the few steps to reach him, marveling at how stupid I'd been. He wasn't an apparition, or a ghost, or even a poltergeist. He was a living and breathing little boy, who had looked and felt so solid because he was just that – solid. Full of life, with his little heart thumping and big blue eyes blinking up at me. My own eyes threatened to tear up, I was so glad to see him for what he truly was.

As I took the bottle of water from him, it crossed my mind that I'd been living in the world of the dead for so long, that my mind now assumes the living are dead. It was easier for me to believe that I was seeing the dead, and so that's where my mind went first. I made a mental note to make sure I get more sleep in the future, so hopefully I wouldn't make this mistake again.

I was glad I hadn't said anything to Andy about any of this – that would have totally freaked the poor kid out. Some crazy girl starts talking to him about how he died, and asking whether or not he could see the peaceful white light. And I can only imagine what he heard me say when I was asleep in the kitchen, dreaming about being buried alive... Nope, I was going to be as normal as possible around Andy from now on.

'Want to hear the whole story about the ghost in the basement?' Andy asked casually.

I choked on my water.

'What?' I spluttered, wiping my chin, 'what was that?' He looked so pleased with himself for shocking me so much.

'The basement,' said Andy, 'the creepy hole in the floor, that feeling like you're suffocating when you're down there – not that you were actually down there, you just dreamed it – do you want to hear the whole story?'

I didn't know what to say – to buy myself a little thinking time, I took another gulp of water.

'It's okay,' said Andy, 'I know that you can hear ghosts, just like I knew I didn't have to hide from you. I can see it. I can see that you are different, and I could see that you wouldn't hurt me. You're a Good One.'

'You can see? What do you mean?' I asked. I was reminded of Audrey's gift and how she could feel people's emotions. Maybe Andy could see them, the way Audrey could feel them?

'I see people in colors,' said Andy proudly. 'I see you like anyone else sees you, but I can also see your colors. You are a rainbow, with bright silver, too.' I imagined myself looking like I'd been splattered in buckets of different-colored paint. 'It's just light,' he continued, 'it shines out of everyone. Some people's colors are murky and gross, and they're the ones you need to hide from. I call them the Bad Ones, or the Poo People,' he giggled to himself. 'The colors around them are always kind of poopy.'

Boys, I thought to myself, mentally rolling my eyes.

'I've never met anyone with colors as clear as yours; it's just like a rainbow. And the silver, that's how I know that you can talk to ghosts, hardly anyone has silver.'

He seemed so eager to talk about his gift, so I asked him how long he'd been able to see people this way.

'Forever,' he replied 'I don't usually tell people about it though, they'd just think I was a freak. I knew I could tell you though – the silver – you're different too.' He paused and thought for a minute, and then he continued, 'Since I've been at this house, I've been seeing ghosts in my dreams, that's how I know the story of the basement – I've been here for a while, so every night I dream a new piece of the puzzle.'

Seems like the dead have been keeping everyone a lot busier – I wondered why that was. Both me and Andy had developed new facets to our gifts since the Darkness had happened. Was it because there were so many more people who needed our help? Or maybe without all the wi-fi and satellite signals flying though the air anymore, our brains were freer to intercept other messages? Eric had once told us that the dead used energy to communicate, and I'd always kind of pictured them soaking up rays from the TV or microwave or something. I remembered science class, where there was a poster of Albert Einstein and a quote about how energy can't be created or destroyed, but can only change its form.

So now that all the computers and cars and cell phones weren't sucking up all the energy, how was it being used; what form had it taken? And all of those people who had died – their hearts had stopped and their bodies had gone cold, but where had all of their energy gone? Were the dead using it now?

Andy broke though my reverie with a more simple question: 'Want some breakfast?'

My stomach growled noisily and we both started laughing.

We made our way back downstairs to the kitchen. We opened a couple of cans of fruit, and I discovered a couple of pudding cups at the back of the pantry. Andy asked me what my favorite breakfast was, and I told him about Sunday mornings, when my mom and I would make waffles or pancakes with syrup and whipped cream and fruit.

'And bacon? I love bacon,' he said.

'Absolutely, bacon,' I answered, 'bacon was the most important part!' We both sighed, lost in memories of the salty, crispy strips of deliciousness.

After we'd eaten breakfast, Andy told me he wanted to show me something. He took my hand and pulled me up the stairs to the second floor. Once we'd reached the landing, I could see two bedrooms to my left, and one straight ahead. On the right were a bathroom, and a big storage closet.

In the first room on the left, there was another beautiful fireplace. Standing beside it was a woman. She was wearing a long dress, and her grey hair was pulled back in a loose bun.

This time, I knew I was seeing an apparition – besides what she was wearing, I could see that she was just a little bit blurry around the edges.

'This is Lizzie,' said Andy.

'You can see her?' I asked him.

'Just her colors,' he replied, 'she's mostly gold with the same silver as you. She's been in my dreams a lot, and she's been telling me stories about this house, and stuff that has happened here. She's the first ghost I've ever been able to see when I'm awake. Or kind-of see. She's just a patch of light to me when I'm awake.'

I approached the woman cautiously; since Andy had turned out to be alive, she was the first actual full-apparition I'd been able to see, too. I wished again that Josh were here to talk me through what I was seeing. Being face-to-face was a lot more difficult than just hearing the Voices – she felt more human to me, more real.

My heart was racing; I felt like I wanted to hide from her. Suddenly I realized what was bothering me about her. Seeing her face. It gave a face to every one of the Voices I'd ever encountered. Every one of those poor, lost souls who had come to me for help. They weren't just sounds in my head, they had been people with mothers and fathers and children. I hadn't wanted to see their faces, so I'd separated myself from them, never imagining them as human. Now they all came back to me. Every one of the passengers from the plane crash. Every person who had lost their life on the ground. Even the kidnapped girl's dad – the man whose life had ended at the hands of the monsters – now came rushing back. I saw his kind eyes, his graying hair, and the grateful smile he'd worn after I'd delivered his daughter to her mother.

I sank to the floor, overwhelmed by this bright new clarity. Breathing deeply, trying to steady myself, I looked at the woman.

'Who are you?' I asked.

'My name is Elizabeth Rose,' she replied, 'but everyone just called me Lizzie. I lived here until several decades ago, when I came to my unfortunate end in the basement.'

Seeing the shock on my face, she smiled and asked me if I'd like to take a seat in a more comfortable place than on the floor. She gestured to an antique armchair in the corner of the room. I got up, walked over to the chair, and then dropped down into the dusty cushions. Andy curled up on the bed against the wall to wait while she told me her story:

'When I lived, I had a gift much like yours, Gracie. In particular, those who had suffered death at the hands of another would seek me out, and I would help them bring their murderer to justice. At first, I worked alone, keeping my secret to myself, but all the while gathering clues that the victims would lead me to. I would give anonymous tips to the police and they would eventually track down the ones responsible. Eventually they tracked me down as well, and asked if I would come and help them with cases from time to time. I was happy to, and together we brought many truly evil people to justice.

'One case was especially gruesome and difficult for us to solve. Several people had gone missing over the course of about a year, and there were hardly any clues. No remains had been found. The only real clue we had were the cigarette butts that were found outside of each of the missing person's houses. One cigarette butt, found on one window sill at each house. It seemed to be part of the murderer's ritual, to smoke and then to leave that bold little hint behind. Obviously they felt they would not be caught, and for many months, they weren't. One day, a body was discovered by some men who were in the forest hunting. Next to it there was a half-dug hole and a shovel that had clearly been hastily tossed aside. The men knew the murderer must be nearby, so they attempted, unsuccessfully, to find him.

'The police brought me to the forest, to see if I could get a sense of what had happened. Immediately I told them to dig more in the surrounding area, and they soon discovered several more shallow graves.

'The victims whispered to me that he was near. They guided me to a spot about twenty meters away, and then they went quiet. As I continued to walk, the sound of my footsteps changed. After a little investigation, I discovered a sort of trap-door in the floor of the forest. I opened it to find the murderer looking up at me, a look of pure hatred on his face. He tried to pull himself out of the hole using the rope he'd attached to the trap door, but luckily the police had been right behind me, and they arrested him before he could attack me. He had an insane, trapped look in his eyes, and what I remember most clearly is the reek of stale cigarette smoke. It surrounded him and intensified with his every movement.

'He was put in jail to serve several life sentences, and I was so relieved to have finally put a stop to his crimes. I took a brief holiday abroad to celebrate and to unwind. I arrived home feeling rested and ready to get back to helping the police. However, when I opened the door to my house, the stink of cigarettes hit me like a punch to the stomach. I turned to run, but it was too late. He paralyzed me, dragged me to the basement, and then started to bury me. He told me that he'd escaped from his guards during transport from the courthouse to jail, especially so he could see me again. He said he was glad to have had so much time to prepare my final resting place while I was on holiday, and that no one would ever find me, or know what had happened to me. He laughed as he worked – a horrible wheezing laugh that haunts me to this day.'

Elizabeth paused for a moment, lost in her memories. She looked over at Andy, who had fallen asleep, curled up on the bed. I wondered if he was dreaming about this encounter right now, adding more pieces to the story. I wondered if his gift would continue to evolve, so that he would be able to hear the dead while he was awake, or if he would only ever hear them in his dreams.

After a few minutes, Lizzie continued, her voice weaker than it had been before.

'The police officer I'd worked most closely with happened to stop by that day, and discovered the murderer burying me in the basement. I had already suffocated, but I was able to watch what happened as I floated above the scene. The murderer tried to hit the officer with the shovel, but missed, and the officer shot him five times, bringing an end, finally, to one of the darkest hearts he had ever come across. Or so he'd hoped. From my position near the ceiling, I saw the murderer's essence leave his body, and it was the murkiest black I'd ever seen. It hovered around the police officer, trying to find a dent or hole in his moral framework, without success. Before it drifted out of the basement, it stopped to consider me for a moment. I felt its hatred and its power and then, all of a sudden, it was gone – off looking for some other weak-willed soul to manipulate.'

I stared at Elizabeth as her words sank in. I had thought that the decline in some people's behavior had simply been because of the Darkness – rules and laws had ceased to exist, so why bother acting like they were still in effect? And I had seen the psychological damage caused by starvation and despair as I'd left the city – people half-crazed, attacking each other to try to save themselves. But was there something more to it than that? The men who had burned my house down hadn't just been after supplies to keep them alive. I knew that they were collecting people too, for what purpose I could not allow myself to imagine. I had thought that the Darkness had just brought out the worst in people, but maybe there was something more sinister at work.

I tried to remember if Eric had ever mentioned anything about malevolent energy, but our classes with him had always been more about how to cope with our gifts. Josh had told me once that he sometimes felt like the things he saw must come from a place of darkness, that sometimes he felt tainted by the visions he was having, but I'd always assumed that he meant that what he saw was horrific, and of course, made him feel awful.

I suddenly felt the weight of the unknown threat. It was as though it had seeped in through the walls, seeking me out, and had come to rest on my shoulders.

Andy sat up suddenly, and let out a little yelp of fear. He was looking around the room in a panic, his big blue eyes not actually seeing what was in front of him. Sure that he was still asleep and just having a bad dream, I got up to go and comfort him.

'Andy?' I said, rubbing his back to try to soothe him, 'wake up kiddo, you're just having a bad dream.' His wide eyes found mine, and locked on them with a frightening intensity. He grabbed my arms and gripped them so tightly that I was sure I'd have bruises later.

'I'm not asleep any more Gracie,' he said, 'but the dream is still going. The colors poured in from the walls and started to drown me. I woke up, but the colors are still here. The room is full of the yucky colors and I can't see anything else. Not even your rainbow...' his small shoulders slumped, 'I want to go home...' Andy started to cry.

'Come with me, Andy,' I said, trying to pick him up, 'let's go outside for a bit, and get some fresh air.' He was too heavy for me to carry in my arms, so I told him to climb on my back. 'I'll give you a piggy back outside, and we can go explore the yard and the stables and see what we can find.'

He clambered onto my back. I could feel him shivering as I descended the stairs. I also felt a rush of anger. This sweet little boy had probably lost his entire family, and now he was being tormented by the dead too. I was glad I'd found him. I made him a silent promise that I'd take care of him in any way that I could, and that I'd do my best to find out what had happened to his family.

As we reached the front door, it crossed my mind that I'd left my backpack on the third floor, but right now I just wanted to get Andy outside. Once he'd calmed down a bit, I would go back in to get it.

As I opened the door, the sunshine and crisp morning air caressed my face, washing away all the anxiety I'd been feeling. When I'd made it down the porch steps, I crouched down to let Andy off. I straightened up, took his hand and started walking toward the stables. I snuck a peek down at Andy's face – the tears on his cheeks were sparkling in the sun, but he seemed to have stopped crying.

'Do you feel better now that you're outside?' I asked him.

He nodded. 'There's something in that house that isn't good for us, it isn't good for anybody. I don't think we should stay here, I don't think we should even go back inside.'

I couldn't face the thought of leaving my backpack behind, and that pile of food in the pantry – it could keep us going for months. I kept my thoughts to myself though, because I didn't want Andy to get upset again. 'Have you always felt this way about the house?' I asked 'You said you've been here for a while – has something changed? Did something in the house change?'

He looked up at me and seemed to weigh his words very carefully. 'It always had a weird feeling to it, I couldn't figure out what it was. When you came in something shifted. It was like every time you moved, your rainbow pushed the gross colors around a little. They were pushed back into the shadows, and they didn't like it.'

I thought about how I'd physically felt the weight of Lizzie's words on my shoulders. How Andy had said the murky colors were drowning him. Was there dark energy gathered in that house? If it was the dead, why couldn't I hear them? What was going on?

We reached the stables and walked inside. The smell of hay and horses and leather was comforting somehow; it chased away the dank and dusty smell of the house. Andy let go of my hand and sat down on one of the wooden benches that lined the walls. He sighed and looked up at me, his long eyelashes still stuck together with tears. 'What are we going to do Gracie? It's never been like this for me, it's getting worse. I used to see people's colors and sometimes I would have dreams, but I never felt like it could hurt me. I'm scared.'

I went and sat beside Andy, wishing I had answers for him. 'I don't know why our abilities are changing, Andy, and I'm a little freaked out too, but I think as long as you and I stick together we can figure the rest out.' Andy nodded. 'We should make a plan,' I said, standing up and trying to sound more confident than I felt. 'We should decide what we're going to do next and then do it. I think the first thing we should do is see if there's anything we can use in here, like blankets or tools or anything – what do you think?'

Andy nodded again, and smiled a little at my exaggerated enthusiasm. He stood up and we started to search. After about half an hour we hadn't found anything promising except a tarp and some leather straps. 'We can use the tarp as a tent,' said Andy, 'if we set it up over some low branches or something, it'll block the wind and keep us dry.'

'I do have an actual tent in the house, and a bunch of other stuff that'll help keep us going. Plus I have a second bag that I could fill with food, I just have to run and get it.' I saw the look on Andy's face and knew this wasn't going to be an easy argument to win. 'We can do it really quickly, together, and we'll be back outside before you know it.' He still didn't look convinced. 'I have to go get my backpack, Andy, I just have to. The only picture I have left of my mom is in that bag, and I just can't leave it behind.'

I was going to suggest that he stay outside while I ran in, but I knew he wouldn't go for it, and I didn't want to be apart from him, anyway. How many times had I yelled at the television screen that people in dangerous situations should just stick together? This did not feel like a good time to split up.

'Okay, fine,' he said, 'but we hold hands the entire time, and we run in, grab your bag and then run out.'

'Agreed,' I said. 'I don't want to be in there any longer than we have to either.'

So we started walking back toward the house. I was trying to think of a way to keep his mind occupied while we ran in and out. My mom and I used to play the alphabet game when we were on a long drive – we'd go through each letter of the alphabet and name a movie that started with each letter. The thought of never seeing another movie kind of depressed me though, so I thought maybe he'd like to try it with the names of food. I explained the game to him as we walked, and started us off.

'Apple.'

He grinned at me, and we both said, 'Bacon!'

'Carrot.'

'Doughnut!'

'Eggs.'

We'd reached the front porch, and Andy seemed distracted enough by the game that I took his hand as he yelled 'French fries!' I pushed open the front door and said 'Gravy for your French fries,' and as he thought about what he would name next, we crossed through the hall toward the stairs. We made it all the way to the third floor, when Andy finally shouted "Ham! Ha! You're going to have to think of a food that starts with "I" Gracie! That's a tough one!'

As we walked into the room where I'd left my backpack, I turned to him and said 'Ice cream!' and I was about to stick out my tongue, but the look of terror on his face stopped me in my tracks.

The room was exactly as we had left it, except for my backpack. It should have been next to the bed where I had let it drop before going to sleep last night. Instead, it was floating in mid air in the middle of the room. As we stared at it, it started to revolve gently.

'We have to go!' Andy whispered urgently, tugging on my hand.

The spinning backpack started to pick up speed. I took a step toward it, suddenly feeling more annoyed than afraid. 'Cut it out!' I yelled. 'Let it drop!'

The bag fell to the dusty floor with a crash, and I dragged Andy forward to grab it. I marched out of the room, down the two flights of stairs and into the kitchen. I pulled the duffel bag out, swung my backpack onto my back, and then stuffed as many cans of food into the duffel bag as I could. When the seams of the duffel bag were straining, I hooked it onto my arm, grabbed Andy's hand again, and marched us back through the entrance hall and out of the front door. I could hear a weird buzzing in my head, as though all of the Voices were speaking at once. I ignored them.

'Are you okay?' I asked Andy, as I directed our path back toward the stables. He didn't answer. He was almost running to keep up with my pace. When we arrived at the stables, he plopped himself down on the same bench as before and finally let go of my hand. I waited for him to say something, terrified he'd been traumatized by everything he had just seen. I set the bag of food aside, took off my backpack and crouched down to his level, trying to look into his eyes. 'Andy…?'

For a moment he just sat there, seemingly frozen with shock. Finally, he looked into my eyes. 'That was AWESOME!' he yelled, jumping up and punching the air. Relief welled up inside me and I started laughing, so glad to see that he was alright. 'Don't mess with Gracie!' he shouted, 'She'll kick your butt!' He paused, 'Even if you don't have a butt anymore! She'll kick it!' He held up his hand for a high-five. Still laughing, I slapped him five and dropped onto the bench he'd occupied a minute before.

'That. Was. Crazy.' said Andy, coming to sit down next to me. 'I was so scared, the room just kept getting more and more dark with the gross colors, and then just before it all went black, you yelled, and I saw a great big flash of light, like the room was full of sparkles, and then the bag fell, and we were out of there! Weren't you scared?'

'I was scared at first, and when it started to spin that really creeped me out, but then I realized that scaring us is what they were trying to do – and it really bugged me that it was working. It's *my* bag, it's *my* stuff. We're going to need it.' I sighed. 'Everything has felt so out of control lately. I'm tired of being scared, I just wanted to be in charge for once.'

'Well, boss, what's next? What's the plan?' asked Andy, grinning up at me.

I laughed again, feeling like I'd just run a marathon – exhilarated, but completely exhausted. 'How about we have some food, have a little rest and then we'll figure out what we're going to do next?'

'Sounds good to me,' said Andy, digging into the bag of food.

Chapter Four

During a small meal that we ate just inside the stables, Andy asked me where I had come from, why I had come to the old house, and how long we would have to travel to get more supplies.

'I'm not sure how long it'll take to find more food – I'm glad we stocked up from the house. There are so many fires in the city now, and besides, there isn't anything left in the stores back home because of all the looting. That's why I made my way here, I was hoping to find more supplies.'

'Fires and looting?' said Andy with an odd look on his face. 'How can the stores be empty?'

I suddenly realized that Andy had never mentioned the Darkness. He had said he'd fallen asleep in his sister's car and woken up alone in the house. No one would have been around to tell him... He didn't know...

'Well... This might sound pretty scary Andy, and a little weird too...' I hesitated, unsure of how to break the news to him.

'What happened, Gracie? It's okay, just take a deep breath and tell me really fast. That's how my sister tells me things, and then I get to ask her as many questions as I want. A few years ago she had to tell me that our dog got hit by a car, but by saying it really fast she got it out quicker and then I got a couple of minutes to try and figure out what she had said. Just say it, it's okay.'

'Okay...' I took a deep breath.

'Thepowerinthecitywentoutlotsofpeoplediedandnowthecit yisbeingstrippedcleanandburnedbythe... Poo People.'

He stared at me, his eyes round with shock. He took a deep breath of his own.

'So... Everything stopped working?'

I nodded.

'And lots of people died?'

I nodded again.

64

And the Poo People… They're destroying the city?'

I sighed and nodded a third time. 'That's why I had to leave. I stayed at my house for a while, but then they broke in and burned it down. I barely got out, and it seemed like everywhere I went, they were there, taking everything and everyone they could find, leaving a trail of fire and destruction behind them.'

'Why are they burning everything?' Andy asked, a frown creasing his forehead.

'I'm not really sure why, it doesn't make any sense to me, either. Maybe they're trying to be in charge of everything, and the less there is left, the easier it is to control.'

'Are they killing people?'

I hesitated again, not wanting to give him too much bad news all at once.

I could see him working out what my silence meant though, and his struggle to make sense of what I had told him.

'It's a lot to hear all at once, I know, it was a lot to deal with as it all happened. Sometimes I still can't believe it. At least we can stick together and help each other, it'll be much better to travel with you than it was to travel on my own. I've come across a few people since I left home, but I mostly avoided them because I never knew who I could trust. You'll be able to tell me who we can trust, and we can figure out food and shelter together.'

Andy was quiet for a while, his eyebrows furrowed as he sorted though the news I had given him. After a few minutes he looked at the two bags of supplies and put back the can of beans he was holding.

'We better not eat too much, just enough to keep going – we don't know when we will find more food.'

'Sounds like a good plan to me, and if we're ever hungry enough, we can always eat dandelions. Clover is safe too, even the flowers, just don't eat it if it's red.'

Surprised, Andy looked up at me.

'Clover, like four-leaf clovers? Like leprechauns and rainbows and pots of gold?'

'Yep!' I said, 'but it can make you pretty bloated too, so if we have the choice we should just stick to dandelions.'

'Eating four-leaf clovers makes you gassy?' said Andy, with a hint of a sparkle in his eye. 'That's not very lucky.'

I groaned and laughed, grateful that he was handling the end of his world so well.

I decided to show Andy everything in my backpack. I laid out the rope, the tent, the sleeping bag, the tarp, the leather straps, the knife, the can opener and the matches. Then I added the little pot, the paper clips, the extra shoelaces and the straw. It was nice to take inventory of what I had, and organize the new stuff. I dug to the very bottom of my bag and found one of the blankets I had taken from my mom's bed. I had forgotten it was there. As I lifted it to my face to see if it still smelled like home, Andy picked up the first aid kit and asked me what was inside. I opened it up and showed him the gauze and bandages, the disinfectant wipes and the tiny scissors that my mom had packed into the little kit years ago.

'Wow! Now I'm extra glad we went back into the house! We have everything we need!' He held up the scissors and snipped at the air a few times. 'We can even give each other tiny haircuts!'

I laughed and grabbed the scissors and tucked them back into the kit. 'My mom was a nurse,' I told him, 'she packed this first aid kit a long time ago, and if she says tiny scissors might come in handy, then they will.'

I showed him the picture of my family.

'This is my mom, she was the best. My best friend and the best mom. That's my dad with us, he left when I was about your age, and I haven't seen him in a very long time. I try not to think about him, it makes me miss him. I wonder where he is now, if he has survived so far.'

I placed the photo back into the first aid kit with Olivia's gym card, and packed the rest of the kit back up.

Andy got quiet and started fiddling with his shoelaces.

'You okay?' I asked him, guessing that he was feeling sad about his own family.

'Can you hear whoever you want?' he asked, 'can you ask a certain ghost to talk to you, if there's someone who wants to talk to them?'

'Usually the dead find me, and then I try to find the person they want to talk to,' I said, 'but sometimes I can really concentrate and find a specific Voice, if they want to be heard and if they haven't gone Beyond already.'

'Beyond?'

'Sometimes the dead have reasons to stick around – they have messages to give or some task they feel the need to finish, and once they do, they seem to disappear from my head. My friends who are able to see the dead have told me that they sort of become part of a bright white light, and they find peace beyond the physical world.'

Andy remained quiet and thoughtful, so I continued to arrange the contents of my bag. I laid out the toiletries and I noticed Andy staring at my toothbrush, and absentmindedly feeling his teeth with his tongue.

'I found a new toothbrush in the house, it was still in its plastic wrapper and everything.' He shrugged, 'I should have kept it in my pocket, I guess.'

I considered Andy, our supplies, and the journey ahead for a moment.

'I want to go back into the house. You're going to need warmer clothes and we can grab some more food and your toothbrush. What do you think?'

He looked scared, but nodded his head. 'As long as we stick together, I think we should get a few more supplies, too. I looked in the closets for clothes that would fit me, and there wasn't much, just some dresses and then some big work clothes for a very tall man. You might be able to wear the work shirts, if you roll up the sleeves and maybe tuck the shirt in.'

'Alright,' I said, 'it's good that you already know what's there, it'll cut down on how much time we need to spend in the house.'

I looked at all of the supplies spread out in front of us. 'Just to be safe, and just in case something happens that splits us up, I think we should divide this stuff up and each have a bag so we can survive until we find each other again.'

I grabbed the duffel bag and emptied it, stacking the cans of food and bottles of water in a pile. 'I'll give you the can opener, and I can use my knife to open my cans. You can take the tent and the sleeping bag too – I'll use the tarp and this blanket I brought from home.'

'I can take the tarp,' said Andy, 'I haven't set up a real tent before, I don't know how. A tarp will be really easy, I just have to wrap myself up in it, like a little fort, I used to make lots of forts at home.'

'OK, for now you can take the tarp, but I'm going to show you how to set this tent up, it's pretty easy once you know how.'

I gave Andy the rope and kept the leather straps for myself.

'We'll get some more food and water from the house,' I said, dividing the pile into two. 'Is there anything here you don't like?'

'I just don't like mushrooms,' he replied, 'if there's any soup or anything with mushrooms in it, I'll trade you for something else. They're just too weird and rubbery. Plus they taste gross. I don't know who the first person was who saw the first mushroom and thought they'd eat it, but yuck, no thanks.'

As I switched out his mushroom soup for some of my tomato soup, I silently hoped that Andy would never be hungry enough to consider eating a mushroom. He had gone from living a normal life in the old world to waking up in the house, which was well-stocked with food, and had not felt real hunger yet. I sincerely hoped he never would.

'So you can't remember anything about how you got here?' I asked him, as I divided the bandages and matches.

'Nope,' he replied, 'all I know is that my sister was driving us home from a visit with our cousins, and I fell asleep in the car. When I woke up, I was tucked in bed in one of the third-floor bedrooms, and I was completely alone.'

He hesitated for a minute.

'I don't know what happened to my sister, but I don't think she made it, because I don't think she would have let me out of her sight.' He reached for the pile of clothes that I hadn't sorted through yet, and as he lifted one of my sweaters, the teddy bear that I had found in Olivia's car rolled out of the pile. I had forgotten about that, too.

Andy picked up the teddy bear with a strange look on his face. He rubbed one of the bear's ears, like it was a comforting habit, something he had done a million times, and I could see that the spot he was rubbing looked a lot more worn than the rest of the bear.

Suddenly Andy's story became painfully clear to me, and my insides turned to ice. I wanted to hide, to run, to protect Andy from yet more terrible truth, but I knew I couldn't do any of those things.

He looked around at the rest of our supplies, his eyes coming to rest on the duffel bag, and then on my shoes.

I waited, not sure if he was going to be angry or hate me or start to cry. I could see him struggling, and I wanted to help, but I didn't know what to do.

I picked up the first aid kit, and found Olivia's gym membership card next to the photo of my family. I held it out to Andy.

'I didn't know she was yours,' I whispered, 'I'm so sorry, Andy...'

He took the card and looked down into his sister's smiling face, his chin trembling and his eyes full of tears.

'I knew she couldn't have made it,' he said, 'I knew from the moment I woke up by myself. I knew.'

'I'm sorry...'

'It's not your fault Gracie, I'm sad, but I'm also glad to know for sure. Did you hear her Voice? Did she talk to you?'

I told him that she had talked to me, and had even appeared to me, so that she could lead me to her running shoes, which I had needed so badly. I told him about finding her gym bag and then about grabbing the teddy because I used to have one just like it.

'She must have known that you would find me, that you could help me,' he said, as he wiped his eyes on his sleeve. 'Do you think she suffered?' he asked after a moment of silence.

'I don't think so,' I replied. I had been asked this question many times before, and for once I could answer completely honestly. 'I think she bumped her head and it would have just been like falling asleep.'

I didn't mention her remains or where the car had ended up, he didn't need to have that kind of mental image of his sister.

I told him about the horseshoe prints that I had seen near the car, and how it must have been the people who had lived in the house who had rescued him.

'I wonder where they are now,' said Andy, still sniffling a little. 'I wonder why they haven't come back yet.'

'Maybe they went to see if they could find anyone else who needed their help,' I suggested, 'maybe they're still going to come back.'

He nodded and hugged his teddy bear to himself, gripping Olivia's gym card tightly in his hand. 'It's nice to have a picture of her, I'm glad you kept it.'

'She saved my life, Andy, I don't think I could have made it much farther without her. I couldn't just toss her photo aside, not after she had given me so much.'

I looked through the pile of clothes and found Olivia's red shirt. I was worried for a second that it would still smell horrible, but it seemed to have aired out enough.

'This will fit you, it was in her bag, she...'

Suddenly I heard the clip-clop of approaching hooves. Andy looked up at me, excited, but as he leaned over to peek out of the stable door, the hope slowly faded from his face.

'Poo People...'

It was all the information I needed. I quickly jammed all of our stuff into the two bags, heaved my backpack into my back and helped Andy slip his arms through the straps of the duffel bag, to wear like a backpack. I grabbed his hand, put my finger to my lips to tell him to keep quiet, and led us to a short stack of hay bales that lined the far wall, thinking I could make us a quick little hiding spot by stacking the bales around us. I had no idea the bales would weigh so much, or that I had become so weak – I could barely even move one, let alone stack them up around us. There was a pitchfork leaning against the bales, so I grabbed it, not wanting to use it on a person, but ready if I had to.

Andy grabbed a shovel he had spotted next to the bales, and held it up, ready to fight.

'This looks like the place they described,' said a male voice, 'I can see the stables from here.'

'Yeah,' said a deep gravelly voice that I knew only too well, 'go tie up the horses and then start hauling the food out of the pantry. I'm going to check the upper floors.'

I was frozen with panic. I couldn't see how we were going to escape this time, there was simply nowhere to hide.

We could hear the first man approaching, muttering under his breath.

'...made him King of the World, he never does anything, we have to do everything, I'm the one who tortured them, I'm the one who made them tell us about this place, but I still have to do all the work and follow all his orders like some pathetic little...'

Clang.

Andy had whacked the man on the side of the head with his shovel as soon as his head had come into view. He had been too busy complaining to check the stables were clear, and he had paid the price for his distraction.

The sound of the shovel meeting the man's skull jolted my body back into action. I grabbed a bucket that was nearby on the ground, flipped it over, and set it down next to the closest horse to use as a step. I grabbed the stirrup that was hanging at the horse's side, and reached out to Andy.

'Climb up!'

'I've never ridden a horse!'

'Me neither! Quick! He's coming to!'

The man was stirring on the hay-strewn floor, groaning and holding his head.

Andy stepped up onto the bucket, put his foot in the stirrup, and tried to haul himself onto the horse. He was just too small. I stepped up behind him and pushed him up as hard as I could.

Just as Andy made it into the saddle, the man grabbed my ankle.

'Well, well, well, look what we've got here,' he drawled, leering up at me.

I kicked out, trying to free myself. Olivia's shoe connected with his nose, which broke with a sickening crack. He swore with pain and let go of my ankle. I stepped up into the stirrup and swung my leg over the horse, misjudging how much force I'd need and almost falling off the other side. I grabbed the saddle to pull myself back up, and settled in behind Andy. I clutched the front of the saddle in my trembling hands, with my arms around Andy's shaking body, and made a clicking noise with my mouth that I had seen people on TV make to get a horse moving.

The horse broke into a slow walk, which almost sent both of us toppling off the side. I clutched Andy more tightly around the waist, and squeezed the horse's body with my legs as hard as I could.

I could hear the man yelling for his leader – we only had a few seconds before they would both be chasing us.

A Voice whispered to me to try to relax, and to sit up straight. It felt counterintuitive; I wanted to stay hunched over, to protect Andy and to be closer to the horse's body, but I slowly straightened my upper body and I could feel a huge difference. I was able to move with the horse instead of trying to clench my whole body in an attempt to stay on. The Voice urged me to press my heels down toward the ground. I did, and the horse sped up to a gentle trot.

I was scared to look back and see if we were being followed, the monsters might be right behind us on the second horse, and they would catch up to us easily.

Suddenly I heard a horse snort right beside us, and my heart started hammering against my ribcage.

I turned, ready to kick and punch the monsters if they tried to grab us, but all I saw was the shining black coat of the second horse, who, riderless, had followed us away from the stables.

I laughed out loud at the sight of the empty saddle, but my joy was cut short by the sound of a gunshot.

Our horse started galloping in fright. It was all I could do to hold on and curl my body around Andy as closely as I could.

I risked a look over my shoulder to see how closely we were being followed, and I saw the second horse thrashing around on the ground behind us. It must have been hit when the monster had shot at us. I felt so sad for the horse, but there was nothing I could do unless I wanted to get us shot, too. I could hear Andy whimpering a little as we raced away from the house.

A second shot rang out and I felt white-hot pain sear my upper arm. I cried out, but I didn't stop. I didn't want to look at it, I just kept my mind focused on getting as far away from danger as possible.

'Are you okay, Gracie?' I heard Andy ask, his voice muffled because he was so hunched over against the horse. 'Did you get shot?'

'I'm okay, it's not too bad, we just have to keep moving for now, I'll take care of it later.'

I wasn't sure how long I could keep going though, I could feel hot blood soaking through my shirt sleeve and dripping from my elbow. I would have to wrap my arm up soon – I didn't want to leave such a perfect trail for the monsters, if they decided to follow us.

After about ten more minutes of galloping, I figured we were far enough away that we could slow down. The only problem was that I didn't know how. The reins were dangling around the horse's neck, but I didn't feel like I could safely let go to free up a hand, and I didn't want Andy to have to try to reach for them either.

Before I could even ask the question, I heard the same Voice as before whisper to lean my weight back a bit. I did, and the horse slowed its pace a little.

'Her name is Patience... She's very gentle... She won't hurt you...'

I thought of the second horse, and wondered if it would be alright. A third gunshot rang out, but sounded much farther away this time.

'His name was Ace...' The Voice let out a quiet sob and then was silent.

I knew that the monsters had killed the second horse, and I felt angry and disgusted at how little regard they had for anything or anyone else. Once again I felt a strong desire to hunt them down and give them what they deserved, but I couldn't just abandon Andy to go on some crazy mission that would surely fail. He needed me to keep my head on straight.

I shifted my weight back a little more and Patience slowed her gait some more. I needed to check on my arm and see how bad the damage was.

'Why are we stopping,' asked Andy, 'what if they come after us?'

'I don't think they'll be able to catch up to us, they'll be on foot and as long as we are quick here, we'll keep our good head start. But I have to bandage my arm, and I can't do it unless we stop for a sec.'

We came to a stop and I swung my leg back over Patience and hopped down.

'Do you want to come down, or just stay up there for now?'

Andy said he'd sit tight, so I opened my backpack and dug around until I found our first aid kit. I opened it up and found a roll of gauze and some white adhesive tape to hold the gauze in place. I took out a bottle of water, pulled out a different shirt and then sat for a minute, willing myself to look down at my arm. I couldn't put it off anymore. I took a deep breath and peeked.

There was so much dark red blood that I almost passed out just from looking at it. I carefully stripped my good arm out of my shirt, and then slipped my head out too. Then I just had the bad arm left to do. I tried to convince myself that it looked a lot worse than it really was, and I peeled my blood-soaked sleeve off of the wound beneath.

It actually wasn't as bad as it looked, the skin and flesh looked pretty ragged, but I could see that it wasn't very deep, and there was no sign of leftover metal from the bullet or anything. I was super glad I wasn't going to have to dig out scraps of metal, I'm not sure I could have faced that without a lot of crying, and I was determined not to upset Andy.

I poured water over my wound and cleaned the area as well as I could, clenching my jaw to keep from making a sound.

I had to use my teeth to unroll the gauze, but I was able to wrap it around my arm pretty easily once I got it started. Now I was stuck. I needed to cut off some tape without letting go of the gauze, but I didn't have enough hands to get it done. I pressed the gauze between my arm and my body, and handed the tape and the tiny scissors up to Andy.

'You get the honor of using the tiny scissors!' I told him. 'My mom definitely knew what she was doing.' I grinned up at him, and he gave me a weak smile in return and cut off a few lengths of tape. The tape held the gauze in place nicely, and I was able, very awkwardly, to put the clean shirt on over my dirty tank top.

I thought longingly of the showers at camp. Eric called them sun showers, because the water was stored in a big black rubber tank, which sat out in the sun all day. We also had the option of baths, but we had to boil the water for that. Either way, it would be a huge treat just to feel clean.

I suddenly realized how thirsty I was, so I took out a water bottle from my backpack and swallowed a few gulps. Then I unhooked the pot from the side of my bag and poured some water out for Patience to drink. I reached out and rubbed her chestnut nose, wishing I had an apple or a carrot or something to say thank-you for saving our lives.

When Patience was finished drinking, I asked Andy if he could hold my backpack while I tried to climb back up. He nodded and took it without looking at me. It took a couple of tries, but eventually I was able to hook my leg over the saddle and haul myself back into place. I took my backpack and eased the straps over my shoulders again, scared that I would topple backwards because it was so heavy.

Once I felt secure, I risked looking behind us, but I couldn't see the tree line that surrounded the house anymore. Comforted a little by the fact that the monsters wouldn't be able to see us at this distance, I clicked my tongue and Patience started walking. I was glad to be moving again. It made me nervous being so close to the monsters, I had no idea if they had the means to come after us, but I felt certain that they would as soon as they could.

I couldn't tell how Andy was doing because his back was toward me, but judging by his silence he was still struggling. I felt awkward and guilty that I had taken his sister's belongings, and that I hadn't figured out their connection sooner. I wondered if he was mad at me, but I was too afraid to ask; I didn't want to hear that the one person in the world that I liked and trusted didn't like me anymore.

We rode in silence for a few more hours and then, feeling like I might nod off, I suggested that we stop for the night. I dismounted first, and then helped Andy down. I didn't know where to tie Patience up, there were no trees or fences and I really didn't want her to wander off, so I asked Andy to hold onto her reins while I pitched the tent. The horse seemed happy to munch the grasses around us, and I was relieved that I didn't have to worry about what to feed her.

Andy looked so small as he stood quietly beside her, and there was a defeated scrunch to his posture that broke my heart a little. He'd been through so much today; I could only hope that our night was peaceful and restful.

Dusk was approaching and I could see the very first star twinkling faintly in the cloudless sky. I felt exhausted and emotionally drained, and put my last burst of energy into getting our camp ready.

Once the tent was up, I took out the rope I had brought from home, tied one end to the horse's reins, and the other end I tied to my wrist, hoping that Patience wouldn't suddenly run off and take my arm with her.

I set up the blanket and sleeping bag in the tent, and then tossed our bags in too, thinking about what we might have for supper.

I looked around, about to ask Andy what he wanted to eat, when I saw the smoke.

So the beautiful old house was gone. The monsters had stripped it clean and it would soon be nothing more than ash. Like my own home. And the city that had once pulsed with vitality, but now lay in ruin, like the ribs of some burned-out skeleton.

The idea of the food from the house's pantry being used to sustain those despicable monsters filled me with rage. I wondered how many of them there were, and how many people they had captured so far. Getting the food back to their base would probably be a priority for them though, which meant that maybe they wouldn't bother following us. Except that they must know that we had food of our own, plus we had stolen their horses – somehow I didn't think they would just let that go. Not when there were supplies at stake. Plus the fun of revenge.

They were coming for us.

'You have time... Sleep... There is time...'

Lizzie was back. She must have watched as the monsters destroyed her house. I wondered what had happened to all of the energy that had gathered there. And I wondered why it had gathered there of all places. Waiting for the monsters to arrive? Waiting to be their guides in this ruin of a world, where it seemed that the only way to survive was to leave your humanity behind?

A sudden thought occurred to me.

'Andy? Did you see any gold or silver around the men today? Are they able to hear what I hear?'

'It happened too fast. I don't know.'

'Okay. That's okay. The tent's ready, we can eat and then get some sleep.'

'I'm not hungry.'

Andy disappeared into the tent. I stared at the column of smoke for another minute, and saw a couple of flares shoot up into the sky. That must be the signal to summon help. They had no way to transport their loot, after all. I felt a moment of satisfaction that we'd at least caused them some delay, but my smug smile faded as I thought of how they might pay us back.

With a sigh, I followed Andy inside the tent, leaving the flap open so I could see what I was doing in the fading light. Andy had already burrowed into the sleeping bag, and I took the hint not to bother him. Instead, I opened a can of soup and settled down to eat. It was tricky with the rope attached to my wrist, but Patience wandered close enough that I could eventually relax. I barely tasted what I was eating – the thought of all that energy from the house was a huge worry. The idea of the leader of the monsters hearing Voices terrified me. He was one person who certainly didn't need any help to be horrible. Before I had heard Lizzie's story, it had never occurred to me that there might be bad Voices – I had never come across any. It was always people asking me for help, or to give messages of love...

'Sleep, Gracie... You're going to need it...'

Suddenly the mental and physical exhaustion seemed to push me down into my blanket, and I was asleep within seconds.

It didn't last long, though. The sound of sniffling woke me up, and it felt like only minutes had passed. For a moment I was irritated to have been woken up, but then Andy sniffled again and my annoyance evaporated.

'Andy? Please talk to me... Please?'

I heard him shift around in the sleeping bag, and assumed that he was trying to cocoon himself even deeper into it, but then I heard him whisper.

'I knew Olivia was gone. I just knew. Having you with me made it a little easier to deal with, like maybe she was still kind of here, with you. Even if she's not with you, you feel like a big sister to me, so that makes it feel like she's here, except it's you instead.'

I couldn't help but smile. 'You feel like a brother to me too, Andy, I'm really glad we found each other-'

'But then you got shot!' Andy interrupted, his voice getting louder and higher as he got more upset. 'If that man had aimed just a couple inches over, he would have killed you, and I would have lost both of you in one day, because I wouldn't have been able to save you. You would have fallen off the horse and I would have been stuck up there, riding around until I died too, because I don't know how to stop, or get down. I'm too small. I'm too small for this scary dark world and it's only a matter of time until I...'

He gasped himself into silence and then started sobbing.

'Stop, Andy,' I said, and I gathered him into my arms, sleeping bag and all. 'You've made it this far, and it's not about being big or small, it's about being smart and helping each other. We help each other, that's how we survive.'

'I'm just slowing you down, you should take my food and stuff and just go, you're better off alone, I'll only hold you back.'

'Do you really think I would ever do that? I'm not one of those monsters, Andy, I need you, and we are going to stick together. I'm so sorry that Olivia died. I know how you feel. I lost my mom when things went dark, and I almost didn't survive it. But I'm glad I did. Because I found you. And now we're a team. We will survive together.'

I couldn't go on, my throat was too tight and I could feel tears about to spill over. Saying out loud that my mom was gone somehow made it more true. I had severed the last link to hope, a link I had not been fully aware that I was clinging to. She was really gone. I felt a new weight in my heart, but at the same time a strange sense of freedom. That last bit of hope had kept me emotionally tethered to the city, but now there was nothing to hold me back.

Chapter Five

Andy's sniffles had subsided at bit, so I tried to get comfortable again. He stayed snuggled close by me, and I heard him whisper that he was sorry about my mom. Then he asked what I missed most about her.

'She was my rock. Whenever things were hard, and whenever things were great, she was always there. Sometimes I would feel like I was floating in space, with no way to control where I went, just drifting around, powerless. But then she'd reel me back toward home and I'd find my feet on solid ground again.'

Andy's breathing had become slower and deeper, and I thought he was asleep, until he said, 'Olivia was really funny. She would make my stomach hurt from laughing so much. She never minded when she had to babysit me, she always made it fun.'

In the silence and darkness, our memories eventually carried us off to sleep.

I awoke with the first light of dawn, my arm throbbing and my stomach growling. All I could see of Andy was the top of his head sticking out of the sleeping bag. I eased myself out of the tent and looked east, where I could see a thin column of smoke still rising from the old house.

We needed to get moving.

I gave Patience some more water, and ran my fingers through her mane while she drank. I was so grateful to have a faster way to get to the lake, Patience would cut our travel time down by a huge amount.

I could hear Andy stirring in the tent, so I went back inside to get us some breakfast.

'Morning,' I said tentatively, not sure if he was still upset.

'Hi,' he said with a smile, taking the can of pears I was holding out to him.

I was so relieved to see that Andy's eyes were free of the sadness and fear I had seen in them yesterday – he seemed to be his usual chatty self again. He asked what the plan was for today, and I told him that after we were done stuffing our faces, we would head west and try to cover as much ground as possible before it got dark again.

'What's out west,' he asked, his mouth full of pears, 'do you know somebody out there or something?'

So I told him about Emily, her gift of foresight, and the text she had sent me.

'Wow, it's lucky you were looking at your phone at just the right second! You might have missed her message!'

'I know, I'm so glad I didn't miss it. But I think I would have headed to camp anyway, even if she hadn't texted me. It's just so perfect there, we'll have everything we need to survive... we can make it our home.'

I thought to myself that we would need to put up some walls or something, to have some kind of defense against what the rest of the world had become. It would be awful to settle at the lake, build a life there, only to be attacked and have it taken away. I didn't say any of this to Andy since he seemed so cheerful, I just wanted to get on the road as quickly as we could.

Andy was full of questions about camp, Emily, and my other friends. I tried to answer them all as we packed up our gear.

'It would be so cool to see the future! Has Emily ever made any other big predictions? Do you think she's at the lake now? Do you think she texted anybody else?'

'I hope she texted other people, and I hope they've all made it to the lake. I'm the one who lives farthest from camp, so we'll probably be the last to arrive. Usually her gift only lets her see a few minutes ahead, but once in a while she can see the outcome of smaller stuff, like once she told me that the wind was going to knock a tree over in the night, and then it did. Once she told me that my friend Josh and I would never...'

I stopped myself, feeling like I had said too much and feeling annoyed by this particular prediction. I tried to think of a change of subject before Andy noticed my discomfort.

'Never...' repeated Andy, extending the last syllable while grinning a mischievous grin and looking closely at my face. 'Hmmm... I've never seen someone's colors change so fast, Gracie. Interesting...'

'You mean I'm not silver anymore?' I asked, knowing I'd probably regret playing along.

'Haha! I meant your face! You're blushing like crazy!' Andy collapsed on the ground in a fit of giggles.

I tried to swat his arm, but missed. He must have had a lot of practice dodging Olivia after teasing her.

I strapped the tent to my backpack, and then it was time to help Andy climb up onto Patience's back again.

He was still laughing on the ground, so I told him, in my most serious voice, that he had five seconds to get moving or he was going to have to walk.

He jumped up, still grinning, and I helped him climb up. I handed him his bag, and he put it on, then I handed him mine. I swung my leg over the saddle with some difficulty – my muscles were stiff and sore from our ride yesterday, but I managed to settle into place behind Andy. I took my backpack back from Andy, and as I was putting it on, he turned toward me a little and said, in a very small and worried voice, 'You're not mad at me are you, Gracie?'

I felt my annoyance slip away.

'Because I was just *josh*in' ya!' And he slumped forward, giggling so hard that I couldn't help but laugh, though I couldn't suppress a huge eye-roll at the same time.

After a while, Andy stopped laughing at his own jokes and asked me to tell him more about where we were headed.

It was a nice way to pass the time, talking about my favorite place and my favorite people; there were so few people who could appreciate what it all meant to me.

I told Andy about Eric and Audrey, and how they would seek out the families who needed them most. I told him about how our camp had started out and about Josh's ability, which Andy found very shocking.

'I'm extra glad I only see people's colors. It would be awful to live in a horror movie like that.'

Andy really liked hearing about the activities we would do at camp, the normal stuff, like swimming and fishing.

There were several fishing rods at the cabin, tucked away behind the canoes and kayaks in the little boat shed Eric and Audrey had built. When we had fished during camp, it was always catch-and-release, but now I was glad to have a food source we could count on. I still wasn't sure if I'd ever be able to kill an animal like a rabbit or a deer, but maybe I just hadn't been hungry enough to consider it yet. Maybe the difference with fish is the lack of cute fluffy fur and that their bodies are already cold. I have never killed a fish before though, I don't know how it'll go when I'm finally face to face with one. It's weird, that I've eaten meat my whole life, but I've never had to do the actual killing. Add that to the list of things I took for granted before the Darkness descended.

Before my mind could wander down even darker paths, I forced myself to tune back into the conversation with Andy. He was chatting about taking swimming lessons at the pool near his house.

'I'm pretty good at diving now too; I was always worried I wouldn't be able to hold my breath for long enough, but I got the hang of it. I used to have dreams where I'd be swimming underwater, then I'd start drowning, but right before I died I would realize that I could breathe underwater! I'll show you how I can swim when we get to the lake, is it deep enough for diving?'

'There is a dock that we would dive from. There's also a big tree on the edge of the beach with a long rope that you can swing on out over the water, and then let go and drop into the lake. I think you'll love it.'

I wondered to myself if it would still be warm enough to swim in the lake once we got there. The hot weather I'd experienced when I had first left the city had not returned, and it crossed my mind that it could be later in the year than I had thought. There was a crisp freshness to the morning air that suggested summer was giving way to autumn, and that meant we were running out of time to travel before the first snow fell. I nudged Patience to get her walking a little faster. I couldn't wait to be farther west, when the grassy plains would give way to forests and mountains. At least we'd have some cover there, better places to hide. I was extremely grateful to be moving faster than we would on foot, but I still felt so exposed and couldn't help but look over my shoulder every so often, to make sure we really were alone.

I asked Andy about his parents – I had been wondering why he hadn't asked if we could try to find them before going west.

'They were in England visiting my grandparents,' he told me, 'me and Olivia were supposed to pick them up from the airport, but I guess the power went out a few days before they were supposed to come home...'

Andy fell silent. I focused my mind on the Voices, urging them to give me any information they had about Andy's parents.

It was Olivia who responded.

'They're alive... The whole world is Dark... But they're alive...'

I told Andy what I had heard, and I could see the tension leave his little shoulders as he relaxed.

'I still might never see them again, right?' He asked.

'There's always hope, Andy, but they would have a very long way to travel without power of any kind.'

I decided to share my own hope with him, however silly it might seem. 'You never know, the power could come back on and I think the world could go back to normal pretty quickly if that happens.'

I realized in that moment that I didn't really believe the world could ever go back to normal, not my world anyway, not after everything I had seen. But Andy hadn't witnessed anything too horrible yet, there was still hope for him, and I wasn't going to be the one to take that away from him.

***

As the days passed, Andy and I settled into a routine of eating, traveling and sleeping. The more I got to know of Andy, the more I liked him. His jokes and stories kept us both cheerful, which surprised me because I couldn't help but dwell on darker things when silence fell. I wondered if he could sense the direction my thoughts were taking during the longer stretches of silence, because he would suddenly come out with a silly anecdote that would get us both laughing and chatting. The instances of silence between us became fewer and fewer, until I found that my voice was hoarse by the end of the day, from answering his endless questions and laughing at his silly jokes. I had never come across someone so witty and so young.

He was very curious about Emily and her father's gifts and asked question after question about the predictions they had made. I told him about Emily's dad knowing that there were going to be huge catastrophic changes coming to the world, and the preparations he had made.

'There's a small percentage of the population who are preppers, they have everything they need to make it for quite a while, like stores of water, food and survival gear.'

'My sister's boyfriend was one too – he loved wearing bowties and loafers with no socks...' Andy turned and looked up at me with a glint in his eye, waiting for his joke to sink in.

I cracked up. 'Not preppy... prepp*er*!'

Andy looked very pleased with himself, and turned around to face the front again.

'Although...' I said, 'I've only met him a couple of times – he could be a preppy prepper, and have a huge hoard of bowties!'

Just as Andy giggled, Patience let out a loud snort as though she was responding to my bad joke, which made us both laugh even harder.

When we stopped for lunch, I told Andy about the shelter that Emily's dad had made for them. I wondered if they had actually hunkered down into the underground bunker he had built, or if they really were on their way to the lake, as Emily had suggested.

'Maybe they hid in there at first,' said Andy, as he opened a can of beans for us to share, 'but maybe knowing that they could survive and make a better life at the lake, they decided to try to get there? Like us at the house – we could have stayed there for a while if it hadn't been so scary and if the Poo People hadn't come, but we would have run out of food and water and then we would have wanted to leave anyway. I hope they will be at the lake, I have a lot of questions for them!'

I smiled to myself, imagining how that conversation would go, and hoping that Andy would get all of his questions answered.

After a brief silence during which we finished our beans and climbed back up onto Patience's back, Andy asked me about the prediction that Emily had made about Josh and I.

I clicked my tongue to get Patience moving again. 'It doesn't really matter, it was a while ago, and...' I let out a long sigh.

'If it doesn't matter, maybe you should just go ahead and tell me, who am I going to tell? And I promise I won't tease you about it again, and I don't think Patience is a huge gossip either, though I still haven't decided about her...'

Patience let out another well-timed snort and we both cracked up.

'Alright, fine. I guess I could give you a little more background about my friend Josh before I tell you the prediction, just so you have the whole story. If you laugh at me or if I even feel like you're trying not to roll your eyes, I'm going to stop answering any of your questions, and I mean that forever. *Forever*. Got it?'

'Absolutely, boss! Let's hear it!'

'Well, I already told you about Josh's abilities, and how the camp was created because of him. He is two years older than me, and camp had been going on for a few years before I started going. I met him on my first day, he was ten and I was eight, he was one of the first people who came to talk to me, and I was so scared and shy, but he made me feel like I had known him for years. From that day on we were pretty much inseparable. He told me about his visions and I told him about my Voices, and we helped each other a lot through some very tough times.

'I had never known someone who understood me so completely before, and it was so nice to have a friend I could really trust. He made me feel safe and normal in a world that I didn't believe I really fit into. We talked almost every day when we weren't at camp, and he's the one I looked forward to seeing most when camp resumed.

'My third year at camp was the year Emily joined. She and Josh and I clicked right away and the three of us spent almost all of our free time together.

'I was still a kid and I didn't care about boys in a romantic way or anything, until I was about thirteen, and at that time I just figured I'd end up with Josh because we liked each other so much and were best friends already. I had never considered anybody else because there was nobody else like him.

'It was in my seventh year at camp – I was fifteen – when Emily made the prediction. We had just finished our classes for the night, and we were walking back to the cabin like we always did, when Josh handed me a fluffy white dandelion and told me to make a wish. I blew the seeds away and Josh asked me what I had wished for. I was so embarrassed.'

I paused, feeling the blood rushing into my face again, just as it had that night so many years ago.

'What did you wish for?' asked Andy innocently, with a hint of a laugh in his voice. 'That Josh would kiss you? Or ask you on a date? Or tell you he loved you?'

Once again I could see that Andy had gained a lot of experience in teasing in his short years, and I felt sympathy for what Olivia must have endured.

'Not even anything that small,' I said, feeling my face growing even more red. 'That night I was feeling super happy and peaceful and the silly vision had just popped into my head of me in a white dress and Josh across from me in a tuxedo. So I wished for him to ask me to marry him. Not right away of course, I was fifteen and in high school, but I was just feeling silly and so I made the wish.

'Anyway, when he asked what I had wished for, I told him I couldn't tell, because it wouldn't come true. He kept asking, but I refused to tell, and so he grabbed the dandelion stem and gave it to Michael, our friend who can get information out of objects through touch, and asked him what I had wished for.'

'Oooh that was a sneaky plan,' interjected Andy excitedly, 'could Michael read your wish from the dandelion?'

'Michael looked from me to Josh and I'm sure he knew what I had wished for, but I shook my head at him, hoping he wouldn't tell everyone and embarrass me even more. He was so kind, and was probably used to being teased himself, so he just grinned and said, "She wished for world peace."'

'Wow, that was nice if Michael, I wonder if he ever told Josh what you had really wished for, or if Josh asked him later and Michael gave him hints. I bet Josh did love you and wanted to marry you, he'd be pretty dumb not to.'

I looked at Andy and grinned. 'Thanks!' I said to him, feeling touched. 'But that's the thing... Later that night when we were about to go to sleep, Emily asked me what I had wished for, and I told her that I wished Josh would ask me out – I didn't tell her the whole truth because I was still feeling so embarrassed. She was quiet for a second, and I assumed it was because she was having a vision of the future, and then she actually laughed at me and said it would never happen.' I sighed, remembering the sadness that had followed Emily's words, and the hurt caused by her callous laugh at my expense – I hadn't expected it from her.

Andy finally spoke, derailing my depressing train of thought. 'But you said that Emily only gets glimpses of the future, minutes before things happen, right?'

'That's how it usually works for her,' I answered, 'I just figured she had caught a glimpse into my future or Josh's future and saw us each dating someone else, or in my case, probably ending up alone...'

'Gracie, that's absurd. You won't end up alone. Even with half the world's population dead, I know you won't be alone. I think Emily was just feeling mean or jealous or something, so she made up a prediction because she knew you'd believe her.'

'But why would she do that, when we had been friends for years? Why would she hurt my feelings like that, knowing how much I'd been hurt in the past by people who were supposed to stick by me?'

Andy thought for a moment, and then spoke, a trace of anger in his voice. 'Maybe she liked Josh too, and wanted you to back off because she could see how much Josh liked you back. She sounds pretty jealous to me, laughing at you like that when you had just told her a secret. Maybe she even had a vision of you two together and she lied about it because she didn't want it to happen, and she thought that telling you it wouldn't happen would make it not happen! She sounds bitter to me, and I bet if I saw her colors, they would have a hint of poo to them.'

I considered his words, but before I could really start to dissect Emily's actions, Andy had another bunch of questions for me.

'What happened after that night? Were you and Emily still friends? Did Josh act differently, like maybe Michael had told him the truth? How did you act around Josh? That all happened a few years ago, so how have things been since then?'

'We are all just friends,' I answered him. 'Josh asked a few times why I seemed sad, and there was definitely a bit of tension between me and Emily for a while, but I got over it and we're all friends.'

I paused, thinking that our little romantic drama seemed so trivial to me now, with the world in its current state.

'None of it matters anyway, because like you said, half the world is dead. I don't even know if he survived, and if he did, I don't know if he'll make it to camp or not. I'm just going to keep my mind focused on our survival and getting us where we need to go.'

Andy seemed to sense that I was trying to end the conversation.

'Alrighty, Gracie,' he said, I won't bring it up again – except I have to say that if he were dead, Josh would come talk to you. There's no way he wouldn't.'

This thought gave me a small amount of comfort, and something made me feel certain that Andy's statement was true.

'Oh, also,' piped up Andy, I think Emily is full of sh-'

'Hey!' I said, laughing, 'just because half the world is dead it doesn't mean your vocabulary has to die a slow death too!'

'Well I was going to say she's full of shenanigans, before you rudely interrupted me. Just because half the world is dead it doesn't mean you can't keep good manners alive...' He looked up at me, grinning.

***

As we continued our journey west, I began to see subtle changes in the terrain that indicated just how far we had come. The flat expanse of the grasslands had given way to gently rolling hills, and though there was no sign yet of mountains on the horizon, I knew that it was only a matter of time until they appeared. I couldn't help but squint into the distance every now and then, sure that I was seeing a deep blue peak emerging into view, only to have my hopes dashed when the clouds rolled in and my lovely mountains turned out to be a thunderstorm.

There were no hints of us being followed by the Poo People, and in time I started to relax and found myself looking over my shoulder less and less, though they were never far from my mind – the shallow wound on my arm had healed over quickly, but the itch of the scab was like a constant reminder to not allow myself to become too complacent. I wasn't completely sure how I knew, but I could feel it in my bones that they were coming for me.

The weather was still warm during the day, though the nights were starting to get pretty chilly. I was grateful every night when we tucked ourselves into our blankets and zipped the tent tightly against the cool air.

Once in a while it would hit me how different my journey would have been without Andy. I remembered the sad, sick girl who had fallen asleep in the grass, wishing on stars, and I would snuggle in a little closer to Andy's sleeping form.

Almost every day, usually in a light, joking way, he would thank me for keeping him alive.

But it was he who was helping me to survive.

It made a world of difference to have someone else to look out for. My attitude, which without him would have been grim, was actually optimistic. I barely thought about my own problems because I was so focused on what needed to be done to help him survive.

I was starting to feel whole again. When I imagined what my heart would have looked like right after losing my mom, there wasn't much left to see – just the absolute minimum necessary to keep beating. Now that I had Andy in my life, I imagined little gnarled twigs growing from the remaining part, forming a twisted but solid foundation, which would never replace what I had lost, but at least reminded me that I could do more than just survive – I could live.

It was Andy who spotted the mountains when they finally appeared on the horizon. He had been pointing out the different species of trees around us, when he looked ahead.

'Uh-oh, Gracie, looks like a pretty big storm on the way...'

I looked ahead too and saw that this time, the storm clouds had beautiful, pointy white peaks with lazy little clouds floating around them. My mountains. Silently they had crept up on us, and now stood proud and majestic against the wide blue sky.

I could barely contain my excitement; we had been traveling for weeks and finally, I was seeing something I had been hoping for with every fiber of my being. Now that I could actually see them, I didn't understand how I could ever have mistaken them for mere clouds.

'We are so close, Andy! We just have to get over those mountains and back down toward the coast a little bit, and we'll find our camp! We just have to stay on the highway! When we see three pine trees growing from one root sticking out of the side of the mountain, we just take the next right turn, and we're there!'

Andy turned in the saddle and looked up at me.

'How do we get over the mountains? I have never climbed anything taller than the climbing frame at the park, I don't know how to mountain climb! What will we do with Patience? She can't climb...'

'Hey, it's okay! We don't actually have to climb anything! The highway cuts right through the mountains. There are a few tunnels we'll have to go through, but mostly it's like any other road.'

'Okay, that sounds better – I wonder if we'll see any wildlife when we're up there, I bet there'll be lots!'

We had seen a few deer in the last few weeks, and a couple of rabbits, and Andy had a great eye for spotting birds and squirrels, but so far we had not seen any major predators. I was grateful, we really didn't have a way to protect ourselves if we needed to, and though we were both a lot thinner than we used to be, we'd still make a pretty decent meal for anything willing to hunt us.

The idea of being hunted brought the Poo People back to mind, though I seriously doubted they would have resorted to cannibalism... Or would they? They had been collecting people... I had just assumed that they would be used as slaves of some sort. But they definitely seemed like the types who would snack on someone once they were no longer useful...

I shuddered and tried to direct my thoughts down a less gruesome path.

'We might see some bigger wildlife once we are in the mountains – I know that at the summit there is a trail you can hike that has a lot of warnings about being in bear territory. Bears are supposed to be afraid of people though, so if we just make a lot of noise we should scare them away.'

I wondered how much I should tell Andy about what we might see. The thing I was most afraid of coming face-to-face with had to be a mountain lion. A few years ago when I was in the car with my mom I had caught a glimpse of one as it crossed the highway in front of us. It was dark and we just saw it for a second as it dashed into the undergrowth, but I had seen enough. The agility, strength and speed were astonishing. Even in the quick sweep of the headlights as it leapt out of sight we had seen its incredible musculature rippling beneath its tawny fur. If there was one creature I really didn't want to tangle with, that was it. I couldn't imagine how a soft, slow human could ever escape such a perfect hunting machine.

As though he was reading my mind, Andy asked me what wildlife I had seen in the past.

I told him briefly about the mountain lion, and about how once we had seen a timber wolf.

'But there are fences all along the highway, and special bridges for the animals to cross, so it's not very likely we'll see too much. Plus, after being so afraid of traffic for so long, I bet the animals still avoid the highway.'

I tried to think of something to tell him about that might take his mind off of predators, because I didn't really know how to reassure him since I was pretty worried about it myself.

'There is a place along the highway where we will be able to see an eagle's nest up in the trees. I've only seen the eagle once, but you're so good at spotting everything, I bet we'll see it this time!'

This cheered Andy up instantly.

'Cool! I've only ever seen eagles in books!' And he was off, chatting about his favorite animals and leaving me with a feeling of relief to have avoided the topic of danger, at least for now.

***

During the weeks of travel so far, we had managed to skirt around the small towns because I was confident that we would find the highway again once we were safely past them. Now that the mountains were in view though, I knew we would have to pass through a major city, and the only route I was sure of was directly through the heart of it.

I tried to put a positive spin on it for Andy, saying that we could have a quick look for supplies on our way through, but deep down I was terrified that we would come across horrors similar to those that I had left behind.

It was after another day and a half of riding that the familiar cityscape came into view, and though there were no longer pillars of smoke rising from the skyline, I could clearly see that many of the skyscrapers were blackened or simply gone.

As we got closer to the city limits, we passed a group of tents that were bordered by chicken wire and military vehicles. I guessed it had once been a refugee camp, but it looked completely deserted. Andy asked if I thought we should check it out for supplies, but something held me back. We had enough food to last a while longer, and we had been lucky with water too, because it had been so rainy lately.

Still, I wanted to make sure we weren't passing by a hoard of supplies, so I directed Patience toward the gate and jumped down. I walked a few steps along the fence, so I could get a better view of the inner area. A breeze swept toward me, bringing with it the horrible smell I had encountered at Olivia's car. As I took a few more steps, trying my best not to throw up or pass out, a vast pile of bulging, long black body bags came into view. There were too many to count, all heaped unceremoniously in a ghastly pile. I turned away and staggered back to Andy and Patience.

'There's nothing here for us. Everything is gone.'

'But maybe in the middle of the camp there'll be-'

'There's nothing, Andy, trust me,' I interrupted, desperate to get away from that overwhelming pile of death.

'Did a Voice tell you?' asked Andy curiously.

'Something like that,' I replied abruptly, still trying to keep my lunch firmly in my stomach.

I climbed back onto Patience and directed her back toward the highway, remembering the girl whose father had been murdered by the monsters. I had directed the girl, her mother and her little brother to the refugee camp that had been set up outside of our city. My neighbors, teachers, and classmates had all headed there. I had even drawn a map so Debbie's crazy sister could find her way there. How many of them had ended up in one of those awful black plastic bags? It was my fault if several of them had. I had sent them to their deaths. I should have at least told the girl and her family to come with me instead. I felt the hot tears roll down my face before I realized I was crying. Debbie's Voice whispered quietly.

'Not your fault Gracie... You tried to help her... We are together now...'

A sob escaped me and Andy turned around, his big blue eyes full of concern.

'What's the matter, Gracie? What did you see? You can tell me, I won't be scared, I promise.'

I sighed, wiping the tears off my face with my sleeve. Andy was so young, but he had proved that he could help before, so I decided to trust that he could handle this, too.

'Sometimes I just get so tired of being the one who survived, Andy, it's really hard to hear the Voices sometimes, and wonder if I could have saved anybody if I had just done something different. There were a lot of people who didn't survive at that refugee camp just now, and a lot of people I know were heading for the refugee camp back home, too. I'm starting to wonder if you and I and the Poo People are the only ones left. Sometimes I feel like we'll get to camp, but none of my friends will have made it, and I really, really don't want to start hearing their Voices...'

I could tell that Andy didn't know what to say, so I suggested we ride for a while longer, but try to get some sleep before we entered the city.

He agreed, and we rode in silence until we found a nice little sheltered area under a group of trees. We pitched our tent and settled down to eat.

'Just so you know Andy, I didn't mean that I wish I wasn't alive, just that I wish I could un-see some of the things I've seen, and that I didn't have to hear the Voices constantly. Sometimes it's hard to feel optimistic because I have a constant reminder of death. But the time since I met you has been great, even when things have been a bit scary.'

'I know you don't wish you were dead, Gracie, I can tell by how hard you've been working to get us to the lake. I just wish I could do something to help you with the Voices; it would be so hard to go around hearing ghosts all the time. I've wondered myself a couple of times how many people there could possibly be left in the world, all the food is running out, and most people weren't really prepared for what happened.'

He paused for a minute, chewing his creamed corn thoughtfully.

'I bet your friends would have talked to you already, if any of them had died. They love you; I don't think they'd leave you hanging. I sure wouldn't.' He chuckled quietly. 'I'm going to be telling you jokes until the day I die, and after that, too!'

'Oh boy,' I laughed, 'my mind will never be quiet then!'

'Nope, and I'll try to make you laugh at the most inappropriate times too, especially when you're not expecting it! People will think you're loony, walking around laughing to yourself!'

'Too bad for you, people already think I'm loony!' I laughed, feeling a lot better about everything. Andy had helped me to see the light in the darkness once again.

Chapter Six

The next morning we packed up our gear and got ready to make our way into the city. I figured it would only take a few hours to reach the other side, if we didn't dawdle too much looking for supplies. We decided we'd only search the stores and areas directly on the road we were on – I didn't want to lose our way by straying too far off course. I was excited to get to the other side of the city; it would mean that we'd head straight into the mountains after that.

The trek into the city took very little time; suddenly we were surrounded on all sides by tall buildings and burnt-out cars. After spending so many weeks under a big open sky, the buildings looming around us had an oppressive feeling and made me feel claustrophobic. We had even lost sight of the mountains. The only sound we could hear was the steady clopping of Patience's hooves, and just the faintest hint of smoke met our nostrils – if there were still fires burning they were not nearby. It felt a lot like being back where I had started, and I had to keep reminding myself that the mountains were waiting for us on the other side.

We realized pretty quickly that the supplies we had hoped to find were in fact non-existent. The broken windows of the stores we passed gaped like the open mouths of starving creatures, black and hollow and forbidding.

I did spy a crowbar in the backseat of one of the burnt cars, and I grabbed it through the smashed window, thinking again of the predators we might meet once we reached the mountains. I wished we had a better weapon, but a crowbar was better than nothing.

I think Andy was pretty shocked to see the city's advanced state of ruin, but he didn't say anything. He asked if we could stop and check out a toy store that we came across. I didn't really want to; I didn't feel as though anything in a toy store could help us survive, and since we had entered the city I had been feeling like we were being watched by unseen eyes.

But Andy didn't ask for much, so I agreed, on the condition that we were super fast about it.

I wasn't going to let Andy wander in to an unknown space by himself, so I told him to sit tight while I did a sweep of the store to check for anyone who might be hiding in there. I told him that if anything happened, and I got ambushed, that he should make a run for it.

Climbing carefully off Patience, I gripped my sooty crowbar in my sweaty hands. I approached the door of the toy store carefully, keeping my eyes peeled for any sudden movement.

I ducked under the broken shards of glass still hanging from the top of the doorframe, and gave my eyes a minute to adjust to the dimness inside.

I advanced a few steps into the wreckage and could see right away that there were very few places to hide. There was one shelf that had been tipped into its side, but the gap underneath was empty. Next I crept toward the till; it stood on a waist-high divider wall and would make excellent cover, but there was no one crouching behind there, either.

There were a few stuffed animals that had been torn from their display cases and trampled under dirty shoes, and a couple other random toys scattered across the floor. Nothing looked useful to me, but I figured Andy could take a look for himself and see if he wanted anything.

I made my way back to Andy and Patience, and helped Andy climb down.

'I'm going to tie Patience to the doorframe, and I'll come inside with you, just give me a sec...'

Once she was secure, I led Andy inside the store, and stood in the middle, where I could keep an eye on him, without losing sight of our horse.

Andy looked around, kicking at the debris on the floor with a disappointed sigh.

'There's nothing here, Gracie, this was a waste of – hey! Come look at this!'

I walked around the toppled shelf and found him squatting in the dust, holding a travel board game, which must have been knocked under the shelf during the looting.

'It's perfect for us! All we do is travel!'

He tucked the game into his bag and swung it back onto his back, beaming up at me.

'*...No...*' Whimpered a Voice desperately in my head.

Suddenly Patience let out a panicked whinny, and we both turned and ran back toward the doorway of the ruined store.

A person, a filthy, emaciated, soot-covered person was trying to gnaw a bite out of Patience's shoulder. Their hands, like burnt claws, were gripping onto the saddle, trying to get leverage for a better mouthful.

Horrified, I swung my crowbar and connected with the fingers clutching the saddle. The person released Patience with a shriek of pain, and collapsed, clutching their broken fingers between their skeletal knees. The person looked up at me, streaks painted down their face where tears had washed the soot away. Their sunken blue eyes shone through matted brown hair, and for a moment, I felt like I could have been looking into my own eyes – she was me; this was some strange parallel universe in which I hadn't escaped the city.

'I'm sorry...' I whispered to the wasted wraith of a girl, 'I'm so sorry...' I reached out toward her, wanting to comfort her somehow, but she mistook my helping hand as an attack. Her eyes turned wild and she swatted my hand away. I thought she was going to lunge at me, so I raised the crowbar again, but she was just trying to struggle to her feet. She limped away from us as quickly as she could, still cradling her damaged hand to her chest. When she reached the doorway of a burnt out computer store, she disappeared inside. Something caught my eye in the second storey of the building, and I could just make out the silhouette of another person, watching us from behind the frayed curtains of a broken window.

The sound of a glass bottle rattling against the pavement in the distance brought me back to my senses.

'We gotta go, Andy, now!'

In his panic and fear Andy had somehow managed to climb back onto Patience by himself, and he sat huddled and shaking, unable to speak.

I checked the horse's shoulder, but there didn't seem to be any damage; we had stopped the girl just in time.

With trembling fingers I untied Patience, and for the first time I felt truly grateful that my backpack was so light these days – I was able to haul myself up without taking it off.

As soon as I was seated, Patience broke into a trot – she was as desperate to leave the scene as we were. I looked back over my shoulder to make sure we weren't being followed, but the girl was nowhere in sight. As we passed by the doorway of an apartment building, I could just make out a human form huddled on the floor inside. Whether they were dead or alive I could not tell, and I urged Patience forward, hoping that we would make it out of the city without meeting anyone else.

I had no idea how anyone could have survived for so long in the city – maybe they were catching the rainfall just like we were, and maybe they had stocked enough food to last this long. Maybe, I thought, as I watched a rat scurry out of an alley and into a burnt-out sandwich bar, they were hunting and eating what they could find in the streets. People had had pets before the Darkness – what had happened to everyone's dogs and cats? I fought back the horrible image of the girl catching and eating smaller animals, the way she had tried to eat Patience. I had never seen desperation like that before, and I knew I would never forget it.

We rode for another hour or so, and as we reached the other side of the city, it hit me that I should have given the girl some food. We didn't have much left, but right now, she needed it more than we did. I could have just left her something on the ground, and she would have come to get it. Instead I had broken her fingers, probably her only hunting tool, and basically left her for dead.

Guilt overwhelmed me and I expressed my remorse to Andy.

'Are you kidding me, Grace?' He demanded, incredulous. 'She tried to *eat* Patience! Alive! She was trying to make a meal out of someone who has saved our lives a bunch of times, and who has carried us for miles and miles, and you feel bad for *her*?'

'I know it sounds crazy, Andy, but she is still a person, in a desperate and miserable situation. We could have helped her a little. Instead we took off, and now I feel bad about it. She looked like me, I saw in her what desperation could potentially do to me, and it scares the living daylights out of me. We've never been as hungry as she is, we haven't been through what she is going through, and it makes me feel sad. I don't want to lose my humanity.'

'Gracie, I don't think you could ever lose your humanity,' said Andy, his voice still shaking slightly after the shock of what had happened. 'I've never met anyone like you, in all my eight-and-a-half years. And even if you were starving like that, I don't think you could just take a bite out of a living animal. You wouldn't want them to suffer like that, I know it. That girl wasn't like you to begin with, I could see it in her colors, and now that there are no rules, she has turned into a savage creature who doesn't care about anyone else at all.'

'You could see it in her colors?' I asked, hopeful that Andy was about to ease my feeling of terrible guilt.

'Yes, Gracie, her colors were so poopy that they almost blended in with the soot and dirt that her body was covered in. I see what people are made of – their deepest selves, not what a disaster turns them into. That girl would have killed Patience, and both of us, without blinking an eye. You can't save everybody, Grace, and I'm telling you, that girl was too far gone to begin with. She only left us alone because she was outnumbered.'

I contemplated what Andy had just told me, still feeling uneasy. I had encountered people who were less than kind before the Darkness, and who would now steal everything you had in order to save themselves; maybe that girl fell into that category. Maybe I needed to be a little more wary of who I was dealing with in the future, and keep in mind that people were in survival-at-all-costs mode. Just because that girl looked a little like me, didn't mean that she felt the way I did. Andy was right – I would never be able to torture a living creature like that, no matter what. I'd want to eat it, no doubt about that, but I'd try my best to end its life in the most humane way possible first.

I understood now how the girl had survived – by taking anything she could get from wherever she could get it. Even if it cost someone else dearly.

'I guess you'll just have to tell me everyone's colors from now on, Andy... It's funny – I went almost my whole life trusting very few people, trying to protect myself from anyone who would hurt me, and yet there I was, trying to help a girl who would have murdered me where I stood if she could have.'

But then I remembered the second figure I had seen in the upstairs window – maybe the girl had someone else to look after. Maybe she wasn't just trying to feed herself, but had someone else relying on her. I looked at the back of Andy's head, swaying back and forth with the motion of our horse, and wondered what lengths I would go to to try and keep him alive... But then I looked down at Patience's chestnut shoulder gleaming in the sun as she bore us ever closer to our destination. I couldn't even think about trying to take a bite out of her. I reached out and gave her a neck a gentle rub, whispering yet another thank you to her for once again saving our lives.

Andy patted her neck too. 'I'm sorry that you almost got eaten,' he murmured, 'I shouldn't have asked to check the toy store, it was stupid.'

I put my arm around Andy's skinny body and gave him a squeeze.

'It wasn't stupid, Andy, we were both hoping for something fun, and you found it!'

I unzipped his bag and found the travel board game. I looked at the box and saw that little magnets would hold all of the pieces in place on the board. I wasn't sure how it would go, trying to play a game while riding a horse, but I wanted to try to cheer him up. I gave the box a little shake so that the pieces rattled around noisily. 'Wanna play?'

***

We traveled until it was too dark to see the road, and then finally made camp. It was challenging to pitch the tent in the dark, but we had agreed to keep going for as long as we could, and to get ourselves as far as possible from the city – just in case we were followed. The strange sensation that I was being watched had not faded as we made our way closer to the mountains. I wondered if I had maybe picked up some new Voices during our brief time in the city, but nothing seemed out of the ordinary as far as what I was hearing. It was just a feeling...

'Want to light a fire tonight?' Andy asked me, as he tossed our bags into the tent.

'How about tomorrow night? I kind of just feel like going to sleep, and putting this strange day behind us.'

'Sure, I'm pretty tired too, I'm just feeling a little spooked out here.'

He hesitated for a moment, looking around, seeing nothing but darkness.

'I have this weird feeling that we aren't alone, you know?'

Surprised, I looked up, but Andy did not notice.

'Maybe it's just because we're so close to the mountains,' he continued. 'We've got a wall of mountains in one direction, and a city with a super creepy horse-munching weirdo in the other direction... Maybe I'm just feeling a little bit trapped.'

I decided to be honest with him. 'I feel it too. That we're being watched. I'm worried someone followed us out here.'

Unconsciously, it seemed, he took a few steps toward me, and continued to look into the blackness that surrounded us.

'How about I keep watch tonight, and make sure we aren't ambushed while we sleep.' I said, feeling certain that I would only toss and turn anyway. 'I'll be able to keep an eye on Patience that way, too.'

He looked over to where Patience was tethered to a tall pine tree. 'Okay, but wake me up in a bit and I'll take over, you need to get some sleep, too.'

We shared a can of cold chili, and then Andy snuggled down into the tent.

I zipped him in, and tried to find a good place to watch from. I pulled the tarp and my blanket out of my backpack. I spread the tarp out on the ground to try to stop any dampness from seeping through, and then wrapped myself in my blanket. Sitting down, I leaned back against a tree stump and stared into the darkness, knowing that if we were attacked, visually I would only have about one second's notice. I tried to quiet the Voices so I could rely on my hearing instead, but knew instantly that it was pointless – the chorus in my head was as loud as ever, and would probably drown out the tell-tale noises of an approach.

I had been excited to gain the cover of the forest, knowing that there were places to shelter and hide, but I had only been thinking about how it would benefit us. Now I realized that we were as exposed as we had been on the grassy plains – though we had lost the benefit of seeing for miles around us. Every tree was a hiding place for a hunter, be it human or animal.

I tried to shake off my increasing paranoia. I touched the crowbar which lay reassuringly beside me, and I took my knife out of its sheath, gripping it tightly in my hand. I would have a fighting chance if something or someone jumped out at me. I decided I needed to change my mentality. Become the hunter instead of the hunted.

I squinted into the darkness, imagining how I would react if someone jumped out of the trees. I pictured myself knocking them out with the crowbar and tying them up with the spare shoelaces in my backpack. They would be at my mercy, and I would be brave and unstoppable...

Suddenly I felt hot breath on the back of my neck. I clutched my weapons, my heart pounding out of my chest. I twisted around, ready to strike at whatever enemy had snuck up behind me. It was Patience. She had wandered over to keep me company, but now looked down at me as though she was quite offended by my greeting. I couldn't blame her, after all she had been through today.

'I'm sorry, girl,' I whispered, standing up to stroke her nose, 'I'm just a little jumpy tonight; it's been a long day.'

She nudged my shoulder as though she understood. Whether she did or not, it was nice to have someone to talk to while I waited for my heart rate to return to normal.

'Tomorrow we'll head right into the mountains; I hope the roads aren't too bad for you. I'm not sure what will happen if we come across deep snow – but I guess there's no point in worrying about something that we might not even have to deal with, right?'

'We could always fashion snowshoes out of twigs for her,' said a quiet voice behind me, making me jump all over again. Andy's amused voice was coming from inside the tent. 'Can you picture that? Patience trying to walk in snowshoes?' Giggling, Andy unzipped the tent and stuck his head out.

I laughed; it really was a funny image. 'Sorry for waking you, go back to sleep, it's not your turn to take watch yet.'

'I haven't slept yet, I'm still too jumpy from what happened today – do you want to try to sleep?'

'Nah, I'm wide awake too. Why don't we start a fire after all and play some more of our new game? I decided that we don't need to be afraid if someone is following us, I'm ready to fight them off with my fancy new crowbar and my dad's old knife.' I did a couple of exaggerated slow-motion martial arts moves, and Andy started giggling again.

We had a slow-motion brawl there in the dark, and ended up gathering wood and starting a fire in slow-motion too. By the time we were huddled next to the fire, we were both in pretty high spirits again. We played our new game for a while, and then Andy started yawning.

'You may as well sleep too, Gracie, it's so late already.'

He snuggled up to me and finally fell asleep. I pulled my book out of my bag and chose a random place to start reading from. I had read it so many times it didn't matter where I began, I practically knew it by heart already. The small black text and familiar phrases worked like a lullaby – before I had even finished a page, I was asleep.

In the morning I awoke, stiff and cold but surprisingly well rested. I was shocked that I had slept so soundly, considering my certainty that we were being followed. Yesterday's events must have taken more of a toll on me than I'd thought. The fire was nothing more than a couple of glowing embers; I looked around, trying to see if there had been any disturbances, or if anything was missing, but everything was as we had left it.

I felt excited to get on the road; I wondered how far into the mountains we would get today.

Andy stirred sleepily next to me, and asked, his voice muffled in the blanket, when the bacon would be ready.

I laughed and extricated myself from our makeshift bed, picking up my dew-dampened book as I rose. I noticed that the cellophane from the board game package was on the ground – it must have fallen out when we pulled the game itself out of Andy's bag. As I bent down to pick it up, I noticed that it was covered in dew drops, and some dew had even pooled in areas. I got down and slurped the sweet water noisily out of the plastic, thinking that if we weren't able to catch enough rain, this might be a way to keep ourselves hydrated. As I was imagining a permanent dew-catching system that we could rig up at camp, Andy's voice broke the morning silence once again. This time, however, there was no trace of humor in his words. He sounded shocked and scared.

'Gracie... Look at this.'

I turned around to see him staring down at our unfinished game from last night. Thinking maybe there was a weird bug or something on the board, I approached and looked at it too.

There was no bug. I felt my mouth drop open in shock and my heart started pounding again. The little lettered tiles were no longer criss-crossed with words we had spelled out last night. They had been rearranged in straight lines on the board to create the message:

YOU SHOULD BE MORE CAREFUL

I snapped my mouth closed and lunged for my weapons, glad that I had practically slept on top of them so they weren't stolen, or worse yet, used to murder us in our sleep. My eyes darted in all directions, trying to catch a glimpse of the creep who had violated our camp so easily. A twig snapped behind me and I spun around, ready to strike. It was Patience. She shook her mane nervously, eyeing me with apprehension. Irritated, I mumbled a brief apology to Patience and asked Andy to start packing up our stuff. He jumped up and started throwing things randomly into our bags.

Gripping my weapons tightly, I started a sweep of the surrounding trees; the hairs on the back of my neck stood up as the sensation of being watched crept over me again.

I looked behind every tree within a short radius, and even checked the branches above me for signs of the creep. The foliage was too thick to see very far above me, and, feeling like getting out of the area was our best option, I made my way quickly back to our camp.

Andy was just finishing packing up our tent, so I untied Patience and led her over to Andy.

'You climb up, I'll pass everything up to you, let's get out of here.'

As Andy used the tree stump to climb onto Patience, I saw that he had left our board game on the ground next to the dying embers of our fire.

I understood why he wanted to leave it behind, but to me that felt like letting the creep win.

Feeling defiant, I gathered up all of the little magnetic tiles and put them in their bag along with the playing board. I zipped the game into my bag and returned to the embers, where I stomped out the last of their life – I wasn't going to be responsible for burning down the forest.

As I headed back over to Patience and climbed up, my eyes continued to sweep the area for any sign of the creep. I guided Patience back toward the highway. We had so far managed to avoid staying on the road, keeping to the trees for cover. Once we were in the mountains though, there would be no option but to travel down the main road – we would have sheer cliffs either side of us where the highway cut directly though the mountainside. Both lanes of traffic had shared the winding path, and I could remember very clearly my mother's white knuckles as she drove us though the pouring rain along an already treacherous path.

When we had put some distance between ourselves and last night's campsite, Andy finally spoke up.

'What was that all about, Gracie? Who wrote that message? Do you think it was a ghost?'

'No I don't think it was a ghost,' I said, without hesitation. 'It would take a ghost a lot of energy to write a message like that, and why would they bother when they could just speak directly to me? Plus, every Voice that has ever spoken to me has been more concerned with their loved ones than with trying to scare me. It didn't feel like a ghost to me, it felt like a person. A creepy person who I think is definitely following us.'

'But back at the house – the backpack spinning – that was to scare us, wasn't it? Maybe there are ghosts who just haven't tried to talk to you before, maybe they're the ghosts of Poo People, and they still aren't nice, even now that they're dead?'

'That's possible I guess, I just wish it wasn't. I wish I could go back to the time when all I was dealing with were messages from loved ones. Things were much less confusing then. Still, I feel like the message was from a living person, and until we know for sure, I think we should behave like we are being followed. I don't want to get sneaked up on again, that was just too creepy.'

'I know,' agreed Andy, 'it's super creepy that they were right there while we were sleeping. They must have been so quiet – that's what made me hope it was a ghost. I would have thought one of us would wake up if someone was moving around so close to us.'

'Yeah, that freaks me out too, I'm usually such a light sleeper, but I didn't hear a thing last night. What a creep to do that to us!' I said, my anger flaring up again.

'Total creep,' said Andy, 'but I guess the bright side is that the creep could have murdered us right there while we slept, but didn't! So maybe he doesn't actually want to hurt us?'

Before I could even reply, Andy voiced what I was thinking.

'But then why be such a creep... Why leave a message at all... Whoever it is seems pretty cracked to me, but I think they're right, too, we need to be more careful from now on.'

I urged Patience to go a little faster, hoping to widen the distance between ourselves and the creep. I wondered how he had managed to keep up with us so far – maybe he was riding a bike or something.

I was so preoccupied with worry about the creep that I didn't even notice we were fully into the mountains until Andy, pointing up, said, 'What's that?'

I looked up and saw netting made out of chicken wire attached to the cliff overhead. It draped all the way down to the ground beside the road, and at the foot of it, was a pile of loose boulders and rocks.

'It's there to catch any falling rocks so they don't roll into traffic.'

'Like an avalanche?' said Andy nervously, his voice a little higher than usual, 'well, I guess I'll keep my yodeling to a minimum then...'

I chuckled and remembered how that netting had made me feel uneasy the first time my mom and I drove through the mountains. I would imagine the whole mountainside rumbling down and squashing our car flat like a pancake. I didn't understand why certain areas had netting and some didn't. It had seemed to me that the whole mountain should have been curtained with chicken wire. Thankfully, I never saw so much as a pebble tumble down.

As the winding road turned a corner, we came across a small red car that had smashed into the guardrail along the drop-off side. The driver would have lost control of the vehicle, and hurtled straight into oncoming traffic full of other out-of-control vehicles.

I steered Patience over to the car and hopped down, telling Andy I was going to check it for supplies.

I peeked over the guardrail and could see a semi truck smashed against the trees lining the cliff. I couldn't imagine trying to drive a semi along these roads under normal conditions – the driver must have been terrified when he lost control, and then swerved as he tried to avoid the oncoming traffic.

Feeling Andy's eyes on my back, I turned my attention to the red car. There was no one inside – maybe the driver had survived and had managed to get help. I tried the passenger door and found it unlocked. There was nothing on the front seats but glass from the broken window. I checked the back seats and found them to be empty too. In the glove box I found a pen and a map of the area. I pulled them out, thinking they could come in handy, and was about to snap the glove box closed when I noticed something sticking out from under the passenger seat. Shocked, I stared at the small handgun, which was mostly hidden by the seat and the shadow cast by the dashboard.

'Gracie? What did you find?' asked Andy from his seat on Patience's back.

I couldn't answer – my mind was racing, trying to decide whether I should take it and tell Andy, take it and not tell Andy, or just leave it and forget about it.

As I stood there debating, Andy took the decision out of my hands. I heard him climb down, and the clopping of Patience's hooves as he led her over to me.

He leaned in next to me, and saw the gun.

'Is that real?' he asked, staring at the matte black metal. 'It's so small, it looks like a toy.'

'I'm pretty sure it's real,' I replied, still unsure of what we should do with it.

'I think we should take it,' Andy declared, and he reached out and was about to pick it up, when he turned to me, mirroring the uncertainty I felt. 'Right?'

'I don't know, Andy. I don't want to kill anyone, I don't want you to kill anyone, even a shot to the leg or something could be a death sentence if the wound can't be treated properly...'

'We could keep it to scare the creep away,' suggested Andy, 'not actually shoot him, but make sure he knows we have it. I would feel safer to have it with us. Plus, if he is following us, he'll check this car for supplies too, and then he'll find it, and maybe use it on us.'

'I'd feel safer if we had it too, I just don't want to be tempted to use it, or to accidentally shoot someone, including myself.'

'We could throw it off the cliff, and pretend we never saw it,' said Andy grinning, 'The image of you hopping around after accidentally shooting yourself in the foot just popped into my head, and it wasn't pretty.'

I nudged him in the ribs with my elbow, grinning too, and then sighed.

'Alright, we'll take it, but only use it if our lives absolutely depend on it.'

I hesitated for another moment, and then picked up the gun. It fit perfectly in the palm of my hand – I hadn't realized that guns could be so tiny.

'Is it loaded?' asked Andy.

'I have no idea,' I said, wishing I had paid better attention during TV shows and movies. I had seen the actors make the little bullet-holder slide out of the bottom of the gun a million times, but now I was at a loss.

'It would be funny if we spent all that time debating about an empty gun. Though I guess we could still wave it around like we mean business, and no one would know the difference.'

I looked the gun over carefully, making sure to keep my fingers away from the trigger. There was a little button on the side; I wasn't sure what it was for, but it seemed like a good place to start. At least I knew for sure that I wasn't going to shoot myself by pressing it.

'A few months ago we could have looked on the internet to find out what to do now, isn't that weird?' said Andy. 'We had all information about everything at our fingertips, and now we just have to cross our fingers and hope you don't end up shooting us both by accident.'

I looked up at him, half annoyed, half amused.

'You know what?' I said, straightening up and glaring into his eyes. 'Oops…'

And I threw the gun casually over the guardrail. We could hear it clatter all the way down the mountainside.

'What did you do that for?' demanded Andy, 'that could have protected us from the creep, and animals and anyone else who might want to hurt us!'

'Yeah, well, I'd never hear the end of it if I shot you, and I'm not really comfortable threatening people with a gun anyway. Don't you feel like that's crossing a line into Poo People territory?'

He thought for a moment and then said, 'I guess you're right, I don't want to become a murderer.'

'Well that's good to hear,' I said, 'there were no bullets in it anyway, so…'

'What? You checked?'

'Yep, around the time you were teasing me about potentially shooting us both by accident because we are no longer able to search for anything on the internet.'

'Ah…'

I giggled. 'Let's get back on the road, there's nothing else here.' I tucked the map and pen into my backpack and helped Andy climb back onto Patience. I was pretty hungry – we hadn't had any breakfast because we left our campsite so quickly, but we had wasted a lot of time at the red car, and I wanted to keep moving.

'Let's keep going for another hour or so, and then we'll stop for some food if you can wait that long to eat?' I asked Andy.

'I'm good for a bit, I just want to keep lots of space between us and whoever is following us,' he replied.

'Me, too,' I said, as I settled myself into position behind him.

***

As we continued along the road, we could see signs that animals were taking back their territory. Chicken wire fences had been erected all along the edges of the cliffs to keep wildlife from wandering into traffic, but here and there the fences sagged right down to the ground. I imagined it would have to be a pretty large animal to push over a fairly sturdy structure like that, but there was no sign of any creatures nearby at the moment, so I pushed the thought out of my mind.

We came across several more crashed cars, but none of them yielded anything useful, and we didn't linger near them for long. I was surprised by the number of semi trucks that had crashed over the side, though the road was so winding and narrow in places that there just wasn't anywhere else to go. Judging by the wreckage, I didn't see how any of the drivers could have survived, though I still listened carefully for any Voices trying to tell me otherwise.

We approached our first tunnel just as the sun disappeared behind the mountain tops – it would still be broad daylight on the other side, but in the shadow of the mountains, darkness descended early.

'Do you want to try to get through before we make camp, or stop, sleep right here, and tackle the tunnel when it's light again?' I asked Andy. 'They are pretty dark even during the day, and that was with headlights to see by – I wonder if we could make a torch or something...'

I looked around for a possible branch to use as a torch, and saw a tall pine leaning out over the ground by the guardrail.

'I think we should go for it right now,' said Andy, peering into the dark tunnel mouth. 'It's still pretty early and I don't feel tired, so it would feel like a waste of time to just sit here doing nothing.'

'I agree,' I said, and I slid off Patience, my eyes glued to the branch that I hoped would light our way.

I pulled my knife out of its sheath; it has a little serrated section on the blade, so I used that to start sawing through the branch. I wished I had thought of packing a saw, it would have been a lot faster and easier, but I was glad to at least have my knife.

Soon I was able to bend the branch back enough to make sure I could see an orangey-brown vein running through the wood – when Eric had taught us how to make a torch, he had emphasized how important this was. The orange part is the sap, and in pine trees it is very flammable. I could see a perfect circle of orange sap in the middle of my branch, and after a few more minutes of hard work, the branch finally parted company with its tree.

I removed any little twigs that stuck out of the branch, and then shaved off the rough bark at the sawn end, so just the smooth white inner bark was left.

I grabbed a rock from the side of the road and positioned my knife over the end of the branch. I used the rock to pound my knife into the end of the branch, splitting it a couple of inches deep, so that I had a decent crevasse. I made another crevasse across the first one, so that eventually I had a deep 'X' cut into the end of my branch. I picked up the bark that I had shaved off the branch, and crammed it down into the splits in the wood as tinder; the orange sap would act as fuel to keep the torch alight.

It was getting dark fast, so I pulled the box of matches out of my bag and struck one against the rough side of the box. I held the match to the end of my torch, and silently hoped that it would catch fire. The tinder did its job – the torch blazed with light. I extinguished the curled, blackened match, crushing it beneath my shoe to make sure it was completely out. Eric had told us that it would take a little time for the sap to really start burning, so I held the torch upside-down as he had shown us, to try to get the fire to spread to the branch itself, before the tinder burnt out.

When Eric had shown us how to do this, he had gathered us at the edge of the lake, saying that these torches were dangerous and that they could potentially burn a whole forest down – each tree would become its own torch, lighting the next, and the next, with all the pine sap fuelling the flame. He had even tossed a burning torch into the lake, so that we could see how long it took to go out – it floated, burning, for at least a whole minute before it finally sputtered and died.

'Nice one, Gracie!' said Andy admiringly as I flipped the torch upright again – I could see the flame had spread to the branch, and knew it would burn for at least half an hour.

'Thanks!' I said, feeling proud of my accomplishment, and grateful that it had worked. 'I'm going to walk ahead with the torch and pull you two along behind me,' I said, looping the rope around Patience's neck and gathering the ends in my hand. 'I'm not sure how long this tunnel will be; driving through it was always pretty quick though, so it shouldn't be too far on foot.'

'Let's do it!' said Andy enthusiastically. If he was scared he didn't sound like it, and I was encouraged by his eagerness.

We headed into the mouth of the tunnel slowly, unable to see more than a few feet in front of us. The sound of Patience's hooves connecting with the pavement echoed back at us from all sides, but it was a comforting sound, and kept the silence of the creepy darkness at bay.

After a few minutes of walking through the tunnel, a sickening and familiar smell met my nostrils that even the smoke from the torch couldn't mask.

Panicking, I squinted into the blackness ahead, trying to ascertain the source of the smell, while hoping that Andy wouldn't be able to see too much.

The torchlight glinted off something metallic a short way ahead, and slowly a pileup of cars came into view.

'Ugh! What is that?' Andy squeaked, plugging his nose. 'Smells terrible!' He paused, and then simply said, 'Oh.'

I guessed the cars had come into view, and he had realized why there was such a strong smell.

We started our passage through the cars, and I did my best not to look in the windows. Mostly I could only see myself and the torch reflected, but here and there I could make out someone's hair, bloody and matted and stuck to a window.

As the light from my torch swept over the cars, I could hear the scuttling of small creatures who had been disturbed by the glow. I tried not to picture them feasting on the remains, but the memory of Olivia's crash site swam unbidden before my eyes, this time complete with greedy rats.

I shook my head, trying to clear my mind of the gruesome image, and suddenly found myself past the end of the pileup. I had been so worried that we would find ourselves trapped by a wall of cars, and that Patience would not be able to get through the entire tunnel. This was our only path through the mountains, and had we found ourselves unable to navigate through the accident wreckage, I had no idea what we would do – Andy and I could easily climb over the pile of cars, but I could not imagine leaving Patience behind.

I wondered if someone had cleared the pathway through the cars – it would have been a tremendous task, clearing away tonnes of twisted metal in such an enclosed space, but it seemed much too convenient that in a sudden and horrifying multiple-car accident that every vehicle would come to rest in such an ideal position... Surely the tunnel would have been completely blocked by the haphazard pile of debris and bodies...

I held the torch low over the surface of the road, looking for any evidence of a disturbance.

There, among the shards of broken glass and plastic, a clean stripe of asphalt was discernible, as though something had been dragged, sweeping a clear path through the detritus. A glint of silver caught my eye, and when I raised my torch I could see several bumpers of all different colors leaning up against the tunnel wall, like a disturbing travesty of a rainbow.

Suddenly I felt like the stony tunnel walls were closing in on me.

I had led us into this dark and stifling tomb which held an unknown number of rotting corpses, and who knew what awaited us at the exit? The people who had cleared the tunnel path could be waiting for whoever tried to reach the other side. We could be ambushed or captured or murdered on the spot... I felt a sudden moment of regret for the rash decision I had made about the gun. But still, I knew I could never have used it against someone else – better to keep it out of everyone's hands instead.

'Gracie?' came Andy's high-pitched voice through the darkness. 'Did you just get super cold? I feel like the temperature just dropped and it could snow or something...'

I turned back toward Andy and my heart almost jumped out of my chest. Hundreds of silvery white figures were floating behind him, above him and beside him. They filled the tunnel with their soft echoing Voices, and as I turned to look toward the exit of the tunnel, I knew I would be surrounded too. Row upon row of figures with whispy white hair and limbs and faces... The faces... Each one staring at me with translucent eyes... Were they accusing me? Condemning me? Did they resent my heaving lungs and pounding heart? Had they come to take them, those most significant of vital signs, away from me? Would they advance, suffocating me, until my heart stilled and I was swallowed by the darkness that had extinguished their lives too? Did they have that power?

As I stood shaking, gasping, frozen with fear, the light from my torch flickered as though wind disturbed it, and then with a hiss and sputter it died. Trying desperately to damper my panic and control my breathing, I focused on the one thing that tied me to life: the rope attached to Patience and Andy. I clutched the rough fibers, willing touch to ground me, to override my other senses, which were threatening to overwhelm me.

Slowly I fumbled my way toward Andy and Patience. It seemed to take an eternity to get back to them. The noise of every step I took was drowned by the echoing chorus of Voices, and the bitter cold surrounding us sapped what little mental strength I had left. I could feel my eyes, wide in the dark, trying to distinguish any shape or movement that would signal my proximity to Andy, but the darkness was as unforgiving as the mountain walls that encased us. The floating figures cast no light – rather they seemed to absorb what little light there may have been, consuming all available energy from our surroundings, making the darkness around us more dense, more forbidding, more suffocating.

Chapter Seven

'Gracie?'

The sound Andy's voice reached me through the solid wall of darkness, and I took the last few steps quickly, stretching out a hand blindly. The comforting warmth of Patience's neck settled my nerves somewhat, and I was able to find Andy's leg dangling over the saddle.

'I'm here,' I said, patting his bony knee. He took my hand and spoke in a shaky whisper, his breath coming in gasps.

'We're not alone, are we?'

'No we're not... Can you see them?' I asked him, wondering if he was getting a sense of who we were dealing with, based on their colors.

'No, but I think I feel them... in the cold...'

I remembered something that Eric once told us, when we had asked why a visit from the dead often left us freezing.

'Eric says that the air goes cold because the dead use energy to communicate with us, or to show themselves. They draw the heat energy out of everything around them, and sometimes it even causes ice to form, because the amount of energy they need is so great.'

I knew there was more to it, that I wasn't doing a good job of explaining, but I could barely speak. It seemed to help calm Andy though, and he squeezed my hand, trying to give me courage.

'Maybe we should get out of this tunnel. I can come walk with you if you want – you don't have to lead us alone.'

I considered his offer. I knew that having him beside me would give me courage, but I wasn't sure what would happen once we reached the exit of the tunnel. I felt that he was safer sitting up there on Patience's back... or did it make him an easier target?

'You are worried about more than ghosts, right?' He asked, and before I could speak, he continued. 'We know we are being followed, that's a fact. Somebody obviously cleared this pathway through these cars, and they could be waiting at the other end, like maybe they claimed this area or something, right? And now, judging by your fear, and how I'm totally freezing, there are more dead people in here than just the ones who died in the cars, right? So we are surrounded on all sides, there is no guaranteed safe escape. So what do we do?'

Once again, before I could squeak even one syllable, Andy answered his own question.

'I think the best idea is to move forward, since we can't go back. The creep is waiting for us if we go back, but we don't know for sure what is at the end of the tunnel. I like our odds better if we go forward.'

He let go of my hand and slid down off the horse. Once he was standing beside me, he found my hand again, and gripped it tightly in both of his own. I jumped out of my skin when suddenly his high voice rang out through the dark.

'It was very rude to extinguish our torch, you know! All Gracie ever does is try to help you, and this is how you treat her? Can't you see she is scared, and tired, and doing her best? Let us through, and stop being so dramatic all the time!'

Andy's voice echoed back to us for a few seconds before the silence swallowed us once more.

'We can do this, Gracie,' Andy whispered, squeezing my hand again, 'we just have to be brave.'

I gave his hand a squeeze in return, and tried to ignore the white figures in my peripheral vision. I had become completely disoriented, so I leaned the dead torch against my leg, and using the rope around her neck as a guide once more, reached out for Patience, knowing that there wasn't enough room for her to have turned around. I felt her strong neck and knew which way to go.

One of Andy's hands released its grip, and I felt him pick up the torch.

'Just in case we can still use it once we get out of here,' he muttered grumpily – he seemed to have taken the ghosts' actions very personally.

I had avoided looking directly at the figures since they had first appeared, but I couldn't ignore them any longer. I looked up, dreading the sight of their eyes shining in the dark, and saw that they were as numerous as before, and that they still blocked our path.

I took a shaky step forward, gripping Andy's hand and Patience's rope so tightly that I could feel my pulse thumping through my fingers. With each step I took, the figures shifted slightly, not disturbing each other, but melding together, becoming brighter as they shared their space, like the crossed beams of two flashlights.

I realized that they were shifting together to make a path for us. I felt hugely relieved that we weren't going to have to walk straight through them, and I quickened my pace, pulling Andy and Patience along with me. I risked a quick glance over my shoulder and saw that once we passed through the clusters of figures, they shifted back into position, resealing the gateway behind us.

The increased volume of the Voices was starting to give me a headache, so I concentrated on the sound of Patience's hooves clopping along the pavement, wishing hard that we would reach the end of the tunnel very soon. If they were not there to scare me, why weren't the figures giving me clues or messages or some kind of guidance? They had all appeared at once, and they had all become louder at once, but there was no single distinct Voice among the noise.

I felt a sudden chill on my cheek and whipped my head around to see the figure of a woman withdrawing her translucent hand – she had touched my face the way my mother used to when she would pick me up from camp. After the weeks of being separated, my mom would always touch my cheek and stare at my face like she was seeing it for the first time, and she would tell me that she had missed me, and she would have tears in her eyes and then she would hug me so tight that my ribs would creak.

With a sob trapped in my throat, I stopped in my tracks, trying to make out her face, trying to see anything familiar in the indistinct misty figure that had materialized in this dismal tunnel. She vanished before I could get a good look at her. My heart pounded and my eyes welled with tears. The sob escaped my throat and I started walking again, desperate to get out of the dark and into the fresh air, where I would be able to think more clearly.

'Gracie?' Andy said again, with worry in his voice, 'What's going on? What happened?'

'My mom... She...' I raised my hand to my cheek, but all I felt there were the wet streaks left behind by my tears.

'Your mom? Are you sure? I'm so sorry...' His last words came out in a whisper, and I knew he understood what I was feeling. Even if they were still alive, his parents were lost to him, too impossibly far away to hope to ever see them again. And Olivia... I raised my eyes, half expecting to see her drifting hazily in front of me, but there was nothing of her in the faces before me.

Fresh tears cascaded down my cheeks for the loss of the girl who had saved my life. Every step I was able to take happened because of Olivia. It was easy to imagine that if we had met while she was still alive, we would have been friends. She might have even accepted my abilities without judgment. She had never pushed Andy away because of his gift; she had loved him and teased him and treated him like he was an average kid.

I squeezed Andy's hand again, and I felt him return the pressure, though he sniffled at the same time.

I started to feel annoyed again.

I wasn't even one hundred percent sure that the figure who had touched my cheek had been my mom. I hadn't seen her face, and she hadn't stayed beside me. In life my mom had always been a source of protection and comfort – so why, in this nightmare of a tunnel, hadn't she drifted beside me, whispering words of love and encouragement? Why had she just dissipated, leaving me feeling more upset than I had felt before her appearance? And now Andy was upset too. It was strange the way the darkness seemed to heighten our emotions – fear, grief, and now anger.

It was as though the distraction of light and sight had kept our minds from dwelling for too long on darker subjects, but we were now defenseless. We had been swallowed by the blackness of this winding crypt of stone.

My anger intensified as we continued to stumble our way through the mass of shifting figures. I wished they would just disappear.

Suddenly I realized that I wasn't afraid anymore. Thinking about Olivia and my mom and the possibility that she had reached out to me had distracted me completely from my fear.

My mom had given me comfort and protection, whether she had appeared before me or not. She had refocused my energy, and though I had gone through a wide range of emotions, from shock to sadness to anger, what I did not feel anymore was afraid.

It reminded me of when I was small and my mom would come into my room because I was feeling scared of the dark.

She would leave the lights off and climb into bed with me, and we would try to decide what the dark shadows really were. I would see a hunched and hairy monster sitting in the corner of my room, and she would squint at it through the dark and say it looked more like a baboon wearing a diaper for a hat. Then she'd go over to the shadowy lump and prove us both wrong by toppling over the pile of stuffed animals I had placed there earlier. She had distracted me from my fear then, and empowered me so much that eventually I was able to bravely peer into the shadows by myself.

Now, with loving memories of my mom at the forefront of my mind, I was able to muster that same courage again. I was able to look up, directly into the faces of those who surrounded us, and see them for what they were. They were not menacing, advancing, ready to snuff out my life, forcing me to join their ranks. They were hovering calmly, permitting us to pass, almost directing our path through the maze of debris within the tunnel.

Their expressions were not twisted in anger or dislike, but rather, each face silently watched us pass by, their eyes serene and without worry.

I heard a faint clank and clatter of metal echo from somewhere far behind us – had the creep decided to attempt passage through the tunnel tonight too?

I looked over my shoulder, but of course, I was unable to see anything but the vague misty figures. The ones who had closed in behind us seemed to have turned their attention to the source of the noise, and were no longer staring at me.

Turning my head forward once again, I suddenly found myself nose to nose with a pale translucent face. I gasped, my heart racing again, my fear returning with a vengeance. The eyes had no irises or pupils, they were solid spheres of white, and they stared intently into mine. The mouth opened; a black slit in the nebulous silvery mask. I focused my mind, breathing deeply to try to slow my racing heart, and leaned in to try to hear what the Voice was whispering.

'...Go...'

There was another clatter from behind us, and this time it sounded closer than before. Someone was stumbling after us through the darkness, and was closing in.

The face drifted back and melted into the mist, rejoining the other figures.

'...*Go*...' said the Voice again, more urgently than the last time, so I tightened my hold on Andy's hand and Patience's rope and urged them to quicken their pace.

After a few more minutes of blundering through the pitch black tunnel, a gentle breeze of fresh piney air brushed my face, and sent my heart racing again, this time with elation.

'I think we can ride again Andy, I think we're almost at the end of the tunnel.'

I helped him clamber back into the saddle, and then hauled myself up behind him.

I wasn't sure how dark it would be once we exited the tunnel, but I hoped that if we were moving fast enough, it would be more difficult for anyone waiting outside to ambush us. I could feel Andy trembling in front of me, whether from fear or cold I did not know, but I gave him a little squeeze to try to reassure him.

I looked over my shoulder again, and saw that the figures were no longer crowding around us: they were now drifting toward the sounds coming from the tunnel behind us. Wishing that there was some way for them to help us escape, I turned my attention back to the road ahead.

We rounded the last bend, the conspicuous clip-clopping of Patience's hooves announcing our approach, and I could see one last car silhouetted against the navy blue of the tunnel mouth. Could there be someone hiding behind it? Or inside it?

Patience began to trot a little faster; I think she must have sensed the closeness of fresh air and freedom and felt as impatient as I did to escape this serpentine mausoleum.

As we approached the crash site of the tunnel's final car, someone, a male, swore loudly in the dark close behind us. Patience had remained extraordinarily calm during our trek through the darkness, but the sound of the angry voice startled her into a gallop, and we cleared the mouth of the tunnel in a few seconds.

We hurtled along the mountain road, passing several more crashed vehicles. I was happy to let Patience put as much distance as possible between us and the tunnel, and as we reached another bend in the road, I could have sworn I heard the same enraged male voice bellow my name into the night.

Andy let out a quiet sob and I urged Patience to run even faster. It unnerved me that whoever was following us knew me, or knew my name at least.

I started talking wildly, keeping an eye on the road ahead as Patience continued to bear us onward.

'Maybe they heard us talking in the tunnel, and that's how they know my name? Or they heard us talking some other time before we knew we were being followed? Maybe they hadn't yelled my name at all just now, maybe they had yelled something that just sounded like Grace? But why would someone walk out of a tunnel and yell trace? Or race?'

'Or brace?' Piped up Andy, and I was glad to hear that he wasn't crying. We continued to come up with as many words that rhymed with Grace as we could, while around us the night sky became steadily darker.

It was when Andy came out with 'hyperspace' that I realized we would have to stop for the night; it was just too dark to see the road properly.

'Okay, Patience, time to slow down your pace,' I said, wondering if Andy would notice that the rhyming game could continue.

'Yes, I can barely see my hand in front of my face,' said Andy, looking up at me, and I could hear that he was grinning.

'Where should we make camp, do you see a good place?' I asked, thinking our only option was to pitch our tent in the middle of the road, since there was sheer cliff wall on our right, and a sheer drop on our left.

'What if we try lighting the torch again, and we keep going?' said Andy, ending the game. I could hear the fear that had crept back into his voice, and it infected me, too.

I agreed to keep going. I definitely didn't want to give the creep a chance to catch up again. I knew that the mountain road would widen soon, and that we would be passing through a few small towns that were nestled in the valleys. My mom and I used to stop and take picnic breaks in the little towns, and sometimes we would explore the shops, or just sit and take in the breathtaking views.

There would be places to hide for a night, we could check the stores for supplies, and there was a shallow river – I didn't want to think about how long it had been since I'd last bathed, and I wouldn't mind washing some of my clothes, either.

I dismounted once again, and Andy handed me the torch. He climbed down too, and held a lit match so I could see what I was doing. I used my knife to shave some more kindling off of the branch's handle, and jammed the curly shreds down between the tines.

The kindling lit easily, and soon the torch was blazing brightly, casting a warm circle of light several feet around us.

Andy decided to walk with me for a while, and took my hand with a worried glance over his shoulder. He was so precocious in so many ways that I had to remind myself that he was also just a scared little kid. I asked him if he would like to play the alphabet game again, but take turns trying to name a movie or TV show for each letter of the alphabet, instead of food, like we had before. The distraction cheered him up instantly, and we were both caught off guard when about a half an hour later, we were suddenly faced with a second tunnel.

I had forgotten that we would have to brave another one before we would reach the first town.

'This tunnel isn't totally closed in, Andy, it won't be like the last one,' I told him, trying to convince myself as much as him. 'It doesn't go straight through the mountain, the tunnel was built into the side, so it has big open windows the whole way.'

I wondered how much longer the torch would burn, and suggested the option of making camp for the night.

'Well,' he said, and he looked all around us, though I was sure he couldn't see any farther than our little pool of torchlight, 'we have traveled a long way since the last tunnel – Patience probably needs a rest after all that running, and I'm pretty tired, too...' He sighed, and I could tell that he didn't really want to stop. 'What if we have a rest and some food here, and then as soon as there is even a tiny bit of light, we keep going?'

'Sounds good to me,' I said, looping Patience's rope around a nearby tree and opening my bag to find her some water, 'I'll take first watch – I think we should just forget the tent tonight so we can move fast if we have to, but we can still get warmed up in the blankets. Do you think we should build a fire?'

We agreed to build a small fire just inside the tunnel entrance. There was one crashed car to block us from view if the creep came along. I guided Patience over to the car, and retied her there, so she would be somewhat hidden too. Thankfully the car was empty; I didn't feel like I could handle the sight of a torch-lit corpse after all we had been through already. Once our little fire was crackling away, I suggested that Andy sleep on the car's backseat. He looked inside and was sold instantly. He settled himself into the plush interior and pulled the sleeping bag over his head, whispered 'Goodnight,' and in less than a minute I could hear him snoring softly.

I decided to wait a while before eating, so instead I sorted through our bags, checking how much food we had left. Five cans. That was it. Five cans of food to sustain us through the rest of our mountain journey. And what if there was nothing to eat once we reached camp? I had been working under the assumption that Eric and Audrey's pantry would be as well stocked as it always was during camp. What if it had been raided? What if the cabin had been destroyed? What if Poo People had claimed it, and we were left with nothing? My mind started racing with all of the possible horrible scenarios, each one starring an Andy who was dying of starvation, looking at me with sunken blue eyes and cracked lips...

I packed our supplies back into our bags and tried to shake the awful images my brain had conjured up, deciding that I had the power to keep Andy from starving. We could fish, we could collect roots and edible plants, I could set traps for smaller animals – if I could just remember what Eric had taught us. I wished I had paid better attention to everything he had ever said, but how could I have known that my life, and now Andy's life, would one day depend on it? If we arrived at camp to find it destroyed or claimed, we still had our tent. It would be a good enough temporary shelter. We could build ourselves a little log cabin and plant a little garden... We would be fine.

I tried not to think about the fact that the ground would soon freeze solid, and be buried under a blanket of snow.

This time, the image of starving Andy included frosty eyelashes and violent shivering, while he slowly turned blue...

I stood up and walked back out of the tunnel, trying to physically remove myself from the disturbing visions that had crept sneakily into my tired mind.

We would be passing through a small town very soon, and we would just have to risk searching the whole place for supplies. There was no other option. I would keep my eyes peeled for edible plants in the meantime, and if we needed to we could snack on pine. I had never tried it, but I remembered Eric showing us how to strip away the soft inner bark, though he had said it tasted best fried in butter. I felt hugely grateful in that moment that Eric had been such an enthusiastic outdoorsman. The fact that pine trees surrounded us on all sides was a huge comfort as well; they guaranteed that I would not let Andy freeze or starve to death.

Feeling somewhat better about our situation, I was about to turn and head back to the fireside when I noticed two bright pinpricks of light shining from the trees above the road.

Eyes.

I was being watched by some unknown creature, and it was impossible to tell how close it was, and whether it was in a tree or on the ground.

As I squinted into the dark, trying unsuccessfully to discern the creature's size, the eyes blinked once and then disappeared.

I took a slow step backward, scanning the dark for any further sign of animals, glad Andy was fast asleep and protected in the car.

I had been so worried about the creep following us that I had temporarily forgotten about being stalked by wild predators as well.

I turned and hurried back to the fire. Looking at the bright flames made my eyes ache, but I added another branch, sending sparks spiraling like earthly shooting stars.

Hoping the fire would keep any animals at bay, I opened the driver's side door as quietly as I could, and climbed into the car, dragging my blanket along with me.

Once inside, I curled my knees to my chest and snuggled under the blanket as much as possible, tucking it under my chin. I pushed down the door lock for good measure, trying my best not to think of the creep, of mountain lions, or of bears, which were sure to be fattening themselves up in preparation for hibernation.

I kept watch for as long as I could, every once in a while adding more fuel to the fire.

I dozed in and out of uneasy dreams, and by the time dawn broke over the mountain peaks, I was ready to get moving.

I whispered to Andy, not wanting to startle him out of a deep sleep, and he rolled over, his bright eyes peering over the top of the sleeping bag.

'You didn't sleep!' He said, and his voice sounded extra loud to my ears after such a long stretch of silence. 'You were supposed to wake me up!' He struggled to sit up, blinking in the soft light of morning.

Andy and I shared a can of cold stew for breakfast while we watched the color slowly return to the mountainside.

In the early light, everything was painted with the same dark blue brush. As the sun rose higher, hints of green started to appear in the dark trees.

We led Patience through the tunnel as morning crept on, looking out over the scenery through the windows created by the tunnel's support beams. Each window was a picture postcard of unbelievable beauty. We reached the end of the tunnel fairly quickly, climbed back into the saddle, and continued along the winding road. I hoped we would reach the first small town by lunchtime.

As we rounded a bend in the road, the sun finally emerged over the eastern peaks. The landscape was suddenly a dazzling sweep of brilliant green trees, jutting mountains of grey, brown and blue, topped in the distance with glistening white snow, and peeking through the trees in the valley floor was a lake of the most vibrant turquoise I had ever seen. It seemed to glow from within: an aquamarine gem stone glittering in the rays of the fresh morning sun.

As I looked out over the magnificent view, I took a deep breath of clean light air and could feel hope surge through my body.

The last few weeks had been so terrifying, and our future so uncertain, that hope felt almost foreign to me. But we had made it into the mountains, we were surrounded by trees and plants that could sustain us if our food supplies ran out, and, most importantly, we were together.

Andy was staring intently at the distant peaks, and I asked him what he was thinking about.

He took a moment before answering, his eyes still trained on the snow-capped summit.

'Just that these mountains have been here forever. And they're going to be here forever. We will change, and move around, and eventually die. Our bodies will decay and turn to dust, and we will be gone, but the mountains will still be standing, never changing...'

He looked back at me and his eyes took a minute to focus on mine.

'I'm just feeling extra small and insignificant. It's weird how much humans have been affected by the Darkness, but the rest of the world is going on as if nothing happened. The loss of power doesn't bother the wild animals – they're probably much happier without all the cars zooming around. The trees and grass are taking back the areas that we paved over, and even the parts that were logged will be growing in again.'

He pointed toward a mountain whose growth of forest had nearly been shaved clean. I could just make out the zig zag pattern carved into the rock where the logging trucks would have driven up and down the mountainside, dangerously hauling the massive tree trunks down toward the main highway.

'It's just so weird to think about – the world as we knew it has ended, but for everything else, it's just getting back to normal.'

Once again I was surprised by the words and ideas coming out of Andy's mouth. He had such deep thoughts for such a young person, though it was true that he had dealt with more in the last few months than some adults had to deal with in a lifetime.

We rode in silence for a while, both of us lost in thought.

My mind wandered to the remote tribes of the world that one of my teachers had talked about. The people lived in grass huts and fed themselves from the land and had little to no contact with the world outside their tribe. They were probably completely unaware that anything had changed for the rest of humanity. When we learned about them I had felt kind of sad for them because I thought they were missing out on so much by being removed from the advances in technology the rest of us were enjoying. Now I felt extremely jealous of their unawareness and of their success, and hoped Andy and I could figure out how to survive in the same way.

The mountain slopes on either side of us gradually became less steep, allowing for a slightly wider road, and I knew that we were about to reach the first little town.

We saw several rockslide warning signs posted along the highway, and when I looked up to scan the cliff top, half expecting to see boulders come tumbling down, instead I saw several long-horned sheep dotting the rocky terrain.

I quietly pointed them out to Andy, who nodded and smiled at me and stared up at the sheep too. They didn't even seem to notice us as we passed by, they just continued to munch the tufty grasses that carpeted the craggy slope.

Around the next bend, the valley suddenly opened up in front of us.

We could see the entire town laid out below us like a map, and I was glad to see that there was no obvious evidence of it having been burned.

'It looks okay!' said Andy excitedly, and this time it was he who coaxed Patience to walk a little faster.

As we drew closer to the town limits, however, the destruction I had been dreading became more obvious.

The town's Welcome sign had been knocked over, and propped back up against the truck that had hit it.

There were rough gouge marks across the area of the sign where the town's population was noted. I could easily make out the numbers beneath: some three-thousand people had once lived here. I looked more carefully at the gashes, and realized that someone had scratched a word into the wood. It now read:

'Population: Lost.'

I stared down at the sign, wondering how many of the Voices I was now hearing used to live here.

There was a sudden rustling behind the truck, and I tensed up, ready to fight, but my opponent turned out to be another big-horned sheep, who looked up at us, unconcerned, and then continued on its way.

A few minutes later we reached a road that ran perpendicular to the highway – the town's Main Street.

Crashed cars lined the adjoining roads, and several were half-buried in the rubble that had cascaded down from the walls they had hit.

There didn't appear to be a single intact store window, and the shelves and remaining contents of the stores lay scattered and broken on the pavement.

'There's nothing here,' said Andy, a note of despair in his voice. 'We should get out of here before someone tries to eat Patience again.'

I started to agree, but the image of our dwindling food supply snuck into my mind, and the urge to at least check the place out won over.

'I think we should take a fast look at the residential area, maybe people fled their houses suddenly, and left food or clothes behind.'

Andy reluctantly agreed, and we continued our wary journey farther into town, keeping our eyes peeled for any sign of movement, our eyes swiveling back and forth as Patience bore us onward.

'I wonder where the refugee camp for this town was?' said Andy. 'There haven't been any signs directing everyone, and we didn't see it when we were looking down on the town... So where did everybody go?'

'...*Lost...*'

The whispering Voice startled me as it rang out loudly over the rest, and I tried to cover up my reaction by rambling off an answer.

'There's another small town fairly close by, we will go through it on our way to the cabin, so maybe we'll find the refugee camp there.'

Andy had not seemed like his usual light-hearted self for the past few days, and I could hardly blame him; we had been through a lot lately. I didn't want to add to his stress by telling him that the whole town had been forgotten, or was dead, or whatever 'lost' meant. Whatever the case, it was not good news, and he was coping with enough anxiety for now.

To try to cheer him up, I decided to tell him about the fruit trees that grow in the orchards near the cabin.

'Peaches and apples and cherries... You can eat them right off the tree and they taste like the sun coated in sugar. There are raspberry bushes right next to the cabin too, and I bet they're all covered in fruit right now!'

I could hear the feigned cheeriness in my voice and somehow it made me feel depressed.

I suddenly realized that the fruit from the orchards would probably be rotten and full of worms by the time we reached it.

This realization made our journey feel even more pointless, and more dangerous than it was worth, since I didn't know for sure that we would even have a good place to settle down. And if we did reach the cabin safely, we were still being followed by the creep... What had I dragged Andy into... It would be my fault, if we, too, found ourselves among the lost...

***

We reached the residential area fairly quickly and dismounted, tying Patience to a new tree after every house we checked, trying to keep her as close as possible.

At first we started out by peeking in the windows, knocking, and trying the doorknobs before entering, on the off-chance that someone would still be home.

Soon though, my crowbar was swinging, shattering glass with satisfying noise, broken shards glittering like diamonds under our feet.

I felt a small amount of guilt for destroying part of someone else's property – was I any better than the monsters who had burned down my own home? But surely one broken window to help us survive was hardly comparable to gutting and incinerating an entire city for personal gain. We were not causing unnecessary destruction: if people ever returned to this forgotten town, they would only have one window to fix, and otherwise would find the houses perfectly livable.

I pushed my guilt aside as we entered our eighth house. So far we had each found several new pairs of socks, and some toothpaste and a toothbrush for Andy. We had been sharing mine up until this point, so he was very excited to have one of his own.

It had taken a lot of convincing to get him to share in the first place, and I remembered the conversation very clearly. The first time had I offered him my toothbrush, he had kicked up a huge fuss about how revolting it was to share. Making grossed-out faces and pretending to throw up between each word: 'Ewwww...' (retch), 'Gracie...' (cough), 'that's...' (gag), 'disgusting!'

Laughing, I had replied, 'No, disgusting would be if all your teeth started rotting out. I know it's weird and maybe a little gross, but times change, and I'd rather share a toothbrush now than have to start pulling out your festering teeth in a few months. So do it for me. Please.'

After a lot more very theatrical fake vomiting, Andy had consented to share my toothbrush.

I decided not to remind him that the one he had found today was not brand new, and that he would be using a stranger's toothbrush. He was just too excited about it as he put it into his pocket. I didn't want to burst his oral hygiene bubble.

We explored house after house and it struck me as we headed for the twentieth house that none of them had been looted before our arrival. Surely other travelers had come through this way in search of supplies? Why were we the first to break the windows? I mentioned this to Andy, and he thought for a moment before replying.

'I noticed that too, Gracie, how nothing is ruined and yet there is no food and most of the clothes are gone. My theory is that everyone decided as a group to pack up and try to make their way out of town together. Maybe they had a big meeting about it, in the early days of the Darkness. Maybe the stores got looted, but before people started turning on each other, they made the decision to leave, together. I noticed that there are no bicycles or strollers or wagons around, and those last two houses definitely had small children living there. So I think they all left, hauling everything they could, and hopefully they all found somewhere to settle together. That's what I hope, at least.'

He gazed, eyes unfocused, down the deserted street, and I knew he was imagining a huge friendly exodus. People helping each other with their kids and supplies, sharing whatever they had... And though I had trouble believing it, why not? This isolated little mountain town might have retained some good, wholesome, help-your-neighbor values that were next to impossible in a big city full of strangers. I was comforted by Andy's belief that there was still hope for humanity.

'So why, according to your theory, are none of these houses ransacked like the stores on the Main Street?' I asked him.

'I think the residents did that so everyone who came through would think the whole town was destroyed. We almost passed through without looking any farther, didn't we? I bet most people wouldn't bother checking things out once they see that kind of devastation, they'd just assume the worst.'

'Well,' I said, 'maybe if the cabin doesn't pan out we could come back here and choose one of these houses to live in!'

'Or maybe we could live in all of them!' He looked up and down the street, appraising each house. Then he shrugged, looked up at me and said, 'Can I break the next window?'

Chapter Eight

After several more hours of searching houses for supplies, Andy asked if we could choose one to sleep in for the night.

Since I had barely slept the night before, I was more than willing to go along with his idea, imagining sinking down into a soft mattress under soft blankets with my head on a soft pillow...

I asked Andy how he wanted to choose which house to sleep in.

'I especially loved one of the first houses we searched,' he replied, 'it reminded me of home, it had the same layout, and I could tell that kids lived there.'

'Sounds good to me,' I told him, 'plus it'll mean we're closer to Main Street, so we can leave a little quicker in the morning. We won't have to find our way back through town before we can leave.' Then I added, 'Although, all I really care about, right this second, is that there is a bed to sleep in. It's been so long since we've had a good solid sleep, I think it'll help us a lot.'

Andy agreed, and after searching a few more houses, we began heading back to where we had started. Dusk was creeping up on us by the time we reached Andy's chosen house, and I was glad we would not find ourselves stumbling through the dark trying to find our way.

I tied Patience up in the backyard so she could munch the overgrown lawn. I spotted a bucket that had filled with rainwater and set it down close by. I gratefully stroked her long nose in thanks – she was truly a member of our little family.

I had checked every backyard we came across for a vegetable garden, and had only managed to recover a couple of potatoes, but still, they would be a feast for us. I tucked one of the smallest potatoes into my bag, planning to plant it when we reached the cabin. I wished that I could have collected some other seeds, but it seemed that the residents had had the foresight to take them, and the ripe veggies.

We decided to save the potatoes until we were back on the road, not wanting to build a fire when we were both already so tired.

So we opened a can of beans that we had found in one if the houses, and sat down to take inventory of our new supplies.

Thanks to our search, we were both decked out in entirely new clothes, and had left our filthy, reeking old ones in a garbage can in someone's kitchen. We had each acquired several new shirts and pairs of pants, and thankfully, warm coats and boots for the coming winter. Our bags were bulging once again, though this time unfortunately, not because of a surplus of food.

In the subsistence category, besides the potatoes, all we had managed to find were a couple of cans of beans, one jar of homemade dill pickles, and a mostly empty canister of powdered infant formula that Andy had discovered in one of the kitchen cabinets. The expiry date was two years ago, so we figured that it had been jammed at the back of the cupboard and forgotten.

I wondered aloud what it tasted like, and Andy said that Olivia had once dared him to try infant formula when they were babysitting their little cousin. 'It was totally disgusting, I don't know how the baby could stand it! Although he did throw up a little bit every time he ate, maybe he was trying to tell us something!' He laughed, and then became solemn as he looked down at the canister in his hand. 'I wonder if my cousins survived...'

He was quiet for a moment and then gave his head a little shake, as though trying to rid himself of yet another worry. He took a deep breath and said, in a voice that was a little too matter-of-fact, 'It's gross, but still, if we're super hungry it might just be the best thing we've ever tasted!'

I looked through a drawer full of jumbled tubs and lids, and found a small container that I transferred the powder into. There was no point in carrying the big empty canister around, it would take up so much space and was mostly made of cardboard so we couldn't even use it for water or anything.

I left it on the kitchen counter, and as I turned back to ask Andy if he was ready to go to sleep, I saw that he was fighting the urge to cry. His face was all scrunched up and his small shoulders were slumped – I could almost see the weight he was carrying on them.

'Let's go find somewhere to sleep, okay?' I said quietly, putting my arm around him.

Together we climbed the stairs to the second floor, and found the master bedroom.

Andy took off his shoes and I stuffed them into his bag, just in case.

I pulled back the covers and we climbed in. It was as plush and comfy as I had imagined. Andy snuggled up to me and finally let the tears come. He cried and cried, and I just hugged him, I couldn't think of a single word of comfort; there really weren't any.

Eventually he sobbed himself to sleep, and I found myself drifting off too. I dreamed that I was younger, maybe six or seven, and I was riding my bike down the street.

The sun was shining and I felt completely happy. My mom called my name; it was time to go home and wash up for dinner. I rang the little bell on my bike to let her know that I was on my way. She called my name again, and again I rang the bell. When she called me a third time, there was urgency, even fear in her voice. I could see her standing there, at the edge of the lawn, calling my name and looking frantic. I rang the bell again, but it had no effect on her, for some reason she just couldn't hear it. I stopped my bike in front of her and grabbed her hand, wanting her to know I was safe, but her hand was cold, it was so cold. I looked up, wanting to see her properly, but instead, she leaned down and put her face in front of mine. The face was no longer my mother's, it was distorted and eyeless and terrifying. She started ringing the little bell over and over, her frigid hand clamped down over mine so I couldn't try to escape...

I woke up in a cold sweat with a scream building in my lungs.

My arm was still pinned under Andy and when I pulled it free I found my hand to be completely numb. I got up and paced around the dark room, pins and needles signaling that blood flow was returning to my hand.

The sound of the bike bell was still echoing in my ears, and I knew I'd never forget the transformation my mother's face had undergone – that horrible image would remain etched on the walls of my mind forever.

I bent down and reached into my backpack, wanting a drink of water to try to wash away the taste of fear. If only I could get the sound of the bike bell out of my head, it made the dream feel too real and too close...

But suddenly the sound started getting louder... I froze, waiting, listening. It wasn't just the dream lingering disturbingly in my mind; there was actually someone outside, riding a bike along our row of houses, ringing that bell in the dark.

The window in the master bedroom looked out over the backyard, so I crept into the room opposite, the one Andy had liked so much because it reminded him of his own.

As the ringing grew louder I parted the thick curtains very slightly, wondering if I would be able to catch a glimpse of the bell-ringer in the dark.

There was just enough moonlight to make out the shape of the person pedaling along the road, though I couldn't make out any facial features. The moon had painted everything with a soft pearly glow that stripped the pigment out of anything beneath it, so I couldn't even tell what color the person's hair or clothes were.

I could see that they looked pretty big, especially pedaling that bike that was obviously too small. Their size and their severe haircut made me think they were probably male.

An enraged scream echoed back to me from the mouth of the phantom-filled tunnel, and I broke out in another icy sweat.

The creep.

Of course it was the creep. He wanted us to know we were being stalked, he had not tried to be sneaky about following us, and besides, who in their right mind would be so obnoxious in times like these, purposefully drawing attention to themselves? He seemed to relish causing fear in others, but felt none of his own.

A true psychopath.

I rushed back to the master bedroom where Andy was still fast asleep, and peeked through the curtains into the backyard. Patience was still tethered where I had left her, and would not be visible from the street, especially in the dark.

I hoped the creep would not notice the trail of broken windows that we had left in our wake, or at least that he wouldn't realize that we were the ones who had broken them. I felt like we had left an easy trail for him to follow, but at least we had doubled back and were now hidden in the first section of houses. He might assume that he would find us where the trail of broken windows ended, and that was at least a few streets away.

The sound of the bell ringing became more and more distant, and I was at a loss for what to do.

Should I wake Andy and try to run before the creep came back? The sound of hooves hitting pavement would be like an alarm in the perfect silence of the night, what if he had a gun and tried to shoot at us? I couldn't sentence Andy or Patience to such a terrible fate.

So we would wait, let the sun rise and give him fewer places to hide... We would still make a lot of noise, but if we could see where we were going, I'm sure Patience could easily outrun a guy on a bike, as long as he didn't shoot us. Again I wondered why he hadn't just murdered us in our sleep that night he had left the message in the game pieces. He enjoyed the sport, perhaps, of terrorizing a teenaged girl and a little boy.

I shook my head in disgust, wondering how I had managed to draw the attention of such a cruel and creepy person.

I looked over at Andy again, his little body snug under the blankets, his breathing nice and even. Peaceful. I felt guilty that I would have to pile more fear and worry on him when he woke up, but he needed to know that the creep was close by. Besides, he knew me so well by now, that even if I didn't tell him, he would know something was up.

I climbed back into bed, thinking that even if I didn't sleep anymore, it would feel nice just to be warm and comfortable. There was nothing I could do right now anyway, and if the creep started searching houses it would take a while for him to find us, especially if he started where the trail of broken windows ended.

I pulled the covers right up to my eyes, remembering how, when I was small, I used to believe that if I couldn't see the monsters coming out of my closet and from under my bed, that they couldn't see me, either. I would tuck my head under the blankets and eventually fall asleep, convinced that I was invisible, hidden by my special armor.

I wished now, as I lay in the dark in a stranger's abandoned house, that the same absolute certainty of safety would carry me off to sleep again. But the bike bell was still ringing in my ears, whether a residual echo or the actual sound in the distance, I couldn't be sure.

I tried concentrating on the slow, rhythmic pattern of Andy's breath, hoping it would calm my adrenaline-spiked nerves. I felt so jumpy and paranoid, though I did have good reason. What I really needed was a solid night's sleep, a sleep free of disturbance from horrifying dreams and stalking predators. A sleep snuggled down in this nice warm bed, safe from monsters and fear and heartache...

***

I blinked in the bright sunlight, wrapped in a warm cocoon of blankets. Andy's smiling face peeked at me over his side of the blankets, and I could see that sleep had completely changed his outlook. His eyes were no longer ringed with dark circles, and they had regained their cheeky sparkle. He looked like he was ready for an adventure, and there was no doubt that I had one lined up for him.

'You're never going to believe what I found,' he told me, looking like he was about to explode with excitement. Slowly he started to shift something out from under the blankets and up in front of his face. The top of a very familiar cereal box came into view, and suddenly the jingle for the commercial was playing in my head. All I could see of Andy were his big eyes peering at me over the top of the bright packaging, and then he started singing the jingle, his voice somewhat muffled behind the box.

'Are you kidding?' I asked him, 'is there actually cereal in there?' I didn't want to get my hopes up too high, but my stomach growled, giving me away.

Laughing, Andy sat up and gave the box a shake. I could hear the contents shifting around and sat up too, wondering where he possibly could have found such a treasure. It was fresh too, the box was still sealed and everything.

'I woke up a while ago and didn't want to disturb you, so I went back into the house next to this one and did a little more searching,' said Andy, as he broke open the cardboard flaps. 'There wasn't anything else, but for some reason I just felt like checking on top of the fridge, so I pulled a kitchen chair over, climbed up, and there, amongst some serious dust bunnies, was this glorious box of goodness that you and I shall now feast upon.'

He grinned at me and pulled a couple of mismatched containers out from under the covers. He ripped open the frosted plastic bag and made a big show of pouring out the cereal.

'My lady,' he said, in a very uppity accent, handing me a bowl of cereal with a nod of his head and flourish of his hand. 'Dinner is served.' And then he crammed a whole fistful of cereal into his mouth. He was barely able to chew with his mouth packed so full, and I couldn't look at him because the sight was so revolting, but somehow he managed to swallow, and then crammed in another handful.

I took a nibble of one of the little squares and the familiar flavor flooded my mind with memories. I looked down at my bowl as I spoke, mostly to hide the tears that had welled up in my eyes, but also to avoid seeing the barely contained, chewed-up contents of Andy's mouth.

'When I was twelve, my mom asked me what I wanted for my birthday. There wasn't anything specific that I needed, or anything that I especially wanted, so I told her that I just wanted to spend the day with her, watching our favorite movies, while eating my favorite cereal. So that's what we did. She wrapped up a couple of boxes of this cereal and a carton of milk, and we lolled around all day, watching movies until our eyeballs ached and eating cereal until our stomachs hurt.' I looked up at Andy, my eyes now dry, and smiled. 'It was one of my best birthdays ever.'

Andy swallowed his huge mouthful, gulped down some water and said, 'My parents used to take me and Olivia to a lake up north every summer for a week. We'd stay in the same rustic little cabin every time, and mom and dad would let us help choose some of the treats we would bring. Me and Olivia would always choose this,' he shook his almost empty bowl of cereal, 'and it used to drive mom crazy because we would always finish it so fast. We would just eat it until it was all gone, we loved it so much.'

We sat munching our breakfast in silence for a while, both lost in memories. When Andy was finished, he pulled the whole bag of cereal out of its box, rolled down the filmy plastic, and then rolled the bag into one of his shirts, to make sure it wouldn't come undone and spill out everywhere. Then he tucked the little parcel into his bag and zipped it up tight.

I finished my breakfast and made the bed, thinking that it felt nice to do something so normal for a change. Then we headed out into the backyard, where Patience stood quietly, living up to her name.

In all the excitement over the cereal I had forgotten all about the creep and his bike bell. I started to tell Andy about it as I untied Patience, speaking more and more softly as the paranoia slithered back into my mind.

As I helped Andy up into the saddle, I caught a whiff of smoke on the air. The smell triggered a panic response, and I started wildly scanning the sky for any sign of smoke.

'What is it, Gracie?' asked Andy, looking down at me with concern. 'Did you hear something? Is a Voice telling you something?'

'No...' I said, starting to lead Patience toward the garden gate, 'the smoke... It means someone is nearby... We should get going.'

I led Patience out of the backyard and into the street, where I climbed up behind Andy, my eyes still raking the sky for the telltale signs of fire. The trees were so tall that I couldn't see most of the horizon surrounding us, I needed to get out in the open, I needed to know where that smoke was coming from. A deep dread that I didn't want to acknowledge had seeped into my bones.

'Is it the creep?' asked Andy, 'does he know we're here?'

I continued telling him about the bike bell from last night while directing Patience toward Main Street.

'So he didn't know exactly where we were, but he knew we were nearby,' said Andy, once I had finished talking. 'He was ringing that bell to try to scare us, and now, do you think he lit the fire to scare us some more? Or maybe it's someone else cooking their breakfast?' he added hopefully.

'I don't know, Andy, it would be nice if it was something as benign as someone cooking their food, but honestly, I have a bad feeling about it.'

'He could have caught me when I went into that other house this morning!' Andy squeaked suddenly, horror in his voice. 'Or what if you had tied Patience up in the front! We're so lucky! I'm glad he didn't find us!'

'Me too,' I said grimly, unwilling to consider what could have happened to my little family if either of those scenarios had played out.

We reached the end of the residential area in under ten minutes, and all the while the smell of smoke grew stronger, making me feel increasingly edgy.

When I turned Patience back onto Main Street, the trees thinned out and I could finally see enough of the sky to ascertain the source of the smoke.

A huge billowing cloud of black and grey was rising up in the near distance. I could tell, from having navigated our way through the streets yesterday, that the fire was burning several houses on the edge of the residential section. It was much too close... My blood started pounding in my ears...

As we watched, the wide column of smoke grew wider still, and now we could see orange flames leaping up toward the sky as the inferno hungrily devoured all that it touched.

The branches of the huge old trees surrounding the burning houses seemed to writhe and stretch, as though trying to keep their dying autumn leaves out of the blaze's reach.

I urged Patience to move faster, the dread that I had been ignoring now threatening to consume me.

Was it possible that the creep had been involved in burning down my house? Was he the second man that I had heard searching it before they torched it? Could he have followed me all the way here, smoking me, like a frantic wasp, out of each new place that I came across?

It was too much of a coincidence that my city had been burned to the ground, and now, here he was, burning this town too. He could have even been there at the stables, when we had first fled with Patience. I had assumed there were only two men, each riding a horse, but it was entirely possible that I just hadn't heard the bike or its rider. That beautiful old house had been devastated by fire, too.

It was just such a strange and wasteful act, and it did not seem like something most people would do. It was almost like the creep was leaving a signature behind – undeniable proof that he had been there, that this was his work... Like an artist, proud of his twisted masterpiece.

But who was he? I knew that the creep was not the leader of the monsters: the scream that had issued from the mouth of the tunnel was definitely not the deep gravelly voice I had heard giving orders to the rest of the group.

I realized with a shiver of horror that if he was in fact the second intruder who had destroyed my home, then he had also beaten a man to death in order to kidnap his daughter.

I didn't understand it, who was I dealing with and why was he following me? There had been photos of me and my family on the walls in our house, so maybe he had recognized me from somewhere, but I could not think of a single person that I had made an enemy of. I had always kept to myself, living my lonely life as a self-preservation strategy.

All of the people that I had come into contact with because of the Voices had always seemed grateful and touched by the messages I relayed to them, as opposed to threatening and obsessive. The people who were uncomfortable at first, even those who were downright disturbed by their loved one's messages, always came around in the end.

I truly had no idea who the creep was, and why he was targeting me. It sickened me that Andy was in danger too, just because he was with me.

We followed Main Street out of town, and were soon racing the mountain wind along the highway. The air turned sweet again, cleansing out the reek of smoke and replacing it with piney freshness.

It felt good to be on the road again, even though I knew the creep would be following us soon. The bike explained how he had managed to keep up with us so easily, and I hoped that if we just covered enough ground in good enough time, we would be able to stay safely ahead of him.

It crossed my mind for a second that it was possible he was riding my bike, the bike I had planned to ride on my journey west, the bike that I had no choice but to abandon, because I had been forced to flee from my burning home. The idea unsettled me and somehow made me feel even more demoralized.

Suddenly my sadness was replaced with anger and purpose. I had Andy to think of... None of this was his fault. I'd brought him into this mess, and I would make sure that he got out... If my last breath was spent saving him from harm, so be it.

***

We reached the second small town after a day of fast travel, and we stopped to quickly search for supplies.

Once again there were no signs guiding the town's residents to any kind of refuge, and I wondered what had happened to them all. It was a much smaller town than the last one, and Andy was shocked to see that there was only a single fast-food restaurant for the whole community.

The houses were in much rougher shape here, and we wondered if the residents of the previous town had ransacked them on their way through, showing them nearly as much disregard as the monsters had shown mine.

There was even less to find in the way of supplies here too, and though Andy now insisted upon thoroughly searching the tops of all refrigerators and cabinets, we still came up empty-handed.

Every now and then I thought I was hearing a bike bell ringing, but I was sure it was just in my head. There was no way the creep could have kept up with Patience, we had made excellent time in getting here.

The mountains had cut off our view of the huge pillar of smoke almost as soon as we had reached the highway again, but here, in this little valley town, we could see it again, rising up against the blue sky and drifting hazily around the mountain peaks like low clouds.

We couldn't decide if we wanted to stay in a house for the night, or keep going and further increase the distance between ourselves and the creep. I wished I knew if he was going to take the time to burn the whole town, or just light a few big fires in key places, trusting the blaze to spread by itself, leaving him free to continue the hunt.

In the end we decided keep going for as long as daylight would allow, and then pitch our tent somewhere along the highway once it was too dark to safely continue. It just wasn't worth it, and I knew, warm bed or not, that I wouldn't sleep a wink anyway, knowing that the house we were in could go up in flames at any second.

When the road got too dark to travel any farther, we pitched our tent and lit a fire, tethering Patience to the guardrail. There was still only the one route through the mountains, and since there was no way to hide our location, with the steep cliffs on either side of us, we plunked ourselves right in the middle of the road, and I set about chopping our two potatoes. I planned to boil them in my little pot and then mash them as much as possible with my knife. Since I had dug them up, I had been craving mashed potatoes, and though I knew they wouldn't be as delicious as the ones my mom would make, with milk, butter and salt, I was really looking forward to them.

I considered adding the smallest potato to the pot instead of keeping it to plant later, but carrying the little brown lump around felt like carrying a physical piece of hope. Plus it wouldn't even add a mouthful to our meal, so I left it tucked away in my backpack.

When Andy dug into his half of the lumpy white mess, he closed his eyes and ate without speaking for several minutes. Finally he opened his eyes, saw me watching him, and said, 'If I concentrate really hard, I can almost taste the gravy. You're a really good cook, Gracie.'

I laughed and continued eating my own lumpy potatoes, closing my eyes and imagining thick dark gravy, maybe some melted cheese on top, and a juicy steak to go with it.

They weren't much, but the potatoes filled our stomachs and we finished our meal with a handful of cereal for dessert. It was nice to feel full, but it also made me more painfully aware of our dwindling food supply. There would be one more town we could check out before the highway ascended through the highest peaks. It was a tiny town, and the highway bypassed it instead of cutting through it. It was likely that fewer people would have entered the town, and there was a small chance that we could find supplies if we took the time to search.

After we passed that last town, we would be traveling through the wildest and highest parts of the mountains, until the highway finally started its descent toward the coast. Once we passed the summit, the terrain would slowly become less steep and more open, allowing us to hide on the slopes instead of forcing us to make camp in between two unforgiving walls of rock.

We settled down in the tent after finishing our meal, and tried, again, to figure out who the creep could be.

'It's weird that the Voices won't just tell you who he is,' said Andy, irritated, 'wouldn't they be all-knowing and want to help us out a little?' As he spoke his voice became louder, and he looked up at the roof of the tent, as though challenging the Voices to respond.

'Hey, Olivia! Remember me? Your little brother? I'm still stuck down here in this dark and scary world and we are trying our best not to join you too soon, so why don't you throw us a bone and tell us exactly who we are dealing with?'

Andy was almost yelling at this point, and I worried that we would be overheard. I was about to tell him to keep it down when he suddenly flung himself down and jerked the sleeping bag over his head. He muttered a grumpy 'good-night' to me, and didn't say another word.

I snuggled down too, pondering Andy's questions and his anger toward Olivia.

He was being forced to work though his grief during an incredibly stressful time. We were tired, running out of food, and being stalked by a nutcase. It was no wonder he was lashing out at Olivia and the lack of information from the Voices. He had lost her so suddenly, and had immediately been thrust into a new dangerous world. He must be feeling abandoned by her all over again.

It made me feel lonely in a way too, that I still didn't know what had happened to my mom. I wondered if I would ever find out. Andy at least had that closure. It had to be sort of comforting... Or maybe he would have been better off hoping that she was still out there, alive.

As for the Voices not giving us more information, I had to assume they simply did not have the answers we were seeking. I couldn't imagine them being unhelpful deliberately, I had only ever felt a sense of love from them; in my experience they were not malicious or spiteful.

I lay awake for hours, my head spinning with questions and fears. Once in a while my thoughts were interrupted by the distant echo of a bike bell ringing, which would start the worries reeling all over again. I knew the creep couldn't have caught up to us yet, it was just my mind playing tricks on me. Wasn't it?

I needed sleep. I was more physically and emotionally exhausted than I had ever been. But I couldn't shut my mind off. As the night wore on, I could feel myself becoming more jittery and paranoid, and finally I unzipped the stuffy tent and snuck out into the chilly darkness.

I took a few deep breaths of the thin fresh air and it helped to settle my nerves. We had put out the fire after cooking our potatoes, and it was just as dark outside the tent as it had been inside. The absolute darkness made me feel disorientated and dizzy, like I could have been standing on the edge of a precipice without even realizing how close I was to falling.

I sat down on the cold pavement so that I could feel the earth under my hands, steady and solid as ever. I wondered how many vehicles had traveled this mountain road, and if any ever would again. Sitting here in the pitch black of night, it didn't seem likely.

It was strange to think of how many times my mom had driven us along this winding stretch of road, while we sang our hearts out to our favorite songs, eating snacks that we had picked up especially for the trip.

I remembered how Andy had looked upward as he had appealed to Olivia for answers, and I looked up too, imagining that I would see my mom looking down at me, about to share life's great secrets with me. But there was nothing. Nothing but more darkness. Even the light of the stars had been extinguished by clouds.

Disappointment washed over me and I felt the first few drops of rain sprinkle my face. I crawled back inside the tent and dug out the pot and the tin cans we had been saving to catch water. I put them outside and zipped myself in, crawling back under my blanket as the rain started to pour.

The sound of the raindrops hitting the tent drowned out the Voices, as well as the worried inner monologue that had been spinning through my head for hours. I fell asleep quickly and slept deeply, until the sound of a crackling fire tore me back to consciousness.

Chapter Nine

I sat up, reaching out for Andy, looking around wildly for the fire, sure that I would see our tent melting before my eyes. After a moment I ascertained that our tent was actually fine, but then it hit me that the whole forest must be on fire, so I leapt up, calling Andy's name to wake him.

'I'm here, Gracie, what's up?' said Andy's voice calmly from outside the tent.

'Fire!' I blurted hysterically, 'the fire!'

I tried to get out of the tent, but my feet were still tangled in the blankets, so instead I ended up sprawled out on my stomach, with the bottom half of my body still inside.

Andy started giggling, looking down at me in disbelief as I tried to extricate my legs from the jumble of blankets, my eyes still looking around, panicked, for the sight of flames.

I couldn't understand what had happened, I was positive I had heard the snapping and cracking of sparks and fire. It wasn't until Andy started to take cautious steps toward me that I became aware that there was a thin layer of ice covering everything around us.

As he continued to walk carefully toward me, I realized that what I had believed to be the sound of a blaze was actually the crunching of ice under Andy's feet. Now that I was awake, the noise was nothing like fire.

I removed my feet from the mess of blankets and finally pulled myself upright, looking around. It was still fairly dark, but I could see that every surface had a weird icy shine to it, though it wasn't like the white glittering hoarfrost that coated the trees back home during winter. This was a flawless layer of clear ice. Andy handed me a branch he had found, and it could have been made of blown glass.

'Wow,' I breathed, 'it's just so perfect. I've never seen anything like this before.'

'Me neither,' said Andy, smiling at the astonished look on my face. He stared at me for a few more seconds before

143

adding, 'You remind me of my grandpa – the one my parents were visiting in England when the power went out. He and my grandma came to stay with us last summer, and my grandpa would wake us all up in the middle of the night because he was yelling so loudly. I asked my grandma about it, because my grandpa refused to talk about it, and she said that he would sometimes jump out of bed, convinced he was still fighting in a war.'

I was dumbfounded. It was nothing compared to surviving a war, but I realized that the events of the past few months had affected me in the same way. Hearing the bike bell when there was no one there; the paranoia; vivid dreams that I was completely convinced were reality. I was also shocked that it had taken the observations of an eight year old to make me aware of the meaning behind my behavior. Andy's grandpa must have been about my age when he fought – I sincerely hoped that I wasn't still dreaming about the creep lighting my world on fire if I somehow managed to survive into my nineties…

***

It was a challenge to pack up our camp with the sheet of ice underfoot, but by the time we were back on the road, the sun had risen over the mountaintops and we were surrounded by the sound of dripping.

It was so peaceful, with the sun casting beams of light through the trees, listening to the ice slowly melt.

As the day wore on, we started to see evidence of old campsites along the road. Little piles of blackened wood and ash dotted the asphalt and empty tin cans and other food wrappers littered the surrounding areas.

Andy was certain that these signs supported his exodus theory, and I couldn't argue. It was obvious that a large group of people had been traveling together, and had made camp together.

'Maybe if your camp doesn't work out, we could try to find this group and ask if we could live with them!' said Andy hopefully.

'Sounds great to me, I love the idea of such a solid backup plan!' I replied, and as I spoke, I felt some of my worry lift. Knowing we might not be totally on our own if my plan turned out to be a failure was a huge comfort. For about the millionth time, I wondered who Emily had texted, and who had actually seen the text before the power went out.

I also wondered if my friends were dealing with changes in their abilities the way me and Andy were, or if they were getting help the way we were. Because I was certain that the dead were not actually trying to scare us. In the tunnel, they had seemed to guide us, while hindering the creep's progress. I felt confident that they had extinguished my torch to make us harder to follow, and I wondered if they had summoned enough energy to knock the creep off his bike as we fled the tunnel, causing him to scream my name in frustration, while giving us a good head start.

Even back at the old house, when my backpack was spinning in midair, now felt like more of a message of warning than a threat. If we hadn't been scared out of the house, we would have been trapped in there, and possibly burned alive, or murdered the moment the monsters had shown up. Maybe the dead had even changed their own colors in order to overwhelm Andy, making us stay out of the house and out of harm's way. It was even possible that Lizzie had appeared, and recounted the story of her death in order to freak us out just enough to make us run when the time came.

The more I thought about it, the more it made sense. I asked Andy what he thought about my theory, and he was very intrigued.

'It's kind of the same way that Olivia saved your life by giving you her shoes! That saved my life too, because then you were able to come find me! Who else have you encountered along the way?'

I told him about the woman in the bookstore, whose sister had led me to my favorite book.

'Well by giving you the book, maybe she saved you from a life of boredom!' Andy cracked up, and I couldn't help but chuckle too – life had been anything but boring lately.

***

We reached the last small town by late afternoon, and did a very fast search of the first few houses, but quickly realized that we weren't going to find anything useful, and that there certainly wasn't any food. The houses had all been stripped and ransacked, and judging by the layer of dust that coated the debris, it had happened quite a while ago.

We got back on the road after only spending about half an hour searching. It was more important now to put more distance between us and the creep.

At least he would have been stuck while that weird layer of ice covered the highway; there was no way he could have pedaled his bike uphill with zero traction. He could have pushed his bike during that time, but he still would have been a lot slower than usual.

Still, we urged Patience to move as quickly as possible, and we reached the summit of the mountain highway as dusk was falling.

There was a restaurant, a tiny museum and a gift shop to mark the apex of the mountain pass, so we decided to spend the night under their shelter since we had the option.

It was obvious that the buildings had been searched and cleared. Boards that had once covered the windows and doors lay splintered on the ground, and in the failing light of day, we could see that the interiors were scattered with debris.

We hunkered down in the restaurant, where there were puffy booth benches to curl up on, and were both asleep within a few minutes.

I had disturbing dreams of war, falling through thin ice into freezing water, and being the last person left on Earth. I felt relieved when the sky started to lighten, and left Andy sleeping while I crept into the other buildings to see if I could find anything.

My mom and me would sometimes stop here on our way to camp, and it felt strange to enter the buildings without her, and to see them so damaged. It felt a little bit like a nightmare, but this one I wasn't going to wake up from.

I entered the gift shop first, remembering how we would stop and look at all of the postcards and wildlife sculptures. A few of them lay scattered on the floor along with the broken glass and trinkets from a smashed display case.

One thing that I had hoped to find in the gift shop was a little specimen box with a magnifying glass lid that I had seen here before. It was supposed to be used as a way for kids to trap and look at bugs up close, but it could also be used on a sunny day to start a fire by focusing the sun's rays through the lens. Eric had shown us how to start a fire this way, and I could remember feeling amazed as the kindling under the little pinprick of light began to smoke and eventually burst into flame. I had a lot of matches left in my backpack, but it would be nice to have a firestarter that would be reusable forever.

My footsteps crunched over the mess on the floor, and I kept my eyes peeled for any sign of the specimen boxes, though I didn't really expect to find one – the place had been turned over so completely I was sure everything useful would be long gone.

I checked the museum over next, and once again didn't expect to find anything – the displays were all just big panels of information about the creation of the highway and mountain railway. I knew there were tracks and tunnels running through the mountains, my mom and me had seen trains zooming along in the distance, and had even talked about riding on the passenger train together so we could see another view of the incredible landscape. Mom always said how she felt like she was missing out on all the spectacular views because she was concentrating so hard on negotiating the treacherous highway. I had offered to drive a couple of times, but more as a joke because I had only been driving for a couple of years. There was no way we would have survived if I had been behind the wheel...

Finding nothing in the museum, I returned to the restaurant where Andy was still fast asleep. I made my way toward the back and into the kitchen, which only had one small window and was almost completely dark. The dining area had huge windows lining the walls so you could look out over the mountain lake and watch the helicopters take people up for tours of the area while you ate.

Standing in the doorway while my eyes adjusted to the dim lighting, I wondered if the helicopters had been on the ground when the power went out. If not, at least the drop would have taken less time than a plane gliding slowly to earth. Then I realized how odd it was for me to find a bright side in crashing to your death in a helicopter.

After a quick search I found that the kitchen held nothing of use, so I went to sit at one of the tables overlooking the lake to wait for Andy to wake up. The view really was spectacular, especially in the fresh morning sunlight.

I couldn't help but feel like the mountains were also starting to seem like an insurmountable hurdle in our journey, especially with our food supplies running out so quickly. At least there wasn't snow on the ground yet; I felt that we should

147

arrive at camp before the snow fell and stayed, if we could keep making such good time.

On my way to camp a few years ago, my mom and I stopped right here for lunch, and as we were munching our grilled cheese and ham sandwiches, big slushy snowflakes had started drifting down from the sky. It was the middle of summer, so we were both totally shocked and finished our food quickly so we could go outside. As we paid our bill, the waitress told us that the weather could change drastically in a split second in the mountains, and that snow in July wasn't really all that uncommon.

We had hurried outside, and as I tried to catch one of the big lazy snowflakes on my tongue, I got hit in the back with a slush ball that my mom had gathered from the grass next to the parking lot.

I had turned to find her doubled over laughing, her hands cradling another dripping slush bomb. Before she could even catch her breath I retaliated. The snow had melted away within a few minutes, but not before we were both soaked and freezing.

The other patrons in the restaurant had stared at us disapprovingly as, teeth chattering, we had giggled our way into the bathroom to change our clothes.

Sitting here now, staring at that same bathroom door, I felt completely detached from that happy, carefree girl. She was as lost to me as my mother.

The memory did serve to remind me, however, that while I had only seen snow in July once, winter was coming, and it was guaranteed that the landscape would soon be blanketed in an icy layer of white.

A sense of urgency filled my mind once again, and I stood up, ready to get back on the road as soon as possible.

I whispered Andy's name a few times, and he woke with a squeaky yelp of surprise.

'Oh Gracie, it's you,' he muttered, rubbing the sleep out of his eyes. 'I was dreaming that we were stuck in that dark tunnel again, and then the ghosts started whispering my name. I'm glad it was actually you whispering!' He sat up, looking around blearily. 'Wish we could order some pancakes...'

We each ate a few mouthfuls of beans and a handful of cereal, and then went outside to find Patience. We had tethered her next to the lake behind the restaurant where there was plenty of long grass for her to eat. As I said good morning and stroked her neck I noticed that her coat was becoming thicker and more fluffy. She could feel winter's approach, too.

As I walked Patience back toward the highway, I noticed a signpost in front of an overgrown trail leading into the forest that I hadn't noticed last night in the dark. I stared at it, and the danger I had left Patience in sunk in slowly and horribly. Andy's voice piped up behind me suddenly, making me jump.

"'You are in grizzly bear territory. Hike at your own risk.'"

I turned and looked at him, and he looked pale and horrified too.

'Yikes.'

He had summed up what we were both feeling with that one word. I couldn't imagine hiking the trail under normal circumstances, but now that there was no tourism noise or constant traffic to scare the wildlife away, it became shockingly clear that we were the ones trespassing, and how risky it was to be here, especially in autumn when the bears would be fattening themselves up to prepare for hibernation. And I had left our horse tied up out on the grass like an all-you-can-eat buffet. Guilt washed over me and I found myself fighting back sudden tears.

Andy took my hand and led us toward the highway, while I dried my eyes on my sleeve. I felt so grateful to have my two traveling companions, and I just wanted to get them safely to camp.

If I hadn't come across Patience, I guessed I would still be somewhere in the prairies at this point, or I would have been caught by the monsters or the creep by now. If I hadn't simply starved to death instead. And meeting Andy had saved my life too, I knew I wouldn't have made it this far without him.

It made me feel better to be back on the road, especially now that we had passed the landmark of the summit. Even though we had at least a week's worth of traveling left to do, the end of our journey felt a lot closer now that I knew we had started the descent toward the coast.

Knowing that we were headed down out of the mountains seemed to have given Andy new enthusiasm too, and his questions and chatter kept my mind occupied, so that I barely noticed the day slipping by. He told me stories about where he grew up, stories about school, and asked me at least a hundred questions about my life and family. He seemed to know that I needed distracting, and I appreciated the effort he put in to cheering me up.

By the time the sun had set behind the mountains, we were both hungry and tired and so decided to find a place to stop for the night. Andy had just suggested that we try eating some pine bark for supper.

'Our food is almost gone, so we need to get used to eating stuff we can find in nature. And at least for today, if it's super gross, we can still wash it down with some pickles, beans and cereal.'

'Sounds like a plan,' I said, chuckling. 'The only pine tree that I'm one-hundred percent sure about is the white bark pine. We learned about recognizing different species of trees in survival training at camp, but I really can't remember what features any of the other edible ones have. White bark pine has long needles that grow in little bunches of five, so if we just make sure to look for that, we should be good to go.'

The road had widened somewhat as we traveled, and the terrain beside it had become more flat and horse-friendly. We had decided a few hours ago to try traveling alongside the road instead of directly on it, so we could benefit from the coverage of the trees. I felt that the creep wouldn't give up until he had found us again, so when we came upon a section of fencing that had been knocked over, we took the opportunity to leave the highway. There was a worn path that ran parallel to the road, so we could stay on course while avoiding being seen.

There were a lot of droppings along the trail, most of which I recognized as deer scat, so I figured it must be a game trail we were following. There were several wildlife bridges across the highway that had been built to allow animals safe passage from one side of the highway to the other. I remembered driving with my mom and seeing deer and big horned sheep crossing overhead as we zoomed along the road. I wondered if we would be visible from the highway if we made camp at the foot of one of the bridges. If he caught up to us, the creep might just bike right past us if we found a good enough spot.

As night truly started to fall, we came upon a large outcropping of rock that looked fairly easy to climb. There were numerous large boulders that created rough steps up to the large flat rock which stuck out of the mountainside, almost like a finger directing us away from the place.

We agreed that it looked like a decent place to make camp for the night, so I told Andy to sit tight while I dismounted to find a safe place to tether Patience.

A low growl behind me ripped through the silence of the evening.

'Gracie!' Andy whispered, panic written all over his pale face.

I froze, staring into his eyes, silently willing him to stay put and not try to help defend me on the ground. Slowly I turned my head to try to catch a glimpse of what I was dealing with. In my peripheral vision I saw a large grey animal slink out from between two trees. I reached for the knife at my hip, but before I could make any further movement, Patience caught sight of the animal and reared up, whinnying in fright, her front legs thrashing dangerously through the air.

I jumped out of the way of her hooves and found myself on the ground. A gnarled tree root had tripped me, sending me skidding headfirst along the forest's mulchy floor.

Spitting out pine needles, I scrambled to my feet but could only watch helplessly as Patience streaked into the trees, bearing a screaming Andy along with her. The wolf that had spooked Patience raced after her, snarling and growling.

The silence that followed their flight was heavy on my ears, which, coupled with the terror I felt, suddenly caused flashbacks of the plane crash. The vivid memories and my sudden solitude paralyzed me.

The rushing sounds starting in my ears warned me that I was going to pass out, so I forced myself to squat down and put my head between my knees, trying to take deep breaths.

I couldn't believe what had just happened. How could I have been so careless... I waited for the lightheadedness to pass, and reached again for my knife. I would follow the path that Patience had taken until I found Andy again. There was no other choice.

I hadn't taken more than two steps, however, when I heard more growling. It seemed to be coming from every direction, and I could not discern the source in the deepening dark.

I knew I had very little time to act. I was probably surrounded by an entire pack of wolves who could pounce at any moment. I leapt for the ledge of rock that jutted out of the mountainside, and managed to clamber my way to the top, feeling tugs on my backpack and shoes as the wolves tried to pull me back down.

Once I was safely positioned on the flat surface of the rock, I looked down and saw at least six wolves jostling at the foot of the pile of boulders, struggling to climb up after me.

I clutched my knife in my sweaty hand, sure that they would be able to manage the climb. They leapt and snapped at me, but their claws slipped off the boulders – they couldn't get a firm enough grip on the smooth rocks to follow me.

I was completely trapped; there was no way I could get down from the ledge without being torn apart. There were a couple of tree branches growing out of the rock face behind me, and I considered cutting one down to make a spear handle. I could use one of my spare shoelaces to tie my knife to the end of the branch and try to stab at the wolves so they would leave me alone. But what if my knife fell off and I lost it? I couldn't risk it. I decided to make a torch to try to scare them away. It was hard to focus on what I was doing with all the snarling and the sound of claws scraping against the rock, but I had my knife ready just in case one of them found a way up.

I finished my torch and lit it with a match, feeling hugely grateful that I hadn't taken off my backpack before climbing down from Patience's back. The light from the torch fell on the wolves and turned them into a swirling mass of flashing eyes and glistening teeth.

I heard a distant scream and my heart dropped into my stomach. It had to have been Andy screaming, but he sounded so far away already. I yelled his name and heard another scream rip through the night. Desperate, I started swinging the torch at the wolves, blinking terrified tears out of my eyes.

Suddenly they backed off as though they had been called, and as one, turned toward the forest. I started to yell Andy's name again, but my voice died in my throat as I heard the hammering of huge paws. Something humungous was crashing through the trees toward me and the wolves. I pressed my back against the rock face behind me, and held the torch up to throw more light into the trees ahead.

The wolves were growling louder than ever, and I could see their raised hackles and bared teeth glinting in the torchlight. I could feel my heart pounding in my throat and squinted into the trees to try to see what was coming, hoping that I was out of its reach too.

Another distant terrified scream pierced my body like a shard of ice, and a sob escaped my throat, just as an enormous grizzly bear finally came smashing through the tree line.

The wolves pounced on the bear, biting at its neck and sides with horrible tearing sounds. The bear bellowed a deep and angry roar, swiping at the wolves with huge paws that ended in long, lethal claws.

The fight was vicious and terrifying and seemed to have no end in sight. It was impossible to tell by the flickering light of the torch which species was being dealt more damage, but I could see that all of the animals had blood shining in their fur.

Suddenly one of the bear's giant paws made contact with a wolf. The force behind the strike sent the wolf flying into the trunk of a nearby tree. The sickening crack and whimper of pain as the wolf's body slammed into the tree could be heard even over the continued battle. The wolf gave one more distressed little whine and then lay still.

A long, high-pitched howl tore through the night and, as one, the wolf pack turned and started running toward the distant sound, leaving their fallen brother behind. The grizzly bear hurtled after them, grunting and snorting as it crashed through the trees.

The animals had taken off in the same direction that Patience had fled, and I didn't know what to do.

I knew that the pack, or some other animal, might come to investigate the injured wolf lying at the foot of the tree, and I did not want to be around when that happened.

The wolf did not stir as I clambered down off the rock ledge, and I wasn't about to pause and see if it was still alive.

I headed in the direction of the highway, hoping to take refuge in one of the crashed cars that lined the road. My footsteps seemed loud as I ran through the trees, and I couldn't help but cry out as branches whipped at my face.

I was running too fast to allow the torch to light my way properly; the flickering light barely gave me a second's warning of what lay ahead. After a branch lashed my face below my eye, however, I slowed my pace, not wanting to cause myself a serious injury.

I could feel blood running down my face from under my eye; first hot against my cold cheek, and then cool as the night air sapped the heat out of it.

I held the torch high in front of me. Where was the highway? When we had entered the forest, the game trail had only been a short distance from the fence, and the highway had always been in view through the trees. I should have reached it by now.

I swung the torch to my left and right, but all I could see were more trees. I took a few more steps in the direction I had been heading. But was it the same direction? Since it had not led me to the highway, it was obviously the wrong direction, so shouldn't I retrace my steps and try to find the game trail again? But that would lead me back to the rock ledge and the site of the fight, which was splattered with blood and would surely attract other predators.

How was I going to find Andy? He and Patience could be miles away by now. And those screams... I was sure they had been Andy's... *Why* had we left the safety of the highway? The threat of the creep seemed like a joke compared to the danger we were in now.

I considered yelling Andy's name again, but I didn't want to attract anything toward me. At least he and Patience were together, hopefully they had managed to run to safety... But where was safe? There was absolutely nowhere that was safe for an eight year old boy who was lost and alone in the mountain wilderness. Patience could only be so much help to him; what if she had been taken down by animals, and Andy was completely exposed and in the dark and terrified...

How would we ever find each other again?

Trying to control my panic, I put all of the negative possibilities out of my mind. I had to figure out the fastest way to find Andy. Right now I was just as lost as he was, so until I caught any sign of him – another scream, or the sound of Patience's hooves – it seemed that my best option for now was to stay put and wait for the sun to rise. I had no idea how many hours away dawn was, the trees were too thick to see the sky, and even if I could, the mountains would block out everything but the sky directly above me, so I wouldn't even be able see when there was a lightening in the east.

All I could do was try not to get even more lost, and hope that no hungry animals stumbled across me as I waited for dawn.

I considered pitching my tent for the night. It would be a comfort to have that sort of psychological barrier between me and the wildlife, but if a curious bear came along I didn't want it to get slashed up, and if I had to leave in a hurry, I didn't want to leave it behind. I knew that bears and wolves were fast, but if I could sneak away somehow, I might be able to avoid meeting them.

I looked up at the trees surrounding me, and though it would be nice to be off the ground, I wasn't sure that the branches would support my weight. Plus, bears could climb trees, couldn't they? A sudden image of a bear pushing over a tree with me it in popped into my head, and I decided I would keep my feet firmly on the ground.

I sat down with my back against a nearby trunk and pulled my blanket out of my backpack. It was a small comfort to know that Andy had food and water in his bag, along with the sleeping bag and warm clothes. Now that I had stopped moving, I could feel the layer of sweat on my skin cooling my body, and a chill creeping into my bones through my contact with the ground and the tree.

I pulled a change of clothes out of my bag and removed my sweaty damp ones, pulling the dry clothes on as quickly as possible. It was a difficult task to accomplish while holding a lit torch in one hand, but I managed after struggling for a few minutes. I put on my coat and wrapped myself in the blanket, hoping that wherever Andy had ended up, he was warm and dry.

I knew he was alive, he had to be, because he had promised to haunt me if he died before me, and there was no sign of his Voice chattering away in my head. I had never felt more grateful for my gift. I just wished there was some way for me to tell him that I was alive too, that I would find him as soon as it was light enough to see where I was going.

The flame at the end of my torch grew smaller and smaller, but I decided to just let it burn out. I didn't want to light a fire on the ground, either, because the trees were too dense and sparks shooting up into the branches would likely cause a forest fire.

After pulling my crowbar out of my bag, planning to use it to defend myself if needed, I huddled deeper into my blanket, and stared at the torch as it slowly died. When the last flicker of flame snuffed itself out, the darkness that surrounded me was deeper than any I had experienced before, though the image of the dying torch still shone white in front of me, as though my eyes were trying desperately to cling to the memory of light.

Chapter Ten

I couldn't remember ever passing a more agonizingly long night, but finally the sky started to lighten enough for me to set out to find Andy. I had been relying on the sunrise to tell me which way was east, but as the morning wore on, the sky remained a perfectly uniform grey, adding to my disorientation and uncertainty.

I had no idea which direction to take, so I tried shouting Andy's name again. Hearing only silence in response, I looked around, trying to decide which way to go. Everything around me looked exactly the same, just trees and those small patches of light grey sky. I remembered something about moss growing on a certain side of a tree being a way to determine direction, but could not recall on what side of the tree it needed to be, or even if the idea was true or not. Plus, I couldn't see much moss on the trees around me, so the theory was useless anyway.

I sighed, at a loss.

Suddenly I heard the faint ring of a bike bell. While it sent a chill through my body, it also gave me hope. Was the sound coming from behind me? It seemed like it, and that probably meant that the highway was in that direction too. If I could just get back to the highway, maybe I could find my way back to the place where Andy and I had entered the forest. There was even a slim possibility that he would have the same idea, and be waiting for me there. If he had heard the bike bell though, my guess was that he would hide, and then I might never find him.

I set off in the direction from which the bell had sounded, determined to find Andy and get the two of us back on track before night fell again.

I gripped my knife in one hand and my crowbar in the other, almost pitying the creep if he had the bad luck to cross my path today. It was because of him that we had been living in constant fear, and it was because of him that we had left the highway. I felt like giving him a little payback. A couple of broken toes would slow him down... or maybe I could steal his bike and leave *him* stranded in the wilderness... But he would find me, wouldn't he. He seemed to be on some psychotic mission to hunt me down. But not kill me... He'd had the chance to kill me already, but he had let me live. I couldn't figure out his motivation. If I made it safely to camp, would I live the rest of my life in fear that he would eventually catch up to me? How could I escape him permanently when he was tracking me so relentlessly?

I couldn't kill him. I could never kill another person.

But as I stumbled my way through the dense forest, I realized that I might have to. It might come to a fight, and if it meant that Andy would be safe, maybe I would find myself capable of murder.

I might also be able to buy Andy's safety by surrendering to the creep, but if that meant leaving him on his own, Andy wouldn't make it for very long anyway. Surrender would be pointless. My thoughts returned to murder.

I stomped angrily through the trees, trying to imagine what it would be like to win a death match against the creep, thereby securing our safety and ending his strange, creepy power over us.

On one hand it would feel great to protect Andy and to be free of the fear. On the other hand though, I would have killed someone. I would have to live with their blood on my hands for the rest of my life, and it seemed a very high price to pay... But maybe Andy was worth what it would cost...

I tripped over a tree root and my rage fizzled out to be replaced by anxiety. I would just have to see what happened and deal with the consequences then. It was a waste of energy to worry about something that might never happen. I picked myself up and continued trekking through the woods, listening carefully for any sign of pursuers. I must be getting close to the highway by now, it felt like I had traveled way farther today than I had last night, even though I was moving a lot more slowly today.

The sun broke through the clouds for a moment, and I caught sight of a glint of silver through the trees. I quickened my pace, thinking I was seeing the sun reflecting off of a part of a crashed car, and that I had finally reached the highway.

As I hurtled excitedly through the last few trees, the scene in front of me opened up to reveal, not the highway, but a wide shimmering lake set into the valley floor created by the

157

meeting of four enormous mountains. The sun disappeared behind the clouds again, just as the realization hit me that I was totally and completely lost. I couldn't remember ever seeing a lake at this point from the highway, so I had no idea how off course I had wandered. Any hope of finding Andy today evaporated, and I had to take several deep breaths before I could begin to consider my options.

The lake was filled by runoff from the mountains, and there wasn't a river I could follow, and without the sun to guide me, there was no way to know which direction would take me back to the highway. I could head back into the forest and hope to find the highway eventually, or I could make camp here and hope that the sun would be shining tomorrow. Not that the sun guaranteed that I would be heading in the right direction anyway; the highway was so winding and in places it even tunneled straight through the mountains, so at this point it was truly possible that it could be in any direction.

I decided to take a short break to rest and eat something, since I hadn't slept or eaten in so long. I sat down on the rocky shore of the lake and opened my last can of beans, taking only a few small mouthfuls, just enough to stop my insides from aching. I transferred the remaining beans into a plastic container I had found in one of the houses we had searched, and stowed it deep into my bag, not wanting to attract any wildlife with the smell. After sipping some water, I leaned back against my backpack and gazed up at the mountain peaks surrounding me, feeling very small and insignificant. This sort of view had once amazed and inspired me. Now all I could see was a cold and unforgiving landscape that had completely isolated me from everything I cared about.

How could I have let this happen? We never should have left the highway. What an idiotic thing to have done. And then to have put so much distance between me and Andy...

Maybe the sound of the bike bell had bounced off a couple of mountains, and what I had actually followed was just an echo. If I had even really heard it at all. It could have been an auditory hallucination – maybe I had finally cracked up.

One of the first doctors that I had mentioned the Voices to had used the phrase 'auditory hallucination,' and had given my mom many significant stares as he'd tossed around the words schizophrenia and bipolar disorder. He had told her about all of the meds I could take to try to correct the chemical imbalance in my brain, and had offered to give us a referral to a psychiatrist.

My mom had very politely handed back the fistful of pamphlets he had given her, thanked him for his time, grabbed my hand and walked us out of his office.

Once we had reached the parking lot, she had scooped me up into her arms, even though I was really too big to carry anymore, and we had walked for several blocks before I felt her shaking subside. We reached a park bench overlooking a duck pond and she sat us down on it, still holding me close beside her. Finally, when she was able to speak again, she told me that, under no circumstances, was I ever to believe that I was crazy or in need of medication because of the Voices. She told me that I was normal and special all at the same time, and no one had the right to tell me otherwise. We had sat there holding hands on that park bench, talking and watching the ducks play in the water, until our bums were numb from sitting for so long, and our fingers and noses were icy from the chilly fall air. That day was one of the first times I truly realized how much faith my mom had in me, and after that I never once doubted that she would always fight for me.

These memories reminded me of Kevin, the little boy whose parents had made the wrong decision and had locked him up in some padded room, despite the enormous progress he had made in those few short weeks at camp. I wondered what had happened to him after the world had lost power. I hated to think that he had been starving and trapped and eventually perished in some padded room somewhere. Maybe he had escaped, or had been rescued, and was even now making his way to camp. It was, after all, the one place that he had felt hope and acceptance – perhaps he would feel drawn to return there, the way I had, and he could be part of our new little community. He would be grown up by now, around sixteen or seventeen years old, so I might not even recognize him if we crossed paths, but I hoped that I would see him again.

***

I'm not sure how long I sat there on that rocky lakeshore, trying to decide what to do. The fact was that I had no way of knowing how to find Andy. If I had wandered this far off-course, then he probably had, too.

Suddenly the Voices went quiet. Once again I was astonished at how loud true silence could be, after years of hearing the constant murmur of the dead. I closed my eyes and lowered my head, wondering if I was about to receive a message from someone, perhaps Olivia, telling me how to go about finding Andy again.

In the silence my ears picked up, not a message from Beyond, but something much closer... The faint sound of twigs cracking across the lake – something large was moving through the trees on the bank opposite me, breaking branches as it came.

I leapt up, thinking I was about to see Andy and Patience appear across the water. To be on the safe side though, I backed into the trees and hid behind the trunk of a tall pine.

I could see the trees across the lake swaying as their branches were brushed aside. Fear replaced hope as I realized that Andy would never make Patience force her way through the scratching branches like that – it had to be something else. I crouched down, gripping my weapons, waiting.

Finally the enormous body of a black bear came out onto the shore, followed by two slightly smaller bears.

A mother and her cubs.

I started to slowly back up, willing the bears not to see me. One black bear alone was scary enough, but a mother with cubs was downright terrifying.

If she felt like her babies were being threatened at all, she would attack. I could run – I had a decent head start with the lake between us, but I knew bears could move very quickly, and they, unlike me, were used to this terrain.

Climbing a tree was out. The trees here looked bigger than the ones I had considered climbing to escape the grizzly and wolves, but I had seen photos of black bears high up in trees, and I hadn't climbed a tree since I was a kid.

I knew that black bears were omnivorous, and would eat any living or dead animal, so playing dead would likely get me eaten anyway.

All of these thoughts flew through my head in less than a minute, and finally I decided that the best thing I could do right now was to keep backing away, and hope that they wouldn't see me.

Still crouching, keeping my eyes on the shore opposite, I took several more careful steps backward, checking over my shoulder periodically to avoid backing into a tree. A few more steps and I would be able to turn around and move a little faster...

A twig snapped beneath my shoe and I looked up, panicked, knowing that the bears would have heard the sound. The cubs looked up, and then stood up on their hind legs, curiously peering into the trees around me. Then, to my horror, they plunged into the water and started swimming toward my side of the lake. The mother bear quickly followed.

Hoping that the sound of their splashing would drown out the sound of my retreat, I turned and ran as fast as I could into the trees, grateful that this time I could see where I was going.

I had no idea where I was heading, and no idea if I would actually find safety. I could still hear the sound of splashing as the bears crossed the lake, so at least I knew they were not chasing me on the ground yet.

I could see that the trees thinned ahead, and hoped that by some miracle, I had stumbled my way back to the highway.

I raced through the last few trees and into the clearing. It wasn't the highway. It was a set of train tracks.

To see something created by human hands in this wild and lonely place gave me a huge burst of hope. I leapt onto the tracks and started running along them, knowing that eventually they would lead to a station and a town

Once I reached the town I would search it for supplies, find the highway, and then double back to find Andy.

Before long I became winded, and had to slow down to a walk, but I couldn't help running some more as soon as I caught my breath. I was excited to see something other than trees and mulch, plus I was putting more distance between myself and the bear family, so I ran as much as I could, feeling more optimistic than I had in weeks.

The tracks gave me a sense of security I had been lacking in the forest, so as night started to fall, I pitched my tent beside them and built a fire.

I ate some beans, and had to stop myself from finishing them. I was certain I would reach a town soon, but I still had to be smart about my supplies.

I remembered Andy suggesting we try to eat pine, so I cut a square into the trunk of a nearby tree and peeled back the rough outer bark. I cut the soft, sticky white inner bark into strips, and then added them, along with some pine needles, into a pot of water. I sat and watched it come to a boil, excited to fill my stomach.

I let the pot boil for quite a while, and then set it aside to cool. When it was cool enough, I took a sip of the warm pine water, and was surprised that it didn't taste too bad. I scooped several strips of pine out of the water, and transferred them into my mouth. It tasted resiny and weird, but I was determined to eat as much as possible, so I chewed. And chewed. And chewed. It didn't seem to want to break down, so finally I swallowed the ball of tough fibers. I felt it stick in my throat, and sipped more pine water to help it go down. I felt it go all the way down, as though I had swallowed a rubber ball.

I looked into the pot, not wanting to eat any more, but feeling as though that would be wasting precious food. Maybe if I only ate one strip at a time it would be easier to eat. I scooped out a single piece and tried it. The only difference was that this time, the lump was smaller and a little easier to swallow. I wondered how my stomach would handle the sudden influx of fiber, and only ate a few more pieces, hoping to spare myself a bad belly ache.

As I sat down next to the fire, I realized the Voices had returned. The sound was a comfort – it was nice to have company again.

The day's activities, coupled with a full belly and warm drink made me sleepy quite quickly, so I zipped myself into the tent and, despite my worry for Andy, I fell asleep almost instantly, feeling somehow protected by my proximity to the train tracks.

It must have been several hours later that I awoke with a start, having heard movement just outside my tent. I sat up, grabbed my knife out of its sheath at my hip, listening intently.

Something or someone was definitely prowling around out there. I heard a deep huff from a set of huge lungs and wondered if the bears had caught up to me. Maybe the smell of beans or campfire or cooking pine had attracted them.

I remained as still as possible, not wanting them to become any more curious about the area than they already were. Suddenly something nudged the side of the tent, and I let out an involuntary whimper of fear. The animal bumped the tent again, and I realized that maybe they thought there was an injured animal inside, because of the pathetic sound I had made.

I jumped up, filled my lungs and let out the deepest, loudest bellow I could muster, and started shaking the tent myself, hoping to scare the creature away by appearing more dominant.

I heard another big huff and a low growl.

I roared again, louder this time, and shook the tent even harder. Silence followed the racket I had made, and I could have sworn I heard the retreat of large paws against the mulchy ground.

Slowly I sank back down, trying to steady my breathing and normalize my heart rate, wishing with every breath that soon I would wake up from this nightmare.

I spent the rest of the night huddled under my blanket, listening for the sound of the animal's return. What if I hadn't decided to pitch my tent? What if I had just been asleep on the ground and had suddenly woken up, face to face with whatever beast that was...

The thought filled me with terror for Andy – how could he possibly survive nights out here, when all he had for shelter was a tarp and some rope? I had meant to give him the tent, taking the tarp for myself, but we had never made the trade. I had completely forgotten, or maybe I hadn't really believed that we would get separated...

Yet his Voice was still absent from the chorus in my head, so he had to be doing alright, wherever he was. Unless he was dying a slow agonizing death somewhere, abandoned and alone and scared...

I sat up, trying to push those awful thoughts out of my mind – imagining the worst would not help either of us survive.

I waited impatiently for daylight to return to the world outside my tent, feeling as though each minute I sat here waiting was a minute that could have been spent finding my way back to Andy. I still planned to follow the tracks to a town, and then work my way back to him.

I tried to think of some way to let him know where I was going. I could leave twigs arranged as arrows on the tracks, pointing him in the right direction, but would he notice them, if he was busy watching out for predators?

I rummaged through my backpack, hoping to come across something that could help me get a message to Andy. My fingers felt something made of paper, that was folded over several times. I pulled it out, examining it with my hands, unable to see what it was in the pitch dark.

The map! I had completely forgotten that we had found a map in that car which had also contained the gun. And hadn't there been a pen as well? I rummaged blindly in my bag some more, and sure enough, right at the bottom, my fingers found the long slim shape of a pen.

I wished the sun would hurry up and rise, so I could examine the map and see what my location might be. Maybe the train tracks would even be charted, and I would be able to find my way back to the highway sooner. I could leave Andy notes along the way, written in pen on... what? Fragments of paper torn from the map? But they might be too small and he would miss them. I could etch messages into trees along the way – but again, if he wasn't looking for them, he wouldn't see them. Plus I didn't want to damage a tree on the off-chance that Andy would notice.

The excitement of finding the pen had vanished, and I slumped down on my side, feeling defeated. Something dug into my ribs, and I reached around to pull it out. My book. My book! I could tear pages out of my book, write messages on them, and leave them in a trail for Andy to follow!

I opened my book, and touched the first few pages, feeling a little heartbroken at having to destroy one of my favorite things left in this world. I practically knew it by heart, but still, losing yet another familiar, comforting item was upsetting.

I rubbed the top corner of the first page between my thumb and finger, and before I could think about it much more, I ripped the page out. The sound wasn't as loud as I had expected, but it still tore at my spirit a little.

Thankful for the dark, I continued to rip page after page out of my book. This would have been a much harder task if I had been able to see what I was doing. Once I had torn out about half of the pages I stopped, planning to write the messages as soon as daylight reappeared.

I would hang them in the trees in little clusters, so they couldn't be mistaken for garbage. If it rained, or if the wind picked up, they might be lost or ruined, but Andy was smart, and I felt that he would know they were meant for him, and that he'd keep looking for more.

After what felt like an exceptionally long night, dawn finally broke, and I could finally check to see if the train tracks were on the map. Of course they weren't. So I folded it back up, and stowed it away in my bag. Trying not to feel too disappointed about the map, I wrote my messages to Andy, telling him to follow the tracks, that I was looking for him, and to get back on the highway toward camp as soon as he could.

I didn't have a concrete plan anymore, there were just too many variables where Andy was concerned. He could be right behind me; he could have found the highway again, and would be at camp before I was; he could be lost and starving in the wilderness.

The first town the tracks brought me to could be days away from the highway, so I couldn't wait for him there. If he was following the tracks, and I went looking for him on the highway, we would miss each other then, too. I could go looking for him at the point where we had gotten separated, but by now he could be in a completely different location. It seemed like the only good option was to continue my journey to find the highway, and once there, I could keep leaving messages for him to meet me.

As I finished writing out the messages, I spoke quietly to Olivia, not sure if she was close by, but feeling it was worth a try. I asked her to help me find Andy, and that she try to help him survive. I hoped that her silence indicated that she was too busy watching over him to communicate with me.

After packing away the pen and my ruined book, I unzipped the tent warily, not completely convinced of my solitude – it was possible that the creature from last night was still lurking somewhere among the trees.

I made as much noise as I could while packing up my tent, hoping to scare away any nearby animals. Once I had all of my gear strapped to my back again, I looked around for a good place to start my trail of pages.

Knowing there was only a slim chance that Andy would even see my messages, I pinned them into the trees nearest the tracks by puncturing the pages with the lower hanging branches. The act of hanging something in a tree brought back razor-sharp memories of my mom and twinkling lights and tinsel, but I pushed those memories aside before they could really take hold, and turned my back on the tree as quickly as I could.

As I made my way along the tracks, I would stop every few minutes and hang a few more pages. Looking back, I could see an obvious trail – it would be hard to miss if Andy came through this way. Or anyone else for that matter.

I traveled along the tracks for the entire day, and by the time night had started to fall, I was starting to run low on pages. My poor book looked so sad, with its cover still hanging on, despite the fact that three-quarters of its insides were gone.

Like me.

I felt like a mostly-empty shell. My mom, my home, and now Andy had all been ripped away from me and scattered across the landscape, and here I was, trying to hold the rest of myself together even though I would never be whole again.

But maybe I would find Andy, and together we could repair some of the damage; he, too, had suffered immense losses. We could both use a few new pages to make up for the chapters we'd lost.

Chapter Eleven

I pitched my tent, finished the last of the beans, and spent an uneventful night tossing and turning.

When it was light again, I continued along the tracks, and started to wonder if I would ever come across signs of civilization again.

At around midday I could see that I was approaching a distant mountain wall. Would the tracks go around it? It seemed too sharp a turn... There must be a tunnel ahead.

I looked up, knowing already that I would not be able to climb over the mountain to reach the other side – I would have to go through the tunnel and hope that no hungry animal was using it as a cave.

As the wall drew closer, I became more and more anxious, remembering the last experiences I had had with mountain tunnels. At that point I had been blissfully unaware of the fact that humans were no longer the top of the food chain. The last few days had set me straight very quickly. Being pursued by the creep was now the least of my worries, as I was easy prey for whatever creature stumbled upon me.

I stopped and made a torch, not wanting to be completely blind once I entered the tunnel, but also thinking that I could use it as a weapon if I needed to.

The tunnel loomed ahead, a great black hole with no light at the end, making me wonder just how long I would be stuck in the dark. There was nothing I could do though, I had to keep moving forward, so I gathered my courage, lit my torch and stepped into the dark. I walked along the side of the tracks, running my hand along the cold damp stone, glad that in this tunnel, at least there wouldn't be a pileup of cars full of dead bodies.

I shivered as I remembered the smell, the horrid stench of rotting meat.

No, it wasn't a sense memory – my nose was actually detecting the same smell, right now, in this pitch black tunnel.

I slowed my pace and kept my eyes glued to the ground, not wanting to fall face-first into whatever I was about to find.

The reek grew stronger, and soon I found myself at the foot of a mound that spanned halfway across the tunnel, and stood about half my height against the wall. I held my torch up, trying to avoid stepping in anything, and saw that the mound was made up of furry lumps and small bones. Some animal had made the tunnel their lair, and had clearly been bringing prey in here to stockpile it and protect if from scavengers. I hurried past the mound, desperate to get out of the tunnel as soon as I could.

It was as I passed the far side of the mound that the torchlight illuminated something that, at first, my mind wouldn't believe. I stopped in my tracks, staring, trying to make sense of what I was seeing…

A human hand protruded from the gruesome pile, and almost appeared to be gesturing to me to stop and turn back.

I fought the urges to throw up and scream and faint and cry, and forced my numb legs to continue carrying my body past the mound. I tried my best not to imagine how that poor person had come to rest in such a remote place, but images of them wandering lost in the woods, or being snatched out of their bed, or simply succumbing to hunger and being dragged here kept filling my head.

Even as a witness to a death match between a grizzly bear and a wolf pack, I had never felt more in danger than I did right now. Not only had I discovered irrefutable proof that humans were fair game to all predators, but I was completely cornered in this tunnel if the animal returned to its hoard any time soon. I had always known that wild carnivores were a danger to humans, but to see the evidence first hand… I let out a short laugh at the pun, wishing Andy were here to appreciate it, and heard my own crazed laughter echo back to me. It snapped me back to seriousness instantly – even though I had seen and survived about as much as I could bear, this was no time to crack up. Bear. I giggled again. Maybe I was just cracking up, and who could blame me, really?

The tunnel seemed to go on forever, and every footstep echoed back to me a hundred times, so it was almost impossible to listen for signs of a returning predator.

The flame from my torch had started to die so I quickened my pace again, hoping to clear the tunnel before it extinguished completely. Just in case, I continued to walk with my hand touching the stone wall, and I'm lucky I did, because my torch sputtered and went out, and I found myself, once again, in darkness deeper than I had ever thought possible.

I stumbled along the tunnel wall still gripping my dead torch, ready to swing it at whatever I might meet.

After about ten minutes of walking blindly through the dark, however, I looked up and saw the exit of the tunnel ahead, and it was clear of any dark, hulking forms waiting to ambush and eat me.

I ran through the last section, needing so badly to get out of the dark, and when I leapt out of the tunnel, the sunlight was so bright it hurt my eyes, but I didn't mind. I'd never been so happy to see daylight in my life. I had been convinced, until this moment, that my body was going to be added to that grisly pile of remains, and that Andy would follow my message trail, and then become part of the pile, too. I breathed the fresh air deeply, thankful to be alive. I left a few extra pages outside the tunnel exit, so that Andy would know I had made it through, and just in case he thought that hand might have been mine. The poor kid, I sincerely hoped he had found another way through the mountains; I didn't even want to imagine the reaction he would have to seeing the hand.

I continued along the tracks, waiting for my eyes to adjust to the brightness, when a crashing sound met my ears. It took me a second to locate the source of the noise. Squinting around, I finally spotted a huge waterfall cascading down from a rocky ledge. It fell into a small pool which broke away into a few narrow streams.

At once I stripped down to my underwear, left my clothes and backpack on the edge, and climbed into the little pool. The water was so cold it was painful, but I didn't care. When I looked down at my reflection in the water, I was shocked to see that half of my face was covered in dried blood. I had completely forgotten that I had cut my face under my eye when I was running away from the grizzly and wolves. I splashed water on my face and scrubbed the blood and other grime that had accumulated there in the last few weeks. Then I waded over to the waterfall and let it crash down on my shoulders. It knocked the breath right out of me, but I felt like it was cleansing me. Looking up, I could see a dark hole in the wall behind the water, and wondered if it was a cave.

I climbed the slippery rock pile at the foot of the waterfall, and found myself standing in a perfect little recess in the mountain wall, with a curtain of water spilling over the entrance. I considered staying in the little cavern for a while, I felt so safe and hidden, but I was already shivering so violently that I might not be able to climb down if I stayed much longer.

The descent was a lot more tricky than I had imagined it would be. Hunger and fatigue had sapped most of my strength, and when I finally reached the edge of the pool again, my thighs were shaking just as much as the rest of my body, but not from cold. I had been traveling for months, and climbing onto Patience's back every day, but still, I hadn't used my leg muscles with such intensity in a long time, and I could feel their weakness as I dressed in fresh clothes.

I washed my dirty clothes in the pool, and attached them to my bag to dry. I stripped some bark off a nearby pine tree and chewed the inner bark as I walked along the tracks, still shivering a little, but feeling refreshed. The pine was just as hard to swallow in its raw form, but I was glad to have something to eat. I needed to replace the energy I had wasted climbing the waterfall, and I needed to warm up.

After another hour of walking, I finally decided to stop and build a fire. My body was still shivering, wasting any precious energy I had left, and the sun would set soon. The nights had been getting colder and I wanted to be warm before night fell, so I didn't have to sit by the fire, exposed to wildlife, in the dark.

I pitched my tent, built a fire, and huddled close to it, wrapped tightly in my blanket. I warmed up pretty fast, and settled down for the night. My exhausted body fell asleep almost instantly, and I was never aware of any nighttime visitors – I slept straight through until the sun filled my tent with light. When I poked my head out of the tent it could have even been close to noon, the sun was already so high in the sky.

I was amazed by how long I had slept, and surprised that I still felt exhausted and weak. All I had eaten in the last few days were some chewy slivers of pine bark, and I was famished. My stomach felt like it had turned inside out, so I drank some water, but it just made me feel nauseated. I coaxed my campfire back to life and made some pine water, hoping it would settle my stomach.

I packed up my campsite while my pine water brewed, and just that small task had me panting and dizzy.

I sat and sipped the hot drink slowly, determined to keep it, and whatever nutrients it might supply, in my stomach.

The brew did give me a little boost of energy, and I set off along the tracks, eating some more pine bark as I walked. I could feel the water sloshing around inside me, and I couldn't help but daydream about all the different meals that I would eat right now, if I could.

Somehow the pine bark just didn't cut it when I imagined digging into a big plate of thick golden waffles smothered in strawberries and whipped cream... With a side of syrupy pancakes... And sausages and bacon and toast and scrambled eggs and fruit salad and milk and orange juice...

Nope, the pine definitely left something to be desired, but at least it should sustain me until I could find something else to eat.

As I continued along the tracks, I became aware that the temperature seemed to be dropping quite a bit. Before long I could see my breath rise in front of me, a swirling white vapor in the crisp autumn air. The unnatural decrease in temperature could only mean one thing. I tensed up, bracing myself for whatever apparition was about to show itself. But nothing happened. I waited, looking around for the telltale glimmer of light to appear, but all that materialized were some fluffy white snowflakes. I had to laugh at my presumption. Cold weather couldn't possibly mean that winter was coming, no, it could only be messages from beyond the grave...

I sighed and kept walking, glad that both Andy and I had found extra winter clothes during our searches.

The snow continued falling as the day wore on, and wasn't melting as it touched the ground. Was this just some crazy mountain weather, or was it actually later in the year than I had figured?

I changed into the winter boots I had found, and though they kept my feet warmer and drier, they were also much heavier than my running shoes, and I could feel the exhaustion in my legs after only a few minutes of walking.

I started to feel frustration too, because I needed to keep going in order to find food, but I needed food in order to keep going.

I didn't want to give up early today, it wouldn't be any easier tomorrow, so I pushed myself to keep walking for as long as I could.

After about another hour though, I started to feel like my muscles were going to give out. I chewed some more pine bark and drank some water which helped, but by the time the sun had started to set, I barely had enough energy left to pitch my tent.

I climbed inside and wrapped myself in my blanket and fell asleep at once.

In the morning when I woke up, it was a surprise that I had slept straight through again, especially because my body still felt so tired. I lay there, wondering what time it was. It was definitely cloudy today – the light that filtered into the tent was subdued, eliminating all highlights and lowlights and making the colors I could see look as flat and as washed out as I felt.

I couldn't seem to motivate myself to get up; I felt like my body weighed a thousand pounds, and the idea of packing up the tent and trekking along the train tracks all day was not remotely appealing.

Maybe I was fighting off a flu or something. Or maybe my body was slowly shutting down from a lack of food. Either way, staying right here in this cozy tent all day seemed like a great idea... Until I remembered that Andy was still out there, fighting to survive.

With a huge effort I hauled myself over to the zipper, and opened the tent flap. The brightness outside blinded me, and for a moment I couldn't understand why – it had been so dim inside the tent. My eyes adjusted to the sudden brilliance, and I finally realized that overnight the world had been covered in a thick blanket of snow.

The sun peeked out from behind the clouds and the scene was dazzling – the snow sparkled, looking like a billion stars had fallen from the sky and now coated everything in front of me. The layer of white was so perfect, so untouched...

So isolating.

In a different world I would have been enthralled and uplifted by such a view, but now all I could see was an added obstacle standing between me and survival. The extra energy it would cost to trudge through the snow in my heavy boots made me want to cry. I let out a sob, but even crying felt like too much effort, so I settled for sitting in the mouth of the tent, staring out into space.

Andy. Andy was out there alone. I was the only person in the entire world who knew that he needed help, and here I was, wallowing in self pity instead of doing everything in my power to rescue him.

Shame and guilt gave me the shove I needed to pack up the tent, and soon I was on my way again. It was lucky that I had the train tracks to guide me; the rails stood out just enough under the layer of white that I could still see which way I needed to go.

With every step I took, more and more snow clung to my boots, so that every few minutes I had to stomp my feet to rid myself of the extra weight. I had worn three pairs of socks, but even so, I could feel the beginning of blisters on my heels. I kept twisting my ankles because whoever had broken the boots in must have walked with most of their weight on the arches of their feet.

I suddenly remembered my coffee-sleeve shoes, and could not imagine trying to navigate this terrain wearing them.

Finally, after stumbling so badly that I almost fell on my face, I switched back to my running shoes. My feet were soaked almost instantly, but I was able to walk more easily, and felt like I was making good time again.

I cut some fresh pine bark out of a tree beside the tracks, and as I started chewing a strip I happened to look down to see huge paw prints in the snow. I hurried back onto the tracks and did my best to put some distance between myself and those prints.

But soon they reappeared directly in front of me, and stretched out ahead as far as I could see. They could have been there since last night, but the point was that I was now following a huge animal along the tracks, and I really, really didn't want to catch up to it. I took my knife out of its sheath, just in case.

Eric had taught us to identify animal tracks at camp, so I did my best to determine what I might be following.

The paw prints didn't seem to have claw marks, so that ruled out wolves, though the prints looked too huge to be from a wolf anyway. The prints all looked pretty similar in size, so that ruled out bears, because their hind paws leave a more elongated print. The prints reminded me of a cat's, but were bigger than my palm... Maybe a mountain lion then? The thought terrified me.

Eric had told us a story about his one encounter with a wild mountain lion, and it had stuck with me for years.

He had been about eleven years old, and his parents had taken him camping. They had a lakeside cabin, but he had decided to sleep on the beach by himself instead of sleeping indoors. He said that he had been staring up at the stars, feeling very grown up and independent, when he had heard a rustling in the shrubs that lined the beach. Immediately he had tucked his head down into his sleeping bag, and tried to stay as still as possible. He could barely hear the animal's approach, and was shocked when he felt its hot breath on the top of his head. He hadn't completely covered himself. He had felt little tugs on his hair, like the animal was munching at it, and then nothing. He had remained there in his sleeping bag, paralyzed by fear, for hours. Finally his mother, worried he was cold, had come out to check on him, and see if he wanted to come sleep inside. He had whispered that something was out there, and his mom had shone her flashlight around the area, and they saw dozens of huge paw prints in the sand surrounding them. They had hurried back into the cabin, and in the morning had gone back out to the beach to investigate some more. They called their local conservation officer, who confirmed that the prints were indeed those of a mountain lion, and that there had been several sightings of a two-hundred pound male cougar in the area. The conservation officer had been completely shocked to hear Eric's story, and said that Eric, who was fairly small and skinny for his age, was lucky to be unharmed, and that hiding had probably saved his life, because most cougar attacks are on children. That incident had been the catalyst that had ignited Eric's passion for outdoor survival skills.

As I continued to follow the paw prints along the train tracks, I remembered seeing cougars at the zoo. One visit in particular stood out, because I had recently heard Eric's story. I was standing with my mom, looking through the glass of the cougar enclosure, when a little blond girl in a purple jacket had walked up to the glass with her parents. She could only have been about three years old, and didn't really seem to care about the animals: there were huge spring puddles on the ground, and she was more interested in jumping in them than anything else. I remembered that the cougar, who had been basking sleepily in the sun before the little girl's arrival, had suddenly leapt up, and was totally fixated on her as she stomped in the puddles. The cougar stared at her, all of its muscles tensed, pacing back and forth, and it didn't shift its gaze from her until the little family had moved on to the next enclosure and out of sight. At that point the cougar had resumed its sunbath, its powerful muscles now relaxed, its tail flicking lazily now and then.

If it was a cougar that I was following now, I could be in big trouble. All I could remember from reading about mountain lion safety and attacks is that no matter what you do, your chances of not getting hurt are pretty slim. There seemed to be two schools of thought on how to behave if you ever encountered a cougar. The first is to stand your ground and act like a big predator yourself, and hope that they didn't feel like you were easy prey. The second is to run. That way they don't automatically see you as easy prey, especially if you manage to get away without faltering. If you do trip and fall, or limp or stumble, they will attack because you look like an injured animal.

All I could do now is hope that I never came across the animal leaving the prints ahead of me, because I knew my instinct would be to run, and I also knew that I was guaranteed to fall flat on my face.

Eventually the prints veered off into the trees, and though I was glad not to be following them anymore, it meant that the cougar could be walking along beside me, stalking me. At least before, I knew it was probably out ahead of me, but now it could be anywhere.

I picked up my pace, walking as fast as my sodden shoes and cold feet would allow, wondering when the train tracks would finally reach a town. And whether I would even make it that far.

That night I harvested some more pine bark and forced myself to eat as much of it as I could. I huddled in front of a roaring fire, which I had made a little bigger than usual in hopes that it would keep any predators at bay. I had set up my socks and shoes to dry beside the fire, and a pot of water and pine needles was boiling away at the edge of the flames. I was looking forward to drinking the hot brew so much – it would feel so good to be warmed from the inside.

I dug some adhesive bandages out of my bag and tended to the blisters and raw areas on my feet that had been caused by the boots. Maybe tomorrow I would try wearing them again. The bandages would give good protection against the poor fit, and it would be nice to travel on warm feet... I really didn't want to lose toes to frostbite. The boots would be a big

175

problem if I suddenly had to run though, I could barely walk properly in them. I decided that a couple of toes versus getting eaten by a cougar was no contest – I would wear my shoes until I knew I was clear of the cougar.

I sat shivering in front of the fire, sipping my pine water and remembering the first few days of my trek. The heat had been almost unbearable and finding water had been a huge concern. Now, I felt like I'd give almost anything to feel the sun pounding down on me, with the open grasslands surrounding me. At least then there had been fewer places for wildlife to hide. And at that time I was unaware of the creep, too. But I also hadn't met Andy yet, and right now he was my main motivation to keep going, so I would just have to put aside the physical discomforts for now, so that I could find him as soon as possible.

The snow started falling again as darkness descended, so I brought my shoes and socks inside the tent, crossing my fingers they'd be dry by morning. I put on every piece of clothing I owned, wrapped myself up in my blanket, and lay there listening to the hiss of the snowflakes that fell too close to the fire.

***

I must have fallen asleep a short time later, because the next thing I knew it was morning. I opened the stuffy tent to find even more snow on the ground, and a small melted circle where the fire used to be. The sun was shining brightly, so I took off a couple of layers and put on my damp shoes. I packed up all my gear and then started my journey for the day, chewing pine bark for breakfast. The tracks were completely buried by snow drifts in some places, but I was still able to follow them because they so clearly cut through the trees, and thankfully there were no more hints of a mountain lion in the area.

For over a week my routine was the same: wake up to yet more snow, pack up my gear, struggle my way through the knee-deep snow while endlessly chewing strips of tough pine bark, make camp again and finally collapse with exhaustion into the tent. I had started to seriously doubt that the tracks would lead me anywhere, and only the absence of his Voice from my head kept me believing that Andy was still alive out there. If he had suddenly appeared in my head, cracking jokes and asking questions, I might have just laid down in the snow to watch the clouds shift by, listening to him chatter until I finally fell asleep forever. As it was, I had no choice but to keep going until I either found him, or I received some confirmation that he didn't need me anymore.

I was starting to wonder if I should leave the tracks and try to find the highway again. I knew it was a terrible idea to wander into the forest when I had this clear path laid out ahead of me, but I just wanted to feel like I was making progress. This struggle through days of endless white was starting to wear me down. I was at the point of giving it one more day along the tracks when suddenly a valley opened up in front of me.

At first I didn't believe my eyes. Could those really be houses and stores and cars I was seeing? Or had my desperate mind finally broken, making me see things that weren't really there. I proceeded along the tracks for a few more minutes, afraid to look away from the town I was seeing, certain that if I looked away for even a second, it would disappear, to be replaced by a continuous expanse of pure white, breaking my spirit at last.

Even as I approached it though, the town stayed firmly in place, looking deserted but mostly intact. I wasn't going to get my hopes up that I would find any supplies, but I would definitely be searching the tops of all fridges.

Before I cleared the trees, I cut out a little more pine bark, and jammed some fresh snow into my canteen and water bottles. I had to stop myself from running through the last section of forest because I needed to conserve my energy.

Just as I was about to leave the last trees behind, movement beside me caught my eye. Something was walking parallel to my path through the trees, slightly behind me, a short distance away.

The cougar must have been stalking me for a while, completely silent in the powdery snow. I kept my eyes straight ahead, trying not to panic. The closest building on the edge of the town was a small barn. If I could just reach it without letting the cougar know I was aware of it, maybe I would find something to use to defend myself.

I slowly unsheathed my knife, knowing it would be no match against the power and agility of a mountain lion. I kept my pace as natural as possible, but knew the cougar was gaining on me. I felt like I was in one of those stupid dreams where you are trying to get to a location, but the harder you try to reach it, the farther away it becomes.

It seemed like I would never reach the barn, yet somehow, I soon found myself within reach of it. I ducked inside and tried to close the big door, but it was completely stuck open by a large drift of snow. I backed into the barn, scanning the walls for any kind of weapon that might help me survive. There was a shovel, a pitchfork and a small hatchet. I grabbed the pitchfork and the hatchet, and stood hidden just inside the doorway, waiting with my breath held and my heart in my throat.

Slowly a huge shadow darkened the doorway, and the cougar peeked its tawny head into the barn. It bared its teeth at me and a rumbling growl grew from deep inside its chest. I had about a millisecond to react before it pounced on me, so I swung the pitchfork over my head, and realized a second too late that in doing so, I had exposed the soft flesh of my torso. The cougar swiped at my belly with an enormous paw, like a house cat playing with a ball of string. I tried to dodge out of the way, but its razor-sharp claws sliced through my clothes and I felt a burning sensation in the skin of my stomach. I knew it had caused some damage, but I didn't know how much. The pitchfork was still over my head, and I brought it crashing down on the cougar with as much force as I could. The tines of the pitchfork only glanced off the beast's shoulder, but still left long gouges in its skin. It spat a terrifying hiss, its mouth wide open, its teeth bared and its yellow eyes glaring at me. But it backed away. It gave me just enough time to stumble to the wall where the shovel stood, before it re-entered the barn. It stood facing me in the doorway, sizing me up, hissing again. Because the barn was dark and the sun was shining outside, I could really only see its silhouette, but it had to be at least two hundred pounds of pure muscle, probably more than double the weight of my skin and bones by now. The sheer size of the animal was astonishing; it had to be at least half my height, and at least six feet long. It hissed at me again, and its long white teeth stood out sharply against its black lips. I could see it getting ready to attack; perhaps it had decided that I was easy prey after all.

It wasn't wrong.

I clutched at my wounds with one arm, and threw the hatchet at the cougar with all my might, not really expecting a hit, but hoping I might scare it away. To my complete shock the handle of the hatchet connected hard with the cougar's skull, and the cougar turned tail and ran back toward the forest.

I grabbed the shovel and hurried over to the door. I could see the cougar standing at the tree line, staring in my direction. I shoveled the pile of snow away from the door with great difficulty, trying to keep pressure over my wounds, and just as I was able to swing the door shut, I saw the cougar leap away from the trees toward the barn again.

I closed the door and swung the latch into place, praying that the wooden walls were not rotten, and that the flimsy latch would be enough to keep the cougar out. I sat down against the door to give it a little more resistance, and soon felt the huge paws scratching at the other side of the door. I thought absurdly of our neighbor's cat, which used to come scratching at our door sometimes.

The barn was too dark to see the wounds on my stomach properly, but I had to do something to stop the bleeding, so I searched though my bag until I found the little first aid kit. There wasn't even close to enough gauze to wrap around my midsection, so I stripped off my ripped shirts until I found the cleanest one. Then I poured some of my water over the cuts. The water was freezing cold because it was mixed with snow, and after the initial stinging sensation subsided, it felt so good washing over the damaged areas. I looked down and could make out four long dark gashes across my stomach, and a new little trickle of blood oozing out of each one. I was lucky, though, the scratches didn't seem to be too deep. The bigger problem was going to be dealing with an infection, since I didn't have anything to disinfect the gashes with.

The cougar started pushing at the door more insistently, so I hastily packed the small amount of gauze against my wounds, packed the cleanish shirt against the gauze, and then tied the makeshift compress into place with the length of rope I had brought from home. I knew my body was filthy, and the shirt was filthy, and that I was just introducing a whole bunch of bacteria into a pretty serious wound. But what could I do? Maybe the cougar would get bored with me, and I would be able to search the town for a pharmacy and some antibiotics.

Of course I wouldn't find any, but I needed a little glimmer of hope to keep me from sinking into the despair that was clouding my mind.

The cougar eventually stopped scratching at the door, but I could hear a deep purr from its massive lungs right outside. It seemed to be waiting for me to open the door, or maybe it was just too interested in the smell of fresh blood to give up so easily.

Very quietly, I got up and checked the barn walls for another exit, or a weak area that I could push my way through. There was nothing. The walls were perfect and sturdy, and the only way I would be able to break through them would be to use the hatchet. I was sure that all the noise I would make hacking at the walls would scare the cougar away, but it didn't seem wary enough of me to go very far. I felt certain that if I escaped, it would come and attack again as soon it caught sight of me.

For the moment at least, I decided that I would resume my position against the door – that way I could keep tabs on the cougar while sitting in the best-lit area of the barn. Slivers of sunlight blazed through the cracks around the door, and I let them shine on my face as I sat and tried to work out an escape plan.

***

Hours later I still hadn't figured out what I was going to do, and I was pretty sure the cougar was asleep outside the door. I had eaten the last of my pine bark, and my water was almost gone. The slashes in my skin were throbbing with every beat of my heart, and I was starting to feel extremely cold.

Night was approaching, and I decided to pitch my tent inside the barn. It would keep me a little warmer than sitting on the cold dirt floor of the barn, but I'd still be able to hear what the cougar was up to.

I wished I could build a fire. Without proper ventilation, though, it seemed like a bad idea, not to mention that there was absolutely nothing in this big empty barn that I could burn, unless I started hacking away pieces of the wall, but the idea was not appealing.

Pitching the tent was one of the hardest things I'd had to do so far – I was exhausted and any move I made shifted the compress over my wounds uncomfortably. I gave up after a few minutes because the pain had become unbearable. I lifted my shirt to check on the compress, but of course I couldn't see anything.

I needed light. I needed to be able to see what was going on with my injury. The dusky light coming through the cracks around the door was not enough to see properly, and I could still hear the cougar breathing outside. I would have to light a fire.

I placed the little cooking pot on the dirt floor, thinking I would light the fire in it, and then I felt through my backpack, hoping to find some flammable item that I had forgotten about, but all I came up with were the remains of my book.

Sighing, I tore out the last few pages and ripped the cover in half so that it would fit more easily into the pot. My poor book. I felt so sad for how completely it had been destroyed, and for the fact that I would never read the familiar, comforting words again. It felt like my one last connection to my past life, and I was about to burn it to ashes... The way the creep had burned the rest of my life to ashes...

Anger flared inside me. How had my life come to this? How, a few short months ago, had I been a healthy, happy high school student, awaiting the end of senior year and looking forward to summer vacation with my mom? And now here I was, starving, freezing, wounded and trapped, probably a few days away from dying of thirst or infection or hunger... If the beast outside didn't figure out a way to get in the barn and eat me first. How did this happen?

The absurdity of my predicament hit me all of a sudden, and I started laughing out loud, my rage disappearing as fast as it had come. The cougar started scratching at the door again, which only made me laugh harder. There was a two-hundred pound wild animal outside my door, and it wanted to *eat me*. For dinner. Suddenly the mental image of a cougar wearing a top hat and bow tie tucking a napkin into its collar and picking up a knife and fork popped into my head, and I could no longer control my giggles. I had gone from being bored at school to being the potential main course for a *lion*. It was just too ridiculous.

My laughter seemed to enrage the cougar, and I could hear it hissing again. I grabbed one of the ill-fitting boots out of my backpack, and threw it at the door. I heard the cougar take off – the sudden loud noise even shocked me, and the pain from such a huge movement sobered me instantly.

I wasn't sure how long my little book fire would last, so I decided to get everything ready before lighting it.

I stripped off my shirts, annoyed that I had been wearing all of them when the cougar attacked, though maybe the extra layers of clothing had saved me from even deeper wounds.

I thought I might be able to bind the edges of the cuts together by using adhesive bandages, so I laid out a few of those too, along with the tiny scissors in case I needed to cut the bandages to size.

I took the lid off my canteen, and took a sip, knowing that my precious water supply was dwindling, but sure that rinsing the wounds could only help.

Finally, I lit a match and dropped it into the pot on top of the last vestiges of my favorite book. I stared as the pages caught fire and the tiny black letters were slowly consumed by an advancing edge of smoldering orange.

I looked down and started to remove the mess of rope, shirt and gauze covering my belly. The thing that had been causing so much extra pain was where part of the rope had nestled its way into one of the gashes, rubbing it more raw with every move I made. I pulled the rope gently out of the gash. The pain was unbelievable, and it made the most disgusting sound as it came out. One of my major pet peeves had always been when people chewed too loudly, or with their mouths open, and pulling the rope out of my wound sounded exactly like that.

The behatted cougar popped into my head again, with his bow tie and cutlery, and he was very politely chewing me up with his mouth tightly closed. A point goes to my imaginary cougar for impeccable table manners!

I must be losing my mind...

I rinsed the wounds with a small amount of water, and then let my skin dry in the open air. My hands shook as I tried to stick the bandages, but I didn't feel cold anymore; maybe the shaking was from being so hungry. Not that I felt like I could eat anything at the moment anyway. Not even pancakes. And the thought of pine bark made me want to throw up the water I had just swallowed. Maybe I was just so totally grossed out by what I was doing that the thought of eating wasn't sitting well with me.

The used gauze was completely soaked in blood, so I didn't see a point in putting it back on. I put a fresh side of the shirt over the cuts, and this time tied it in place with a long-sleeved shirt. It would be much more comfortable to lay down without the rope around my waist, and the shirt wasn't likely to cause as much chafing as the rough rope if it got stuck in my wounds.

With my work done, I sat and watched the fire consume the rest of my book. I tossed the used gauze into the pot too, trying not to think of my mom, and how the first aid kit that her loving hands had packed years ago was now almost completely empty.

Just before the fire died, I wrapped myself in my blanket, and then lay on top of the flat tent, glad to have the layer of nylon between me and the cold ground. I sipped the last of my water, and fell asleep worrying about how I would get more, with the cougar right outside... and the little town burning around me...

Or was it the barn that was on fire? Or just me? I woke up suddenly. My skin felt so hot and yet I was freezing. Snuggling deeper into the blanket did nothing to chase away the chill, and I couldn't remember what the rules were for a fever. Was I was supposed to try to cool myself off? Or stay warm to try to help the fever cook whatever germs my body was fighting? I dozed off again, wishing my mom were here to tell me what I needed to do.

I drifted in and out of consciousness, dreaming about both the living and the dead. My mom was always there in the background, and Andy stood silently, holding my hand. I knew by his silence that he was just a dream, the real Andy would be talking my ear off, telling me about his adventures of the past few weeks.

Eric was there, whispering with a man I recognized as the one who had set my injured arm when the plane had crashed. I hadn't thought about him in months, why was he here all of a sudden?

Eric looked like he had aged at least twenty years since I had last seen him, and Audrey stood by his side, as ever. Emily and Josh came and went, always together, and every time I saw them leave, I would slip back into darkness, too annoyed by the image of them together. I dreamed of fire and blood and loss, and all the while the cougar scratched at the door.

I wasn't sure how long I stayed there on the barn floor, lost in feverish dreams and nightmares, waiting for the darkness to consume me, and allow me to finally find peace.

Chapter Twelve

Finally the pain began to subside, and the heat trapped by my skin began to dissipate. I realized slowly that I wasn't actually curled up on the cold dirt floor anymore, but that I was actually in a clean bed, between crisp sheets. A needle in the back of each of my hands was delivering clear fluid into my bloodstream, and a blood pressure cuff lay nearby on a table. Where the hell was I? Where was my backpack? The only photo I had of my mom was in there! I was about to sit up and try to take the needles out of my hands when I looked across the room at another small table standing under a window. The photo was there, propped up against a glass cup full of dandelions. My backpack was on the floor in front of the table, right next to Andy's duffel bag. I blinked in disbelief, staring at the dirty bags, unable to understand how they could possibly be sitting there together in this strange room. I must still be dreaming, or maybe I had finally died and this was some weird version of Beyond.

But no, I could still feel the pain on my stomach where the cougar had slashed at me, so I couldn't be dead. All of the Voices I had communicated with always said that a release from the physical shell meant an end to all pain.

I looked under the sheet and saw a clean wrap of gauze over my stomach. Where had all of these supplies come from? Who had put the needles in my hand? *Where the hell was I?*

Once again I started to get up, determined to have the upper hand if someone came into the room. I would grab my knife from... Wait, where was my knife? And my crowbar? I couldn't see them anywhere, and it looked like my clothes were gone too. Someone had stolen my stuff! Surely the first aid kit would still hold the tiny scissors, and they might buy me enough time to escape if I managed to poke them in someone's eye...

I was still struggling with pulling the needles out of my hands when Andy walked into the room. *Andy...*

He stood in the doorway, staring at me with disbelief, looking skinny but otherwise clean and healthy. The look on his face quickly turned into joy, and he bounded across the room at me.

My first instinct was, oddly, to try to protect myself from him, but it disappeared in a second. Here, finally, was the boy who had kept me alive when all I had wanted to do was give up.

I opened my arms to him and he climbed carefully onto the bed and snuggled up beside me.

'Hey kiddo,' I whispered – my voice didn't seem to be working properly, maybe from not speaking for such a long time, or maybe because it was difficult to speak with such a huge lump in my throat. I tried to fight back the tears, but then figured there was no point, and soon both of us were sobbing unrestrainedly, releasing all the worry and fear and pain of the last few weeks.

Eventually I was able to speak again.

'What happened to you, Andy? How did you survive? How did you find me? How did we get here? Where the hell are we?'

Andy giggled, drying his tears on his sleeve, and looking up at me with those big blue eyes that I had missed so much.

'Who's asking a million questions now, hey Gracie?'

I smiled as Andy rested his head back on my shoulder and told me his story.

'As soon as Patience took off I knew I was in big trouble, especially with that wolf chasing us, but I was glad it did, otherwise it probably would have stayed behind and attacked you.'

I decided I would tell Andy about the rest of the wolf pack fighting the grizzly bear later, if ever.

'Is Patience okay?' I asked, worried.

'She's totally fine,' Andy replied, 'she's outside grazing. She got a few scratches from the wolf and she had some pretty bad sores under her saddle, but she's healing now.'

I sighed with relief.

'Anyway,' said Andy, and I could tell he was excited to keep talking about his ordeal. 'The wolf chased us for quite a while, until it scratched Patience's leg, and she just happened to kick back at the right second, and almost knocked the wolf's head off. She was awesome.' He paused, lost in the memory for a moment.

'So anyway, there we were, lost in the forest without you. I had no idea what to do, or how we were ever going to find you. Just as I was about to try to retrace our path back to you, a group of people came through the trees.'

Andy looked up at me again, and his smile couldn't have been any wider.

'You might remember that I did a lot of screaming, as me and Patience were being chased by the wolf.'

The sound of Andy's distant, terrified screams was something I would never forget, and the memory of it turned my blood cold.

'It was because of all of my screaming that Eric found me so fast.'

Andy was still looking at me, smiling, watching my face as his words slowly sank in.

'Eric?' I said, 'What? Eric found you?'

'Yep!' Andy said, putting his head back on my shoulder to finish his story.

'When I saw all the people come through the trees, I thought I was a goner. They all had weapons, like axes and knives, and they were all bigger than me, and I started to wonder if maybe they ate kids or something. But then I looked at the man at the front of the group. He was carrying a torch and I could see that his face wasn't angry or hungry, but concerned. And then I noticed that his colors are very similar to yours, Gracie, and I knew right away who he was, because you had told me so much about him.

'So I said "Eric?" and it didn't even freak him out! I thought it might have, because he'd never ever seen me before, but he just said, "Hi, Andy," which totally freaked me out!' Andy laughed, and the sound filled me with joy.

'So after a second, Eric asked where you were, and I told him how we had just gotten separated and so he took Patience's rope and we all walked back to the rock ledge where you and me had first seen the wolf.

'We found another dead wolf on the ground, and there was a lot of blood splattered everywhere, but the whole group knew it wasn't your blood, and that you were still alive.'

Andy paused again, so I quickly told him a censored version of the grizzly and wolf fight, because he seemed so upset.

'I know, Gracie,' he said, 'I know exactly what you went through because they were all talking about it as we stood there. They pretty much gave me a play-by-play of your whole journey. They weren't trying to be mean, they were just trying to find you, but listening to them talk about how wolves were biting at your legs, and how a cougar was stalking you, and how you were slowly dying from infection was probably the hardest thing I've ever had to listen to. I hated that I couldn't help you, and I hated that you were dying all alone.' He was quiet for a moment, and then spoke again. 'At least with Olivia, I didn't know for sure what had happened to her, and I didn't know exactly what she was suffering at the very moment that she was suffering it. Her death, for me at least, was quick, because one second I had hope, and the next second I didn't. Listening to them talk about you was so much worse. We all felt so helpless.'

He reached up and touched the place under my eye where I had cut myself running through the trees.

'Some kind of bacteria got in, they weren't really sure when, but something was making you pretty sick and they were getting more and more serious about the possibility of not finding you in time.'

'How *did* you guys find me?' I asked, 'I was so lost, even following the train tracks felt useless because I didn't know if they would ever lead me anywhere...'

'Emily,' Andy replied. 'Eric found Emily right after the Darkness happened. She and her dad were hiding in their bunker, just like you thought they would be. Eric knew that they would be there, and that Emily would be able to guide them to the rest of the group. They had bikes, so they were able to cover a lot of ground pretty fast, and since they all knew the power wasn't coming back on, they were able to gather a lot of supplies before the rest of the world panicked and cleaned out the stores.'

'Who did they find next?' I asked, trying to sound nonchalant, knowing that Josh lived closest to Emily.

Andy looked up at me again, and the light of mischief was shining in his eyes. I had forgotten how his eyes would twinkle when he was up to no good.

'Well Gracie, funny you should ask. The person Eric collected next, who lived a short distance from Emily's city, a stone's-throw, you might say, barely a day's ride by bicycle, even while pulling a wagon full of supplies behind you, creating extra drag because the added weight would add so much resistance, thus requiring extra exertion to… ouch!' (I had poked Andy in the ribs), 'Okay, okay! The next person Eric chose to attempt to locate was a young man named… Joshua.'

'They found Josh?' I asked, unable to keep the worry out of my voice. 'Is he okay?"

'They did find Josh, yes.' Andy's cheeky grin slowly faded. 'He's doing fine physically, but he's struggling a bit otherwise. His gift…' Andy shuddered involuntarily. 'It's been a rough time for him with more than half of the world's population putting on horror shows in his head…

'Everyone will be so excited to know you're awake though, I should go tell them.' He started to get up, but I stopped him.

'I don't want to be alone again,' I said, and I was surprised to hear the panic in my own voice.

'Okay, Gracie, don't worry.' Andy snuggled back down next to me, and we stayed there, holding each other, for a long time.

After a while, a thought occurred to me. 'How on earth did you guys get rid of the cougar?'

'Oh right! I haven't even told you the rest of the story! So after you found the train tracks, Emily saw that you were leaving behind pages of your book to try to guide me in the same direction. We had already found our way back to the highway though. Emily's dad saw that you would reach the town by following the train tracks, we just didn't know where you would end up. The plan was to reach the town, and then follow the tracks back into the mountains until we met up with you. But you got cornered in the barn before we could reach the town, and then we had to figure out how to not get eaten by the cougar ourselves. They think you were already delirious by then, so you couldn't hear us telling you that you were being rescued.

'In the town we met up with another one of your camp friends – he said he'd been waiting there for a while, but knew we would come eventually. He figured out a plan to get rid of the cougar. He asked us if we had anything flammable so we could scare it away using fire, and he got super excited when he looked through my bag and found a straw and the baby formula. He said we should wait until dark so that it would have the biggest visual effect. I'm not even really sure how he set it up, but he used the straw to blow the formula out over a torch, and it was like a huge cloud of flame! It looked so cool! And it totally scared the cougar away so we could finally get into the barn and to you. I'm glad it worked, because nothing else we had tried would scare the cougar, and we had wasted so much time...' He looked at me, pain written all over his face.

'While the group was trying to deal with the cougar, Eric rigged up a stretcher to pull behind his bike, and he pulled you all the way here. And to answer your question from before... We're here, Gracie. We're at your camp. We made it.'

I looked at him, still trying to absorb the story he had just told me. Then I looked around the room again, but it all seemed unfamiliar to me. 'I've never seen this room before, are you sure this is camp?'

'It's Eric's room. Eric has been sleeping in one of the bunk beds so you could be more comfortable.'

I realized that I hadn't ever seen where Eric and Audrey slept. Of course they didn't sleep in the same little rooms as we kids did, they were a married couple – of course they wouldn't sleep in a bunk bed. I felt silly, and guilty for the inconvenience I had caused everyone.

'Well I'm doing fine now, so Eric and Audrey can have their room back, I'm totally fine on a bunk bed.'

Andy was looking at me sadly, and suddenly a very familiar Voice whispered louder than the rest in my head. *Audrey...*

'... It's okay, Gracie, don't be sad... Everything happened the way it was supposed to... Eric will be okay too... Be strong...'

I couldn't help the tears that welled up in my eyes. Poor Eric, to lose the love of his life...

'What happened? How long ago did Audrey pass away?' I asked Andy, blotting my eyes with my sleeve.

'I'm not sure, I didn't want to ask. She was gone before I met up with Eric though.'

'Why didn't she ever talk to me before now?' I wondered aloud.

'Maybe she was trying to spare you the pain of knowing,' said Andy, 'maybe she knew how much it would hurt you, and just wanted you to be able to focus on surviving.'

I lay there in silence for a long time, heartbroken and shocked.

Andy stayed with me until I fell asleep again, which I really appreciated because the idea of being on my own, alone with my thoughts, was too much.

At one point I could hear people whispering in the doorway, but I just pretended to sleep, not ready to face my friends yet, and hear their stories of loss. Andy's even breathing next to me settled my nerves, and I drifted off to sleep again.

When I woke up the next day, the first thing I was aware of was Andy beside me. I assumed we were back in the tent, and I was about to wake him up so that we could get an early start on our traveling for that day. Then I opened my eyes and remembered that we had reached our destination, and that we were safe.

Suddenly my stomach growled so loudly that the sound seemed to bounce off the walls, breaking the peaceful morning silence into a million pieces.

Without looking up at me, Andy started laughing. 'Morning, Gracie.'

My stomach growled again as though answering him, and he sat up, still laughing.

'Who needs an alarm clock when you're around, hey?' He yawned and stretched. 'Do you feel like walking? You should see the pantry here, it'll blow your mind! The doctor said it would probably be best if you just had a little bit of broth at first, but it doesn't sound like anyone else is up yet – I say we go make some pancakes!' He laughed again after seeing my eyes widen at the idea of a pancake breakfast.

'For pancakes, I definitely feel like walking!'

I sat up slowly, careful of the tubes sticking out of my hands, and swung my legs over the side of the bed. Standing up was tricky; my legs felt like they were made of both lead and jell-o, and I almost collapsed taking my first step. Andy was right there though, ready with a supporting hand. He wheeled the pole that held the bags of fluid, and made sure we didn't tug on the tubes as we walked. He chatted about all of the people that were staying at the cabin – he thought there were about fifteen, but said that it was hard to tell for sure because people kept coming and going to try to find supplies.

Memories flooded my mind as soon as we left the hall that led to the bedroom. Seeing the big open main room of the cabin, with its wood burning stoves and huge wall of windows was like coming home. All of the anxiety I had felt about seeing my friends again disappeared: this was where I belonged.

Andy helped me over to the kitchen and sat me down in one of the chairs. He opened the pantry door with a big smile and a flourish and laughed as he saw my jaw drop.

'It's pretty useful to know someone who knows when to stock up on supplies!' Andy joked, pulling pancake mix out of the pantry. 'They're not from scratch or anything, but all we have to do is add water and we'll have a nice, fluffy stack of pancakes. Can you believe it? Seems like we were just talking about eating pine to survive!'

I shuddered at the thought of eating pine bark again. Andy noticed, and apologized for mentioning it.

'Don't worry about it, it kept me alive – I just hope I never have to eat it again. I feel like it's still stuck in my throat.' I made an exaggerated hacking noise, like a cat coughing up a fur ball. Andy cracked up, which only made me hack and splutter more enthusiastically.

At that very moment, Josh walked into the kitchen.

We were both laughing so hard that at first it didn't register with me who I was seeing. But there he was, looking just as I remembered him, his sandy blond hair tousled from sleeping, his brown eyes lighting up to see me and Andy goofing off.

'Gracie,' he said, as he approached us, his eyes fixed on my face with an intensity that made me blush.

Praying that Andy wouldn't make some embarrassing comment about my changing colors again, I stood up slowly. All I could muster speech-wise was a quiet 'Hey, Josh...' and then I found myself wrapped in his arms.

The months of worrying about whether he was alive and whether I would ever see him again caught up with me in that moment, and I found myself fighting not to cry.

He finally released me, but kept hold of my hand. I was glad for the continued contact – I was feeling as though the whole room could evaporate any second, but holding his hand kept me tethered to the scene, so if the cabin did suddenly dissolve, at least I would go with it.

Josh looked into my eyes again, and I was surprised to see tears in his. I squeezed his hand and managed to whisper that it was good to see him, which felt like the biggest understatement in the universe, but I was having trouble collecting my thoughts, and was glad to be able to speak at all.

He just kept staring at me as though worried I might disappear, but eventually asked how I was feeling. I was just about to reply when Emily walked into the kitchen and, squealing with delight, ran the short distance to hug me.

I hugged her back with my free arm – Josh did not seem willing to release my hand just yet. I felt another wave of relief to see Emily healthy and whole, and I thanked her for texting me right before the Darkness fell.

'You're my best friend, Grace, as if I wouldn't text you to warn you about the end of the world!' She laughed, kissed my cheek and sauntered toward Andy, who was busy mixing batter in a big silver bowl. 'What's for breakfast, Andy? Were you right? Did pancakes make her get out of bed finally?'

'Yep!' said Andy, pouring batter into a frying pan on top of the woodstove, 'too bad there's no bacon, hey, Gracie?'

I had been at the point of introducing my friends to Andy, before I remembered that they had been traveling with him for weeks while they searched for me. Plus all of the time that I had already spent here, unconscious. It was weird how their friendships made me feel like the odd man out. But I supposed I was. I had missed a lot. The old feeling of not belonging crept into the back of my mind, which was especially upsetting considering where I was – the one place that I had always fit in.

'Gracie, why don't you go sit on the couch and we'll bring your breakfast to you?' said Andy, looking a little concerned. 'You look like you could pass out...'

Josh, still holding my hand, led me over to the couch which faced the big windows. We had spent a lot of time sitting here over the years, telling stories and drinking hot chocolate. The view outside the window looked exactly the same, except that I could see piles of sheet metal and wooden pallets stacked in the distance.

Seeing what I was looking at, Josh explained that they had spent the last few days collecting materials to build a fence around the area.

'Eric was worried that the fruit trees will attract bears, and we all thought it was a good idea to have some protection against Poo People.'

I looked into his eyes, smiling at his use of Andy's phrase. He grinned back, and for the first time I noticed the dark rings under his eyes. There was no other word but 'haunted' to describe how he looked, and I remembered what

Andy had told me about how much Josh was suffering these days.

I wished silently that I could help him somehow, and as I squeezed his hand again, vivid images started flashing through my mind.

Death. Death was all I could see. Bloodied bodies; the moans of the dying; it all flooded into my mind in shocking high-definition, and then just as quickly, vanished.

I gasped and realized that I had somehow invaded Josh's mind, and had seen a tiny portion of what he was seeing all day, every day.

Still panting from the shock, I told Josh what had happened. He didn't seem surprised, but did pull his hand out of mine.

'All of our abilities have increased since the Darkness,' he said, 'you must be able to read minds or something now, like Michael, remember? He had to wear gloves to protect himself. Eric thinks it's because of all of the energy that has no place to go anymore.'

I tried to take his hand again, but he resisted. 'I don't want you to have to see what I see, Gracie, it's pretty horrifying lately.'

I took his hand in both of my own and held it tightly.

'We are in this together. How are we supposed to make it if we don't stick together? I can't do it alone, not anymore.'

I felt more tears welling up in my eyes, and tried to blink them back, embarrassed by my show of weakness. Josh let go of my hands, but gathered me up in his arms, and held me close until an annoyed voice nearby cleared their throat ostentatiously.

'Ahemmmm… Break it up you two,' said Emily, 'it's time to fatten this girl up!' And she handed me a plate stacked high with pancakes dripping in golden syrup.

Everybody else's plates only held one pancake, and I realized that, of course, the supplies would have to be carefully rationed to sustain such a large group through the upcoming winter.

I ate a few bites of fluffy delicious pancake, but knew that my stomach wouldn't hold much more anyway, so I insisted that everyone take their share of my stack.

Slowly others began to join us for pancakes; some people that I knew well from camp, and some that I had never seen before. Each person had a story to tell, and of course each had suffered loss. It was a shock when the girl who had almost been kidnapped by the monsters walked into the room with her mother and little brother. They came and hugged me, and the girl sat down beside me and apologized for not thanking me properly before.

'I was so scared and relieved and sad all at once, I should have thanked you, but I didn't. I'm so glad you're okay. My name is Lindsay, by the way, and I've been wanting to ask you if you have heard anything else from my dad?'

Lindsay's mom started to reprimand her daughter for being so blunt, but Emily got there first.

'Give her a day to feel better why don't you? She's been through hell and hasn't even been awake for an hour!' She turned to Josh and her anger was written all over her face. 'See? This is why I told Eric we shouldn't allow ordinary people into camp! They either treat us like freaks or use us for our abilities, and I'm sick of it!'

She turned back to Lindsay, who looked angry too, and as though she was about to retort.

'No!' said Emily, now trembling with rage. 'You obviously don't know how lucky you are to be here! If you hadn't run into Eric when he was looking for Grace, you'd probably all be dead in a stinking pile somewhere, which means that Grace has saved your life twice already! Did you know that she lost her own mother? No? You lost your dad, but you still have your mom and your brother. Grace has no one! Her mom was at a café on her coffee break when a plane fell out of the sky and hit...'

Emily couldn't suppress an angry sob at this point and I sat frozen with shock at her words, my brain numbed by the revelation. I finally knew what had happened to my mom, and the tiny spark of hope that I had carried with me had just been stamped out. It was too much, I started to feel faint. Josh took my hand again and tried to get Emily to stop, but she seemed to be on a rampage.

'Look at her! Can't you see she's still hooked up to meds and that she can barely sit up? Did you bother to ask her how she is doing? Did you bother to see if there's anything you could do for her? Of course not! You only care about yourself! She saved your life twice, has been unconscious for days after almost dying, and all you think of is to ask more of her! I'm so sick of ungrateful people!'

194

And Emily stormed out of the cabin, leaving an extremely uncomfortable silence in her wake.

Lindsay looked at me, whispered a quiet apology and walked slowly back to her room.

Andy took her place beside me on the couch and told me he was sorry, too.

'She said she saw what happened to your mom just after she sent you that last text, but it was already too late to warn you because the power went out right after. I told her you didn't know for sure that your mom was even gone, but maybe she assumed that I told you when you woke up or something. I'm sorry you had to find out that way.'

It took a while for me to find my voice again. I knew Andy understood though. He understood the strange denial that you hold in your heart, and he understood the painful relief of finally finding out the truth. And he understood the isolating feeling of having no one left.

But I wasn't completely alone, not anymore. I grabbed Andy's hand and told him I was alright. Holding hands with two people that I loved gave me the strength to look into Lindsay's mom's eyes.

'Your husband told me how to get Lindsay back to you, and once he saw that you were reunited, I felt his presence lift. I used to think that if someone went Beyond, into the light, to Heaven, or however you want to phrase it, that they were gone forever, but now I'm not so sure. If he shows up in my head again, of course I will tell you as soon as it happens. But know that the most important thing to him, and his last request, was to see you three reunited. And in that moment at least, he found peace.'

She looked at me sadly for a minute. 'Thank you, Grace... for everything. Come on, Toby,' she said, drying her eyes and taking her son by the hand, 'let's go help with the fence.'

I was about to ask Andy and Josh to help me back to my room when I saw Eric through the windows, walking toward the cabin with a man I didn't recognize at first. As they drew closer, I realized that the second man was the one who had set my arm after the plane had crashed. He must be the doctor that Andy had mentioned before, and the reason that I had survived.

As they walked into the cabin, they were still deep in conversation about how to reinforce the fence. Both men saw me sitting on the couch at the same moment, and both of their faces lit up. Eric hurried over and squatted in front of me, looking into my face with relief and happiness.

'Gracie…'

But before he could say much more, I was crying again, thanking him for working so hard to find me, for bringing me to the cabin, and for saving Andy too.

'And I'm so sorry about Audrey, Eric, I…' But I couldn't say anymore after that.

He understood though, and said he was sorry about my mom. He gestured to the man standing behind him.

'This is Doctor Joseph Albert, Grace, I believe you have met him before…'

The doctor held out his hand to shake mine. 'Call me Joe – how are you feeling today?' He peered into my face, and I hastily dried my eyes on my sleeve.

'I'm fine, just a little tired.' I replied, feeling self-conscious. Looking at him reminded me of the day the plane had crashed, and the sadness I had seen in his face as he realized who I was. 'How did you know my mom?' I asked him.

'We worked at the hospital together – and honestly I had been wanting to ask her out for months. I finally did, and we were supposed to meet for a coffee… that day… she said she needed to talk to you before we went to dinner together or on an actual date, but she agreed to a coffee… now I wish I'd never asked her… but she was just such an incredible woman… I'm so sorry.'

I didn't know what to say, so I just thanked him for saving my life.

'Joe was able to get a lot of medical supplies out of the hospital after the power went out,' Eric told me, 'we're so lucky we ran into each other. Your mom had told him a lot about our camp, and he was headed here anyway. We found him working at the refugee camp, and Lindsay overheard us talking about coming here, and wanted to join us.'

'All of the other doctors and nurses I know ended up at the refugee site, but I knew you needed care, and I couldn't just let that go,' said Joe, 'Lindsay told me that a girl who fit your description had saved her life, and saved her family's lives by sending them to the refugee site. We left to find you as soon as we could, but it was a while before we could get out. The camp had become somewhat of a prison. One of the guards eventually realized that the death toll was just going to keep rising – food was running out and the conditions were becoming increasingly unsanitary, so he let us out. We couldn't get close to your neighborhood because of the fires, but it didn't matter because we knew you wouldn't be there anymore anyway.'

'Emily had seen you enter a big old house, and we were so excited to have a new lead,' continued Eric, 'but when we finally got there, all that was left was a smoking ruin and a dead horse. Emily told us that you and a boy had escaped on another horse, but seeing the horse's wounds was a shock, and knowing that someone armed with a shotgun might be following you was terrifying. We traveled as fast as we could, but it wasn't until we heard Andy screaming in the woods that we actually caught up, and at that point you were nowhere to be found.'

I sat in silence, trying not to slip back into a state of panic at the memory of Andy's screams and at the thought of my time alone in the woods.

Andy saw my discomfort and chimed in. 'We met up with Kevin almost as soon as we reached the barn where you were trapped. He was the one who figured out how to scare the cougar away...' He watched my face closely as I absorbed yet more shocking news.

'Kevin?' I turned to Eric. 'Kevin? The same Kevin whose parents had him locked up because of his gifts?' Eric smiled at me and nodded. 'How?' I asked. 'Did he escape? Had he been released? How did he get away?'

'He thinks that someone, most likely one of the hospital staff, let everyone out once they were sure that the power wasn't coming back on. He said that he was in the dark for quite a while, and then his door was suddenly unlocked. He left his room and discovered the rest of the patients wandering around the hospital. Kevin thinks that someone must have wanted to give them a chance to survive, instead of leaving them all to starve.' Eric sighed and continued, 'I'm sure there are a lot of hospitals and prisons where the patients and inmates were not so lucky.'

'Kevin said that as soon as he had made sure that his parents hadn't survived, he set out to find Eric and the rest of you,' said Andy, 'you were the only people who had ever accepted him, and he knew that camp would be a good place to try to start a new life.'

'He's out on a supply run right now,' added Eric, 'but he told us to tell you that he's really looking forward to finally seeing you again.'

I tried to imagine what Kevin had been through, and it made me feel completely exhausted. Joe, who was looking at me with concern again, told me that it might be a good time for me to take a nap. 'You look pale, Grace, we will all be just outside working on the fence, and we'll wake you up for lunch.'

I nodded. Josh and Andy helped me to my feet and back to my room. 'Do you want me to stay again?' asked Andy, after I had climbed back into bed.

'I'm so tired that I think I'll be okay now,' I replied, 'but thank you.'

They wished me a good sleep and left, closing the door behind them. After a few minutes I started wishing that I had asked Andy to stay after all; he was good at settling my mind down when it started going in circles, like it was right now. Josh, Emily, Lindsay, Eric and Joe had all given me a lot to think about, and though my body felt like I should be able to sleep for a year, my brain simply refused to allow it.

A gentle knock at my door distracted me from my anxious musings, and Josh re-entered the room, this time alone.

'I thought you might need something to help you sleep,' he said shyly, holding something out for me to take. My book. He had brought me a new copy of my favorite book. I stared down at it, extremely touched.

'You said once that reading it always helped you sleep, even if you had had a really bad day.' He hesitated, uncertain all of a sudden. 'That was a few years ago though, I don't know if you still...'

I still didn't know what to say – it was one of the most thoughtful gifts I had ever been given, especially because I had convinced myself that I would never find another copy.

'Thank you,' I whispered, and I told him about having to tear most of my copy to pieces, and then finally use the rest as kindling.

'Wow, that must have been hard for you. Now I'm extra glad I made the group wait for me while I found it in the library of one of the towns we went through.'

I took his hand, said thank you again, and hugged the book to my chest. Then I set the book in my lap and riffled through the pages. 'This means a lot to me, Josh, I'm never going to be able to say thank you enough.'

He was quiet for a moment, and I wondered if maybe he was having a vision. As though I had summoned it from his mind, I saw a brief flash of myself lying unconscious on a dirty floor.

Finally he spoke.

'The search for you was one of the hardest things I've ever gone through,' he said, avoiding my eyes and staring at the book in my hands. 'I didn't think I'd ever see you again, and when we finally found you, I couldn't imagine how you would survive. You were so sick, and your wounds...' He shuddered. I got another brief glimpse of myself, this time unconscious and bleeding on a makeshift stretcher, being dragged along behind Eric...

'I've been so worried...' He looked up at my face, and I was struck again by how haunted his eyes had become. I wondered if his nightmares were allowing him to get any sleep.

Still holding my hand, Josh leaned in slowly, looking intently into my eyes, and my heart started to race.

'Get some rest, Gracie,' he said, and he kissed my forehead.

I stared at the door after he closed it behind him, surprised at his abrupt departure.

Looking at the book in my hands, I also felt surprised that he had gone to so much trouble just for me, and that he had remembered such a small detail about something I had mentioned in passing years ago. His actions didn't align very well with the prediction Emily had made about Josh and me – that we would never be together as anything more than friends. Or maybe he had found the book for me simply for that reason – because we were friends. We had known each other since we were kids, after all, and the bonus of being gifted had bonded our group even more tightly.

I felt silly for thinking he was going to kiss me. He had never kissed my forehead before, but I'm sure he was just glad that we were all safe, so he had decided to give me a friendly peck on the forehead.

He said he had been worried about me, but how could you *not* worry about someone you've been friends with for over a decade, especially when you're getting a gruesome play-by-play of everything they are suffering?

Whether it was romantic or not, giving me the book and kissing my forehead had achieved one thing at least – I was no longer consumed with worry about Kevin and Joe and Lindsay and what they had been through.

I opened the book's cover and just seeing the familiar title page relaxed my entire body and my mind. I managed to turn one more page before my heavy eyes started fluttering, trying to stay open to at least read the first sentence. I registered one last thing before I drifted off to sleep. There was a hand-written note on the blank page facing the opening chapter.

For Grace,
To help you sleep.
Love Josh.

Chapter Thirteen

I slept straight through the rest of the day and the following night, and woke up to the distant sounds of hammering.

I felt great. Just really, really hungry. I laughed out loud at the thought of what Andy would say if he could hear my stomach rumbling right now.

It wasn't until I was getting dressed that I noticed that the needles were no longer in my hands – Joe must have removed them when I was sleeping. Having them gone cheered me up even more.

Walking was still a challenge, and I could feel my newfound energy being sapped as I made my way into the kitchen. On the counter I found a note from Andy attached to a can of beef broth. It read:

'I could hear your stomach rumbling from outside. No pancakes today, doctors orders! Come outside when you feel like it!'

He had signed it with a smiley face, and then had drawn a series of stickmen. The first had a long dark ponytail like mine, and its belly was big and round with big claw marks across it, and he had written the word 'rumble' about six times around the little person. The rest of the stickmen were all plugging their ears, and had expressions of intense pain on their faces.

I smiled, and as I muttered, 'Very funny,' the artist himself walked into the cabin.

'Morning, sleepyhead!' he said, and grabbed a can opener to help me fix my breakfast. 'Nothing but the finest for you,' he laughed as he plunked a spoon into the can.

I laughed and tasted the broth. It was salty and cold, and absolutely delicious. I gave up on the spoon and just started drinking out of the can.

'Joe says that if you can keep down that whole can, you can have something a little more substantial for lunch. I think he doesn't want you to start barfing all over the place because you haven't really eaten anything in such a long time. And I agree, it would be a tremendous waste of our pancake supply if you couldn't keep them down. I should have thought of that yesterday, but hey, I was more worried about getting you up off your butt, lazybones.'

I was halfway through swallowing my last mouthful of broth, and started laughing at Andy's cheekiness. I choked on the broth and Andy slapped my back a few times.

'Are you alright?' said an amused voice behind us. Why did Josh always have to walk in the room when I was doing something embarrassing?

'I'm fine,' I croaked, feeling my face turn red.

Josh smiled at us both and when I looked into his eyes I was struck by how clear they were. He no longer looked haunted and exhausted, but more like the boy I had known in the past.

'Did you have a good sleep?' I asked him, curious at the change.

'I did! I slept like a baby! With you here and safe and sound I was finally able to sleep, it was great!' He laughed and hugged me, and once again took my hand. I was surprised, but happy to see him acting like himself again, and of course I was happy to hold his hand. The butterflies in my stomach churned the broth up a little bit, but I ignored them and agreed to come outside when Andy asked me if I felt up to it.

'You've got to see the fence, Gracie,' he said, 'we've only been working on it for a week or so, but it's almost finished!'

'Andy told us all about the creep who was following you, so Eric made the fence a priority,' said Josh, holding the door open for me and Andy. 'We're getting a lot of our supplies from the two closest towns – I never noticed how many wooden pallets are just stacked up everywhere, behind stores and restaurants and stuff. The metal siding is a little trickier because it's not as easy to take – usually we have to use tools to remove it from its original place, but the extra work is worth it, because it's so strong and won't burn.

Andy and Josh glanced at each other nervously and I guessed why – Andy had probably told Josh about my house being burned down, about the creep burning down the towns we were hiding in, and the nightmares the fires had caused.

'I'm fine,' I said, 'being back here... I feel more safe now than I have in months.' I took a deep breath of the fresh piney air and soaked up the surroundings, feeling as though just walking this familiar path was restoring my health better than anything else so far.

I could see the lake sparkling through the trees, and knew that the old site where we would have our nightly campfires was nearby. There was no snow on the ground yet; the cougar and I must have gotten hit by some of the crazy mountain weather. There was a definite chill to the air though, winter was right around the corner.

As we continued down the path, the sound of hammering got louder. In the distance I could see Lindsay and her family working, and beyond them were a man and a woman who Josh pointed out.

'That's my mom and dad,' he said, waving to them. They put down their tools and walked toward us. I had never met Josh's parents; he had always arrived at camp before me, and they were always gone by the time I got there.

'Grace,' said Josh's mother, as she wrapped me in a hug, 'we've heard so much about you over the years, it's wonderful to finally meet you.' I hugged her back, wishing I could find the right words to thank her for being so supportive of her son, especially during the days before they had met Eric. It must have been terrifying for her. Of course, no words came to me, so I tried to just show my feelings through the hug.

Josh's dad shook my hand and congratulated me for being such a trooper. 'I can't believe I'm shaking hands with someone who wrestled with a mountain lion!'

I noticed that he and Josh had the same playful smile, though there was a layer of fatherly concern underneath his teasing.

I smiled. 'It's great to meet you both, Josh has told me a lot about you, too.' Before I could start to feel awkward, Josh's dad started chatting to us about the fence and how it was coming along. I felt relieved that I didn't have to think of something else to say. Small talk is not something I'm good at, especially when I'm so aware that both parties have so much prior knowledge of each other.

I felt embarrassed that Josh grabbed my hand again once the introductions were over, but his parents just smiled at me and continued chatting, so I tried to ignore my self-consciousness.

After a few minutes, we left Josh's parents to their work and made our way over to where Eric was pounding a fence post into the ground; he looked up and smiled at our approach.

After I had assured him that I was feeling much better, he gave me a brief explanation of how they were using bikes, skateboards and a lot of rope to haul the fence supplies back to camp.

'And now that we have Patience to help us too, the work is going a lot faster than I had hoped!' Eric said enthusiastically.

'Kevin should be back soon with more supplies,' he continued, 'and he thought he had seen signs of other survivors, so he might see if they want to come live here with us.'

'Bad idea,' said Emily behind me. I turned around to see her and her dad walking toward us.

'I don't see why we should let a bunch of strangers into our camp,' she said bitterly. 'Nobody helped us along the way, did they? All of the people we met on our way here either tried to steal from us, or kill us, so why on earth would we invite them to come eat our food and sleep where we sleep?' Emily looked close to tears now. 'Dad has even seen a vision of the whole camp on fire; people running and screaming and burning... We can't just ignore that!'

I started to feel dizzy at the thought of losing this place to fire, and the possibility of it happening was all too real. The creep was still out there somewhere, still hunting me, and if he found me, he would find my friends. Andy grabbed my elbow to steady me; no one else noticed me sway because they were all staring at Emily.

'What exactly did you see, Roger?' Eric asked Emily's dad.

'Basically just what Emily said,' he replied, 'a lot of destruction and injury. I saw people I didn't recognize swarming through the fence, and the cabin swallowed by flames.'

Roger's words sent me over the edge, and I suddenly found myself back in bed with Andy sitting in a chair by my bedside. I must have passed out.

'Hey again,' said Andy when I turned my head to look at him. 'How are you feeling?'

'Sore,' I replied, and groaned as I tried to sit up.

'Just take it easy, you're not supposed to get up again until tomorrow, it's doctor Joe's orders.' He handed me a pack of saltines. 'Are you hungry?'

'Very,' I replied, ripping open the packet with my teeth and sending the crackers flying everywhere.

Andy laughed and helped me gather them up. 'Cheers,' he said, holding a cracker out. I touched it with one of my own, and we both took a bite.

'What happened after I fainted?' I asked, 'are they making plans to reinforce the fence and rethinking allowing strangers into camp?'

'Well, we pretty much just got you back in here, the doctor checked you over, and asked me to sit with you, and then they all left again.' He nibbled his cracker, looking thoughtful. 'I don't think Eric would ever turn anybody away though, do you?'

I shook my head in agreement, and reached for another cracker.

'We can't just ignore Emily and her dad, though, can we,' I said. 'Their predictions have helped us all in the past, and the one we just heard is pretty huge.'

'Emily's predictions,' muttered Andy quietly, and he made a scoffing sound under his breath.

'Pardon me? Do you have something to say over there?' I asked teasingly.

'Yeah I do!' said Andy, and suddenly he seemed too agitated to stay seated – he stood up and started pacing the room.

'I asked Emily about the prediction she made about you and Josh, because all Josh ever talked about was you, and I know you like him, so it just seemed weird to me that you guys would never get together.' Andy caught sight of the alarm in my face. 'Don't worry, I didn't ask when Josh was around, I didn't want to embarrass you, or give your secret away,' and then Andy muttered under his breath, 'though you'd have to be blind not to notice the way you blush whenever he is around.'

'Andy…' I said warningly.

'Well it's true, Gracie, you have zero poker face.' He paused, looking at my face and waiting for a retort. But of course he was right. Even now I could feel my cheeks turning red at the thought of blushing. Andy looked smug. I sighed.

'Fine, my ambition of being a world champion at poker is ruined. While I try to figure out what I'm going to do with the rest of my life, now that my gambling dreams are over, why don't you tell me the rest of your conversation with Emily?'

Andy smiled. 'Where was I,' he said, obviously enjoying himself. 'Oh yes... So... I told Emily that you had mentioned her prediction, and I said how weird I thought it was, because you and Josh are so perfect for each other and you obviously like each other. I asked if there was maybe some catastrophe that was going to keep you two apart. Well, she got pretty defensive and started rambling about how you guys aren't actually right for each other, and how any person with half a brain could see that, and Gracie, it was the weirdest thing, that as she kept talking and talking, her colors started to change.'

I looked at him, surprised. 'Really? Does that happen?'

'I've never seen it before, but it was really clear. She went from having the usual light, translucent colors with a bit of silver for her gift, to having gross murky Poo People shades woven in with the bright ones. It scared me a little. But as soon as she stopped talking the murky colors disappeared. The same thing happened outside just now, when she was telling Eric we shouldn't let normal people into our camp.'

'Wow,' I breathed, looking at Andy in wonder. 'It sounds like you have a new facet to your gift...'

'Maybe... Or maybe Emily struggles with right and wrong, because she ended up telling me that when she first met you she saw a future with you and Josh as a couple, but she didn't want it to happen, so she lied to you about it.'

I frowned, feeling a weird mix of joy and betrayal.

Andy looked apologetic now. 'I'm sorry Gracie, I almost didn't want to tell you because you've had trouble with trusting people you thought were your friends in the past, but I want you to be happy, and being with Josh will make you happy. Emily was just jealous of the friendship and spark between you and Josh. She doesn't like being a runner-up, but I've seen Josh when he's around you, and I'm telling you, he's crazy about you.'

I could feel a new blush creeping into my cheeks.

'The whole time we were looking for you, Josh's colors were dim and always kind of stormy, and then we found you, and they brightened for a second, until we realized just how sick you were. Since you've been up and feeling better, his colors are almost as bright as yours, with lots of gold and silver. No sparkles though, you're still the only one who sparkles...'

He grinned at me. 'You're also the only one who blushes like that. You're an open book, Gracie.'

'And apparently you're a human lie detector... Too bad the world ended or *you* could have been poker champion of the universe.'

He giggled. 'Anyway, the point is that you and Josh are meant to be together, so you can stop wondering if he's just being so friendly because you're just friends. It's hubba-hubba romance central around here now. I even have my barf bucket ready so I won't make a big mess when you two finally get it together.'

I couldn't help but laugh. Andy, as usual, had managed to cheer me up at a time when things seemed so bleak. I was so lucky to have met him, and once again my thoughts strayed to Olivia and the fun she must have had with him. I wondered what her defense tactics had been with him, when he really got smart-aleckey.

'...*Tickle his ribs*...' said a Voice I recognized as Olivia's.

'Andy, could you please grab my book from on the table?' I said, hoping to draw him close enough, but trying to be casual.

'Sure!' he said, and jumped up to get it for me. As he came back around to the side of the bed, he stopped and stared at me. 'What are you up to?' he said suspiciously. 'Your colors tell me that you are being sneaky about something.'

'Oh right, the human polygraph thing. Well you're not the only one with tricks, kid, Olivia just told me how to keep you in line when you get sassy like this.' I grinned at him gloatingly, and saw surprise cross his features.

'No fair!' he said to the ceiling. 'You're my sister! You're supposed to be on my side!'

'Too bad, so sad,' I said at Olivia's suggestion.

'Wow, she really is here.' Andy smiled, and then stared at me with mischief written all over his face. 'You think you know sass? You ain't seen nothin' yet, chickie!'

And then his face grew more serious. 'Why is Olivia still hanging around, though? Shouldn't she be Beyond by now?'

'That's a good question – I've been wondering lately if anyone ever goes Beyond, or if after I help them, they just move away from me, or go quiet, or maybe they follow their loved ones around so I don't hear them anymore.'

'But then wouldn't your mom be talking to you night and day?' He said tentatively, as though scared of upsetting me.

'That's the only problem with my theory,' I said, smiling at him to show I wasn't upset at the mention of my mom. 'I know she's around somewhere, and that's very comforting. She's just keeping a low profile, I guess.'

'Maybe she's keeping an eye on things somewhere else, and she'll give you a heads-up once she knows what you need to know,' Andy suggested.

'Maybe,' I agreed. Andy's idea brought us back to the reason I was back in bed in the first place.

'What do you think about letting strangers into camp?' he asked me. 'I think I already know the answer, because you were all ready to become best-friends-forever with that girl who tried to take a bite out of Patience...'

'Ha, ha, very funny,' I said with an eyeroll. 'I guess it'll be on you to tell us if they are Poo People or not, so make sure your Poodar is working.'

Andy cracked up and actually snorted with laughter, which got me laughing too. Boys and bodily functions – it never fails.

'What's so funny?' asked a voice at the door, and Josh poked his head into the room.

'Oh, Gracie just coined the best name ever for my ability,' said Andy, still laughing, 'I can spot Poo People a mile away, like I have a radar for them, so she just called it my Poodar! Get it? Poodar!' And he collapsed in a fit of laughter again, holding his sides.

Josh laughed too, but I think mostly at Andy's hilarity.

'Andy was just asking whether I thought it was a good idea to let strangers into camp,' I said loudly, trying to make myself heard over Andy's renewed giggles. My question sobered him up pretty fast.

'Yeah, Josh, what do you think about it?' Andy asked, with a slight hiccup. 'Do you think it's safe to bring in people we don't know? What if they just take over? We don't have any guns, how do we protect ourselves from a big group that might just want to take what we have, and what if they don't care about what happens to us? What if they try to kill us?'

While Andy's questions were all very serious and I could see the worry on his face, I couldn't help but smile to myself. I had missed his chatter and his questions so much, it felt like being reunited with a part of me that I had lost.

'Well,' said Josh, 'we are trying to figure all of that out. The fence is the first step, so at least we can delay anybody from entering until we get an idea of what they're about, and your abilities will definitely come in handy then. Emily is trying to create weapons from materials we have around here, like spears and arrows and clubs, but I'm not really sure if she's actually really considered having to use one on somebody...

'Our trip to get here was pretty uneventful because our group was fairly large, with quite a few adults, and we did a lot of our traveling before things got really out of control. Not many people tried to mess with us, and I'm not sure if everyone here really understands how bad it is out there.' Josh paused, looking out the window.

Once again, the wretched girl who had tried to bite Patience popped into my head. Her deplorable physical and mental state, and the lengths she had taken in her desperation. How could we defend ourselves against a group made up of unstable people like that? And yet, how could we just turn them away? To do so would be as much of a death sentence as firing a gun at them.

'Honestly, though,' continued Josh after a few moments, 'I have no idea how we would defend this place if we were attacked by a bigger group, especially if they had guns or knives. Kevin said he would be on the lookout for weapons during his supply run, but we're all so sensitive to death, and the effect it has on people, it feels weird to think about traveling down a road where we might actually cause it...' He trailed off, his familiar worry lines etched deeply into his forehead.

We sat in silence for quite a while after that, all three of us lost in thought, yet none of us able to come up with any kind of solution.

***

The next few weeks passed uneventfully for our camp, and though the worry of Roger's prediction was never far from my mind, I couldn't help but feel happier than I had in months. I was back in the place I loved, with people I loved, and for the moment we were all safe and sound.

My strength returned slowly, and though I didn't yet have the energy to haul and hammer fence materials, I offered to be on torch duty, making as many torches as I could. It was tiring work, but I was able to sit while doing it, and it felt good to be of use.

Eric kept a campfire burning day and night. There was a watch-duty schedule around the clock, and part of the task was keeping the fire burning. I had given my remaining matches to Eric, but everyone agreed that they should be kept for emergencies, and as long as we kept the campfire alight, we shouldn't need to use them.

Eventually I was added to the watch rotation, though at first I always had a partner to make sure I could handle it. We would walk the perimeter inside the fence and add wood to the fire as needed.

Eric had stockpiled a huge stack of firewood over the years, and part of the daily work for the group was to go beyond the fence and chop more to keep from depleting the stack. A constant campfire ate up a lot of wood, not to mention the wood stoves in the cabin, and with winter approaching, we needed to be sure we could keep ourselves warm. The wood stoves only had to be lit for a few hours a day and it would heat the whole cabin, and after a day of working in the chilly air outside, it was always wonderful to feel the cabin's warmth wash over me.

Most nights we would all gather in the common area around the main stove and make plans and discuss the day. Sometimes it felt like the old days, with Eric leading our lessons, but the holes left by the people we were now missing made it hard to really enjoy. There was just too much grief in the room.

***

Soon, there was a thick layer of snow on the ground, and a thin layer of ice forming on the lake. With the fence completed, we turned our attention to food preservation. We had been eating a lot of fish and we had the equipment to fish all the way through the winter, we just needed the ice on the lake to thicken up so it could bear our weight and we could drill holes for ice fishing. We even had a little shack that we could drag out onto the ice so we could stay a little bit warmer while we fished.

Despite the earlier tension, Emily and Lindsay seemed to have settled into a close friendship, and were rarely separated during the day. I had never confronted Emily about her fake prediction, but our friendship had definitely cooled since our last summer at camp. We were still amicable toward each other, but the breach of trust stood between us like a wall. I spent most of my time with Andy and Josh, who behaved like a pair of brothers, laughing and joking and teasing me whenever possible.

Andy's need for a barf bucket did not arise for several more weeks.

Eric entered the cabin one morning after completing his night of watch, took off his parka and boots, shook the snowflakes out of his hair, and joined all of us at the breakfast table.

'You know what?' he said, after wishing us all good morning and helping himself to some oatmeal, 'by my count, Christmas and New Year's Day should be sometime around now. I'm not sure which days exactly, but I was thinking we could have a little celebration tonight, decorate a tree, and ring the New Year in in style. We can begin a new calendar tomorrow, have a fresh start and leave the hardships of the last year behind us. We've all worked really hard to get to this point, and I think we could all use a little party. What do you guys think?' He paused for a moment, nodded toward the door and then added, 'Plus, there's one more thing we need to celebrate...'

The cabin door opened again, and among a swirl of flurries came a figure heavily cloaked against the cold. Everyone jumped up with cries of welcome except me – I had no idea who was hidden behind the woolen scarf and fur-trimmed hood. Even after he had removed all of his outerwear, and I had a clear view of his face, I still had no idea who I was looking at, so I stood up, about to introduce myself, when he smiled at me and said, 'it's been a while, Grace, it's good to see you.'

I shook his hand and as I looked into his eyes my memory flashed back to a scared little boy sobbing in front of the campfire, terrified that his parents were going to lock him up because of his gifts. There was almost no trace of the boy I had known left in his features. He would be around seventeen or eighteen, but he looked at least thirty-five. He looked like he had suffered many lifetimes of pain.

'Kevin...' I said, and I stepped forward to hug him. 'It really has been a while... ten years? I'm so sorry about everything that happened to you, are you doing okay?'

'Ten years, yeah, sounds about right. It got hard to keep track in there. I'm probably one of the only people on earth who is happy that the power went out.'

As I pulled back from the hug I caught a whiff of stale smoke; the smell instantly filled me with panic, but I did my best to hide it – he had obviously spent a lot of time huddled over campfires to keep warm during his journey, every one of us probably smelled the same after being on watch duty. I really needed to get my panic triggers under control. I did my best to act naturally and breathe normally. He had been out on the supply run for weeks; he didn't need me acting like a weirdo for no reason as soon as he walked through the door.

'I'm glad you're back,' I said, and I was happy to hear that my voice sounded pretty normal, 'Eric said you might try to find more survivors while you were out there – did you have any luck?'

'Yeah I did,' he replied, as he sat down, grabbed a bowl and filled it with oatmeal. 'They're a few days behind me because of the snowfall – I wanted to get back here as soon as I could, to let you guys know I'm okay, and to allow us to get prepared for an extra twenty people...'

'Twenty?' said several people at once.

Eric's voice held surprise and excitement at the thought of so many survivors.

Emily's voice sounded unhappy with a trace of fear, while next to her, her father said nothing, but shook his head almost imperceptibly and continued to stare down at his breakfast.

'We have lots of room, and lots of food,' said Eric, 'and as long as they all pass our screening test, they are more than welcome to live here.'

'Screening test?' asked Kevin, his brow furrowed in confusion, 'what screening test? These people have traveled for weeks, hauling supplies for this camp, with the promise of shelter for their families when they arrive. How can you even think if denying them after that?' He had half-risen to his feet and was looking around the table at each of us, incredulous.

'It's not a difficult test,' said Eric easily, taking a sip of water and winking at Andy over his cup, 'and if you are vouching for them, I'm sure there won't be any problems.

We've had a couple of alarming predictions crop up in the last few weeks, and measures must be taken to protect ourselves. We don't know who we're dealing with, and it's possible that you don't even know their true colors, so until we find out for sure, we need to be careful about it.'

Kevin nodded and said he understood, though there was still a slight coolness to his manner.

I was staring at Andy, wondering what he thought about being solely responsible for vetting such a large group of people, but Andy was watching Kevin curiously.

Once breakfast was finished, I asked Andy to come to my room to help me with a fake task, so I could ask him what he thought of Kevin.

'He's another one whose color pattern I've never seen before,' he told me speculatively. 'It swirls really fast, and it's hard to see specific hues. I didn't notice it before, because I was so worried about you and getting you to safety, but now that I've had a proper look at him, I'm not really sure what to make of it.'

'And you never talked to him about your abilities?' I asked.

'Nope, there just wasn't time, I barely spoke to him at all.'

'And Eric never told him?'

'I guess not…it almost seems like Eric doesn't quite fully trust him… I wonder if Eric knows something we don't know?'

'Maybe, but you'd think if Eric had any misgivings about him, he'd let us know, or he simply wouldn't let Kevin stay… it's weird.'

'I think so, too,' agreed Andy, 'you and I can keep an eye on him. I'll watch his colors, and you can listen out for any Voices that might have warnings to give.'

'Sounds good,' I said, 'he's definitely different from the little boy I remember, but maybe that's what happens to you when your parents lock you up for ten years. He never stood a chance.'

'And maybe that's why Eric is giving him the benefit of the doubt, even though he's a little strange these days.'

'Or maybe we're reading a whole lot of something from a whole lot of nothing.'

Andy laughed. 'Yeah, maybe we're the ones being weird!'

'Well it wouldn't be the first time, would it?' I said, poking him in the ribs to make him laugh some more.

Josh poked his head in the room. 'Hey, you two! We're on balloon duty for tonight!' He threw us each a package of balloons and we followed him back out into the common area. Kevin was already sitting on a couch, looking through a small box of party decorations.

'Wow!' I said, picking up a roll of blue paper streamers, 'Eric meant it when he said we should ring in the New Year in style! I had no idea we had such a great supply of decorations!'

'Eric said they were Audrey's,' Josh responded, 'he said the New Year's party was her idea; she wanted to celebrate the fresh start of being safe in our new home. I think it's his way of honoring her.'

We were all quiet for a few minutes, as we looked through the box of decorations that Audrey had so carefully collected. There were brightly colored streamers, sparklers, and more bags of balloons.

Josh held up a package of balloons. 'We should save some of these for the summer! We could have a big water-balloon fight!'

'Yeah!' piped up Andy, 'we could break up into teams and see who can stay the driest!'

I pictured the two of them working out their strategies to soak the rest of us. I smiled at the image; it was such a normal, happy thing to plan for.

'One of the kids I was locked up with filled balloons with alcohol to light his opponents on fire,' said Kevin quietly, 'kind of like a Molotov cocktail for kids...' He looked up at us when we didn't respond. I realized that my mouth was hanging open, and I snapped it closed. 'It didn't work,' he said hastily, 'no one got hurt. But that was the last straw that made his parents finally lock him up and throw away the key.'

'Yiiiiiikes...' whispered Andy finally.

'Sorry,' said Kevin, looking down at his hands, 'I should keep that sort of thing to myself.' I looked at his hands too, and noticed that they were scarred and rough-looking. What on earth had happened to the little boy I had cared so much about? Why hadn't his parents tried harder to protect him? Why hadn't I?

We blew up balloons in silence for a while, and then Kevin, clearly feeling awkward, offered to go outside to get the ladder so we could start hanging the streamers.

'Holy guacamole...' said Andy as soon as the door had closed behind Kevin. 'No wonder he seems a little odd – it would mess anybody up to be stuck with a bunch of actual psychopaths for ten years. No wonder his colors are so confusing...'

Josh let out a quiet whistle. 'I wonder what other horror stories he had to listen to when he was in there. And then knowing that he was never really safe from the people he was locked up with... And knowing that it was his parents' choice to have him live like that...'

I felt an enormous amount of guilt for not trying harder to rescue him when he was first committed. And again, I felt a huge wave of gratitude for the love and support that my mom had always given me.

'Poor Kevin,' was all I could add to the conversation, and once again, I resolved to try to help him as much as possible. It gave me a sense of déjà vu, but this time would be different; ten years ago none of us had any say in what happened to him. Now, we could all work together to protect him, and heal him, and no one had the power to hide him away and punish him.

Kevin came back in with the ladder, and I offered to help him string up the streamers. He seemed relieved that we weren't shying away from him after hearing such a grim story. Soon Andy and Josh had Kevin joking and laughing, and I could see hints of the happy person he could have become.

Today would be a day for laughter and fun, but maybe tomorrow we could talk to Eric about resuming our fireside classes. I felt sure it could benefit all of us, but no one more so than Kevin.

***

That night the cabin looked spectacular. We lit a few oil lamps and a few candles, and with the decorations we had hung up, you couldn't even tell that we were having a party without power. Andy had decorated a tree that Eric had brought in from outside, and we even sang a few Christmas carols while we prepared our party snacks.

The food was still limited, but we each had a plate of crackers topped with some of the weirder items from the pantry.

'Ugh,' said Andy, putting his cracker topped with caviar onto my plate. 'Even when I was at my hungriest I don't think I would have eaten this!'

I laughed and gave him a cracker topped with canned ham in exchange. 'As long as it isn't pine bark, I'm never going to be picky again!'

Eric had also brought out a small bottle of champagne. It was so tiny there was really only enough to have a sip each, but it added to the feeling of celebration when he popped the cork and it bounced off the ceiling. He poured a splash into each of the tiny paper cups he had lined up on the table, and handed them out.

'Since we have no way to know when it is actually midnight,' he said, finally taking a cup for himself, 'why don't we start a countdown right now and make a toast to the New Year on our terms!'

Everyone agreed, so Eric continued, holding up his tiny paper cup. 'Merry Christmas, Happy New Year, and here's to a fresh start!'

Each of us held up our tiny cup and shouted 'Cheers!' Suddenly everyone was hugging and singing, and we all lit our sparklers from the candle flames.

'Wow! Check that out!' shouted Andy over the noise. He was looking up at the night sky through the big windows. All I could really see was the reflection of the light inside, so I opened the cabin door to get a better look. Everyone followed me, so I took a few steps outside into the chilly night, and looked up.

The whole sky was alight with dancing colors: turquoise, pink, yellow and white all swirling amongst the millions of stars, bordered by the perfect black silhouettes of the surrounding trees.

There were sighs of appreciation and wonder, and I felt overwhelmed by the incredible beauty of the scene. It made me miss my mom terribly. She would have loved the chance to see this. But maybe she was part of it, swirling among the stars in a beautiful night rainbow...

I felt someone take my hand and assumed it was Andy. He had such a knack for knowing when I needed a little emotional support. He based it on my changing colors, I supposed. I squeezed his hand and turned to smile at him, to let him know I was okay, and received a surprise when I saw that the concerned face looking back at me was not Andy's, but Josh's. The butterflies started fluttering away again, and I felt so silly for not immediately noticing the size of the hand that now held mine.

The people behind us had started drifting back inside, shivering and complaining about the cold.

'Want to take a walk?' Josh murmured to me. I wasn't sure if it was the cold or Josh standing so close beside me that was making me tremble, but I nodded and we set out onto the path.

We had only taken a few steps when Josh muttered for me to wait a minute, and he went back into the cabin. I stood there in the cold, staring at the sparkler in my hand as the last few seconds of silvery sparks showered down over my skin. The sparkler fizzled and died but when I looked back up at the aurora, I could still see a hint of its light shining in front of the swirling colors.

Josh returned a moment later with my coat and mittens and a fleecy blanket. I put them on and he took my hand again, both of us automatically heading toward the campfire.

When we arrived at the fire pit, Josh threw a couple of logs into the flames, and a shower of golden sparks swirled around us and into the sky. I sat down on one of the long logs that we used as seats around the fire, and arranged the blanket over my legs.

It was so peaceful sitting there in the quiet darkness, with the heat of the fire warming my cold nose, and it felt completely natural when Josh came to sit beside me and put his arm around me. I rested my head on his shoulder and he laid his cheek on the top of my head. We sat there for several minutes before he finally spoke, his voice a whisper, his breath misty in the freezing air.

'Remember the dandelion?' he asked, and I could feel heat creeping into my cheeks that had nothing to do with the fire.

'Yes,' I responded, glad that he couldn't see my blush in the dark. 'And I thought Michael would keep it a secret...'

'He did... mostly,' said Josh. 'When I told him last summer about a prediction that Emily had made about you and me, he said that it didn't sound right, based on the dandelion. That's all he said.'

'Emily told you her prediction?' I asked, feeling hurt all over again at the lengths she had taken to keep us apart.

'Yeah,' said Josh, 'she told me a few years ago when I told her I was going to ask you out.' There was a slight growl to his voice now, and I could feel his annoyance as he lifted his cheek off of my head. 'I wish I had never listened to her...'

I looked up at his profile, surprised by the intensity in his voice.

'When we were traveling here and trying to find you, she had me half-convinced that I would never see you again. It almost drove me insane. All those years I had wasted, never telling you how I felt from the moment I first met you. The thought of never seeing you again... Of you never knowing that I... I...'

Josh looked down at me, tears and firelight shining in his eyes, unable to continue.

I reached up and touched his cheek. 'Me, too...' I whispered.

He looked into my eyes and slowly lowered his face to mine. His lips were unbelievably soft and warm and suddenly I felt like I might be floating among the stars, too.

***

On our way back to the cabin a little while later, I felt like I was walking on air, and the only thing keeping me tethered to earth was Josh's hand holding mine.

As we entered the cabin I was relieved to see that Andy seemed to have gone to bed already; I didn't need a lot of vomit jokes tarnishing my perfect evening.

Josh walked me to the door of my room, kissed me once more, and whispered good night.

I knew I would never be able to fall asleep without help, so after I had changed into my pajamas and climbed into bed, I lit a candle on my bedside table so I could read for a while.

As usual, the moment my eyes focused on the text of my book, I started to feel sleepy. Just before I drifted off, I blew out the candle and hugged the book to my chest.

The next thing I knew, sunlight was pouring in through the window and my stomach was growling noisily. I sat up, feeling happy and excited about the day ahead. Josh and I were planning to do some ice fishing in hopes of supplying a feast for dinner later.

As I climbed out of bed I knocked my book to the floor. It landed open and a bunch of pages fell out. I stooped to gather them up, feeling a rush of sadness that I had ruined the gift that Josh had given me. As I straightened up with the loose pages in my hand, I realized that they were punctured and had handwriting all over them. *My* handwriting. The pages I had torn out of my old book and hung from the trees as a way to leave messages for Andy...

My blood turned cold as I stared at the pages, trying to figure out how they had ended up here. I looked around the room. It was possible someone had come in through the window, or even that they had just walked straight in through the cabin door when we were all busy.

The photo of my family stood where it always did, but there was something else there, too. Another photograph. One that I recognized easily because it had been part of the display my mom had arranged on our living room wall. It was a picture of me that my mom had taken a few years ago, but something had been done to my face in the photo.

I walked over to the little table where the two photos were propped up, and saw that one of the little plastic board game pieces, the letter 'X,' had been glued over my face.

My heart racing, I picked up the picture and turned it over. There, in messy black handwriting was a message that almost made me faint:

'Time to burn like mommy.'

Fighting the urge to throw up, I ran across my room and threw the door open, planning to show Eric or Joe or anybody what I had found.

The main room of the cabin was empty. Everyone must still be sleeping off last night's party.

Frantic, I ran over to the windows to see if maybe Eric was outside working. It had clouded over and looked like it could snow any minute. I couldn't see anyone out there.

Just then, Kevin came out of his room, yawning and looking bleary-eyed.

'Morning, Grace,' he said, and shuffled over to the kitchen.

I was just about to go and show him the pages and the photo, when suddenly the Voices in my head started screaming and crying all at once.

I sank to my knees, clutching my head. I must have yelled out, because suddenly doors were flying open and the sleepy occupants of the rooms were rushing out to see what was going on.

Andy reached me first. 'Gracie? Gracie, what is it?' He grabbed my arms, trying to pull my hands away from my head. 'What are you hearing?' He then noticed the stack of papers I had dropped on the floor. He picked them up. He read the back of the photo. 'What the – Gracie, where did these come from? Eric, look at this...' He handed the stack to Eric, who looked at the pages briefly and then leapt into action, ordering everyone to get dressed and get ready to search the area for the intruder.

Andy tried to pull me to my feet, but he was too small to manage it. Joe and Roger helped me up, and sat me down on one of the couches. After making sure I was physically fine, they hurried away to get dressed so they could help search the woods.

Andy knelt down in front of me, and Josh sat beside me, both trying to figure out how and when the pages and photo could have been planted. The only person who hadn't moved a muscle was Emily. She stood frozen, staring into space.

'It's the creep, it's got to be,' said Andy, 'who else would have taken the time to collect all of the pages that you left for me, Gracie? And the letter piece on your picture, he would have stolen it when he left us that creepy message while we were sleeping... And the photo itself... You were right... He must really have been following you since he burned your house down.'

I could barely follow what Andy was saying; the Voices were still screaming, and getting louder by the second.

I looked up at Emily, who was still staring at a vague spot on the wall. 'What are you seeing?' I said, realizing that I was probably shouting to be heard over the din in my head. 'What is it? What is coming?'

Emily blinked and slowly turned her head toward us. Her eyes found mine and I could see the terror she was feeling as she tried to regain control.

I stood up, still clutching my head, and walked over to take her hand. 'Em, please, tell us what you saw.' She seemed unable to do more than just stare at me.

I squeezed her hand. Suddenly, images started racing through my head. It was chaos. People running through burning trees, screaming, with flames erupting left and right. Our fence being toppled under the sheer weight of the advancing crowd. The images I was seeing did not match up with the Voices I was hearing – though the Voices were still connected to the people in the images somehow. The dead seemed to be screaming for the living.

The images from Emily's mind stopped as suddenly as they had started, and as we stared at each other, an understanding passed between us. 'How much time?' I whispered.

She looked at me desperately as she responded, 'Now.'

Chapter Fourteen

Before Emily had even finished speaking, Josh and Andy jumped up, both looking out the windows. 'What is that?' Andy yelled, running toward the window to get a better view.

The Voices went silent for a moment, and I was able to hear distant rhythmic crashes.

'They're trying to knock the fence over, they'll make it through in a minute... We need to...'

But what? What could we possibly do to defend our camp and ourselves against such a big, angry group?'

Josh threw us each a coat and told us to get our boots on. 'We're sitting ducks in here, we need to get outside and see what we can do to help.'

'I told them we needed weapons!' Emily had found her voice again. 'I've got a few spears and sticks out by the shed, but not enough for everyone. How many times did I say we need to be able to protect ourselves? And now, what? We're all going to die because no one would listen to me!

'Is that what you saw?' said Andy, panicked. 'We're all going to die?'

'No that's not what she saw,' I told him, glaring at Emily as I took Andy's hand. 'But Josh is right, we need to get outside and find the others so we can make a plan.'

We left the cabin and ran out into the trees. We passed the pile of torches I had made, but after seeing the prediction in Emily's mind I was not about to arm my friends with fire.

Josh shouted that he could hear Eric in the distance, and led us in that direction. Soon we met up with most of our group. I gave them a brief summary of what Emily had seen, and Eric started to suggest what we could use as weapons, besides what Emily had made.

Before he had made it any further than telling us about the axes in the tool shed, however, there was an almighty crash. The fence had given way.

The silence that followed was ominous and heavy. Each of us was holding our breath.

Suddenly the shrill chime of a bike bell ripped through the silence.

My heart started pounding and a black fog started to cloud my vision. He was here. The creep had found me. I could only gasp while I tried to fight back my panic.

I was vaguely aware of my friends pulling me back toward the cabin. They didn't understand. Nowhere was safe. The creep had followed me across half of the country. Hiding in the cabin wasn't going to stop him. He would burn it to the ground, with all of us inside it.

I saw a purple streak fly past my head, and suddenly a ball of fire erupted on the ground next to me.

'Hide! Hide! Hide!' yelled Eric, and I was pulled behind a tree. I realized that the person holding my hand was Andy, and seeing the fear in his eyes snapped me back to myself. 'Are you okay?' I asked him, searching his face for signs of physical pain.

'I'm okay,' he replied, and he threw his arms around me in his relief. 'I thought you had finally cracked. I thought he had finally broken you.'

I fought back the lump in my throat and hugged him tightly. 'Takes more than a jerk with a dumb bike bell to break me.' I pulled back and held his face in my hands. 'We've got this.'

He gave me a small smile, nodded, and took my hand again.

This time a streak of green shot through the trees and exploded with a burst of flame. *Balloons. Molotov cocktails for kids...*

The truth hit Andy and me at the same second. *Kevin.* We jumped up and ran for it, coming to a stop behind the tool shed. Another balloon exploded beside us, dousing the shed with whatever flammable liquid he had used in the balloons.

'How could it be Kevin?' I panted, peering around the side of the shed to see if I could spot him. Another fireball hit the shed. We ran into the trees again, and out of the corner of my eye I could see several people moving through the woods toward the cabin. I changed direction, pulling Andy along behind me. We had survived too much, and suffered too much, to allow our new home to be taken from us.

We reached the cabin before the intruders, and I stood in the doorway, without a weapon or any cover.

'Get out of the way, Grace,' came a deep gravelly voice through the trees. It shot terror thought my veins. It was the same voice I had heard in my house just before it burned, and later, giving orders as I crouched hidden on top of a school bus. Maybe Kevin wasn't behind everything after all?

'We have guns; we are taking this cabin and everything it holds.' The man stepped out from behind a tree. He had dark hair and stubble and was wrapped in a heavy parka. He had a couple of rifles slung casually over his shoulder and a handgun held loosely at his side. He seemed completely relaxed, almost smug. 'There's no point in trying to stop us, I think you know that.'

Several more people appeared from behind the surrounding trees. Each of them had a gun trained on me and Andy. I stepped in front of him, trying to shield him with my body. I couldn't see any of my other friends, and had no idea where they were and whether they were hurt or not. Snow had started falling in big fluffy flakes, further obscuring a possible view of my friends.

'Get out of the way, and maybe we'll let you live,' growled the man.

One of the Voices in my head rose above the rest, and a misty figure appeared next to the man.

'Gary,' I said quietly to the man, trying to stop my voice from shaking, 'your grandmother, Rose, would like you to know that she is not impressed by what you are up to. She says it is not how she raised you.'

Gary froze, staring at me with shock all over his face. 'Shut up,' he snarled, and then he turned and addressed the trees behind him. 'What did you tell her about me? How does she know my grandmother's name?'

'Nobody told me a thing about you, Gary, except for your grandma,' I said. 'She is standing beside you, as she always did in life. She says she is very touched that you have carried her necklace with you all this time, and she is sorry that she had to leave you when you needed her most.'

Gary raised his gun and pointed it at my head. 'Stop it.'

Another figure appeared next to a woman who stood on Gary's left. The woman looked haggard and filthy, and started when I addressed her. 'Lisa,' I said to her, at the figure's urging, 'Amanda says you need to cut this out, and try to remember who you were when you were together. She says she misses her twin, and doesn't recognize the person you have become.' Lisa lowered her gun slightly, and looked at me with shock and uncertainty.

'If Amanda is really here,' challenged Lisa, 'then you'll be able to tell me-'

'About the matching seahorse tattoos each of you had on your left foot? And how you got a second one to keep the first one company after your sister passed away?'

Lisa dropped her gun into the snow. 'I'm sorry,' she whispered, and held her hands out to me. 'I'm so sorry.'

'We are willing to take in new people,' I said to her, 'you are welcome here, if you will agree to live peacefully with us. There is plenty of food and space for everyone.'

Gary still had his gun aimed at us, and there was still so much anger and suspicion in his face.

'Gary,' I said gently, scared of aggravating him farther, 'your friend Tommy is here, too...'

Shock registered on Gary's face, and it caused him to lower his gun. 'Tommy...' he whispered. 'I haven't spoken to anyone about Tommy in decades... How do you know...'

'Gary, I'm so sorry about Tommy. He wants you to know that it wasn't your fault, and he never blamed you for a single minute, and he wants you to stop blaming yourself. The water was too deep, and you were both too small... He is happy you survived, and he only wants you to be happy, too.'

Gary's face crumpled and he gazed at me with sadness in his eyes. But there was something else there too... Something that was directed at me, rather than inward... Regret?'

I seized the opportunity to address the whole group of intruders, now that I could see that Gary wasn't going to be an issue anymore.

'Each and every one of you, right now, has at least one person standing beside you, wanting to communicate with you,' I shouted, to make sure I was heard by the people at the back of the group. 'If you will let me, I will sit down with each of you and give you their messages.'

'Gracie...' whispered Andy from behind me,' 'I can see their colors changing... Their most fundamental colors... are shifting... You are changing them!'

The shrill note of a bike bell suddenly split the silence again. I looked around, frantic, for the source. I heard Andy gasp behind me.

Kevin had sauntered out from behind a large pine, and was cradling a red balloon in his hands. There was an unlit sparkler attached to it like a fuse. In his other hand he held a bike bell.

'Recognize this?' he taunted me, his eyes alight with insane pleasure, ringing the bell again. 'You should. It's from your very own bike, Grace. It's been fun following you across the country. I couldn't believe my luck when I saw the pictures of you at your house. And then to see you running away as it burned... Oh, that was a good day. I'd been hoping to see you again for over ten years, and there you were, alive, and free as a bird.'

I just stared at Kevin, whose face was completely unrecognizable, and so full of hate.

'I should have been free, too,' Kevin continued, putting the bike bell into his coat pocket and pulling out a lighter. 'All of you here, at this camp, you told me you would help me. You told me that I belonged with you and that we could do great things together. Well, that didn't work out so great, did it? Not for me, at least. It was all lies. And now you're lying to all of these people, these good people, who are just trying to survive. You're playing with their vulnerabilities, just like you played with mine. You left me to rot in the dark alone. '

He turned and addressed the group behind him, pointing a long scarred finger at me.

'She's saying she can communicate with dead people, and you're all just going to allow that? She's a freak! All of the people living here are freaks! Ever wonder why they have so much food and how they all managed to survive so easily? It's because they can see the future! They knew this was going to happen! This apocalypse, or Darkness, or whatever you want to call it. They saw it coming! They saw that half of the world was about to die and decided to save themselves rather than try to help anybody else!'

There was some muttering among the people behind him, but Kevin had turned his attention back to me.

'Just like you couldn't be bothered to try to help me once you found out that I had been locked up. Oh, I got your letters, your sad letters full of wishes that there was something you could do. But you never even tried.'

He held up his balloon. 'It took me a long time to perfect these... I just couldn't get the fuse right. Matches didn't work, lighters didn't work, but sparklers... Perfection.' He paused for a minute before continuing.

'My parents didn't understand me like all of you pretended to; they just thought I was some kind of freak who had blackouts and liked to play with fire. They caught me experimenting with the neighbor kids,' he held up his balloon like he was performing a soliloquy to it, 'and they decided that I needed to be removed from society.' He laughed a harsh and hollow laugh, still admiring his balloon creation. 'Well, as soon as I got out of that loony bin, I tracked them down, and removed *them* from society. It was easy after all of those years of picturing it. They really shouldn't have given me so much time to think...'

I didn't know what to do. Kevin was obviously insane, and felt that he had a score to settle. I could feel Andy shivering behind me, clutching at the back of my parka. The snow had started to fall more heavily now, and it was impossible to see all of the people in front of us, let alone ascertain where my friends were hiding.

Movement caught my eye. Gary was edging carefully toward Kevin, raising his gun slowly as he went.

All I could do was try to distract Kevin so he wouldn't see Gary coming. I raised my voice and spoke to the group first.

'My friend can see the future, it's true, but she sees things with less than a minute's warning, and once the power went out, it was a lot harder for her to communicate what she had seen. And her dad sees events that are coming, but his visions are way too vague to ever be able to warn anyone. Believe me, if any of this could have been prevented, it would have been. All of us have suffered losses – I lost my mother. She just happened to be in a café that a plane crashed into. I was only a few blocks away. If I could have prevented that, don't you think she would be standing here with me now?' I gestured to Andy. 'His parents are stuck overseas, and his big sister was killed when she lost control of her car, and he was in the car with her. If there had been some way for him to save her, he would have. One of my oldest friends lost his beautiful wife. The list goes on and on. And we already have people here who were not part of our little group of "freaks." You are all welcome here.'

Gary had stopped advancing while listening to my words, and I could see the remorse on his face.

I turned to Kevin, and saw Gary nod at me from behind Kevin's back.

'I think your parents understood you better than anyone, Kevin. You pulled the wool over our eyes, but they saw the real you. The potential damage you could cause. The damage you *have* caused. Murdering your own parents. Looting and burning everything in sight. Collecting young girls for purposes I don't even want to think about. Murdering innocent men for trying to protect their daughters. And whipping up this mob to help you do it. There isn't a word strong enough to describe how despicable you are. And, honestly, how pathetic you are. I don't doubt that you had fun terrorizing us across half the country. But I'm over it. Your dumb little bike bell and your creepy messages in the woods… I just feel sorry for you now.'

Kevin glared at me and looked like he could easily kill me. 'Your time is up, Grace…' He lit the sparkler. 'Say "Hi" to your mother for me…'

'Drop the balloon,' growled Gary suddenly in his deep gravelly voice. He and most of the group now had their sights securely trained on Kevin. 'Drop it, or I'll-'

'What?' Kevin smirked, his voice almost bored, 'open *fire*?'

And he lobbed the balloon at Gary.

The fireball exploded at Gary's feet, dousing his lower body in flames. His screams tore through the air and seemed to bounce back at us through the trees. The rest of the group seemed frozen, too horrified by what they were seeing to act. Gary dropped to the ground and started trying to suffocate the fire under the snow. I started to advance toward him, thinking only of helping him, when Kevin's voice rang out even louder than Gary's panicked shrieks.

'STOP!' he screamed, and I froze in my tracks, turning my head to look at him with disgust. He had a gun pointed at Andy. 'You're all so used to loss, right? So it probably won't bother you if I take out one more of your freakish little group?'

I suppressed a whimper, not wanting him to see that he had succeeded in causing me more pain. Andy's eyes were huge in his chalk-white face. But there was a defiant set to his jaw too. 'Go ahead,' he said, 'I wouldn't mind seeing my sister again, anyway. Death doesn't scare me. You don't scare me. I'm a little bored, to be honest.' He hopped down the steps, and walked over to Gary to help him smother his legs in snow.

Kevin watched him go, disbelief on his face. Only the surprise of Andy's boldness kept him from shooting, but I could feel his anger radiating out of him, and knew we had only seconds before he finally lost it.

Suddenly a shot rang out, and I screamed and reached out for Andy, sure that it was Kevin who had fired. But it was Kevin who crumpled into the snow, writhing and bleeding and screeching in pain.

I looked around, trying to figure out who had shot him, but there were so many people with their weapons aimed at him that it was impossible to know. I ran over to check on Andy, but he was completely fine. Gary's legs were no longer on fire, but I could see that the damage was severe.

'We have a doctor here, Gary, he saved me when I was half-dead, and he'll be able to help you too.' He nodded his thanks, unable to speak through his panting.

The group in the woods had started to advance, and I asked some of them to stay with Gary while Andy and I went to look for Joe. They gathered around Gary, and Lisa took his hand to try to calm him.

Andy got up and grabbed my hand, and we looked around the trees, still unsure of where our friends had gone. The snow was falling thicker than ever, and a freezing wind had picked up too – a blizzard was upon us and we would need to get under cover as soon as possible.

The snow had stopped the fire bombs' flames from spreading through the forest, though there was quite a bit of damage to the tool shed and the trees that had taken direct hits.

Andy and I started calling out our friends' names, and soon heard them calling back. It turned out that they had climbed onto the roof of the cabin, and we found some of them hidden behind it; they had witnessed the whole exchange.

Being so close to the scene, I wondered why they hadn't come to back us up, especially when the danger had escalated so quickly. Granted, they didn't have any weapons to threaten anyone with, but half of them were adults, and maybe could have intervened a little.

Maybe they could see the disquiet I was feeling written on my face, because Eric was quick to explain.

'We were going to come and stand beside you, Grace, but Emily had a vision that our interference would only exacerbate the situation. She said Gary and Kevin would open fire on all of us, and it became clear very quickly that you had it under control.'

I looked at Emily, who had just climbed down from the roof. She would not meet my eyes.

'I'm so proud of the way you handled yourself, Grace,' Eric continued, putting a hand on my shoulder. 'You saved all of us. You saved all of them. That took a massive amount of bravery and selflessness. I know your mom is very proud of you, too...'

Eric's words meant a lot, but I could not tear my eyes away from Emily. She was still looking anywhere but at me. After everything we had been through, I didn't want to think that she had actually made up another prediction to benefit herself, leaving me and Andy completely vulnerable to the whims of a psychopath.

I felt Andy tug on my hand and I looked down at him, hoping he would be able to shed some light on what really happened.

He looked pointedly at Emily, and then shook his head. I mouthed the word 'poo' and he nodded. So she had thrown us into the fire to save her own skin.

I continued to look at her, feeling as though I was seeing her true colors for the first time. I had called her my best friend for years... I had trusted her with my heart and my secrets... The lie about Josh I could understand, I supposed, if she had been jealous enough. But this? Potentially allowing me and Andy to be murdered... Which would also have resulted in everyone else's murder anyway, if I hadn't convinced Gary, I knew that for sure. He would have burned down the cabin with all of my friends trapped on the roof without blinking an eye. The hold Kevin had had over him was too great: Gary had been like a puppet, with Kevin manipulating the strings.

Emily's betrayal cut even deeper because she had basically sacrificed Andy, too. And then used her gift as an excuse, not only to let it happen, but to actively prevent anyone else from trying to help. She looked like a different person to me now... Cowardly, selfish and cruel.

But my issues with Emily would have to wait. I realized suddenly that no more people were climbing down from the roof. And Josh was nowhere to be seen.

'Where did Josh go?' I demanded, panicked, looking around to see who else was missing.

'Here, I'm right here,' said Josh's voice, as he and his parents ran up behind me, followed by Joe. 'We were with you guys at first,' Josh continued, 'but we had to dodge a couple of fireballs and then we almost ran into a group of the strangers and had to take off in the opposite direction. We heard the gunshot and came as fast as we could. What happened?'

I flung my arms around Josh and felt relief flood my body. He was alive, he was safe. Andy filled the others in on what had happened in front of the cabin, and the horror on Josh's face was almost too much to look at.

I turned away from Josh and addressed Joe. 'There's a guy out front who is badly burned and really needs your help,' I told him. 'Kevin is out there too; he's been shot, but I'm not sure where or how bad it is. He should have people standing guard over him, but just watch out for him, he is still very dangerous.'

Joe nodded and hurried into the cabin's back door to grab his medical supplies.

Shouts from the front if the cabin rang out through the snowy air, but the wind was whipping so fiercely that the sound was distorted and somehow muffled.

I grabbed Andy's hand again and all of us ran around the side of the cabin, to see what was going on.

The first thing I saw was a large pool of blood, shockingly crimson against the fresh white snow. A trail of blood drops led away from the pool toward the lake, and I could barely make out footprints left by whoever had stumbled along, bleeding.

There was a large group of people still gathered around Gary, and several who were huddled together on the porch of the cabin, trying to keep warm in the blizzard, but clearly feeling unsure of whether they had the right to enter the cabin.

One of the men from the new group ran up to us, a shotgun slung over his shoulder. 'He's gone!' he yelled, struggling to be heard over the roar of the wind, 'I checked him over and thought he was dead, but when I turned around a few minutes later, he was gone!' He ran off, following the trail of ruby droplets into the trees.

Kevin, shot and bleeding profusely, had managed to escape. I found that I felt more annoyed than scared. Sure, Kevin would obviously love to kill me, and that made me feel a little vulnerable, but his elusiveness and his persistence just made me feel like sighing and rolling my eyes. His creepy stalker act had gotten old.

Eric rallied a bunch of the other newcomers, and we all headed off into the trees, spread slightly apart so we could cover more ground. Andy, Josh and I stuck together, trudging through the knee-deep snow, keeping our eyes peeled for stray footprints or random drops of blood. The bitter wind whipped snowflakes at our faces and felt like a million white-hot needles piercing our cold skin.

When we finally reached the shoreline of the frozen lake, we could see a clear path of red droplets stretching out into the middle, and then nothing beyond that. The man who had followed Kevin first was walking out on the ice, taking slow cautious steps along the trail of blood. He turned back and saw all of us watching him. He waved for us to stay where we were, and started to make his way slowly back to us.

'He fell through,' he told us as soon as he was close enough. 'There's a big hole where the blood trail ends. He must have fallen through a patch of thin ice and then couldn't find his way back out again. He's gone.'

I didn't know what to feel. Sadness for the little boy I had once known. Horror at such an awful way to die, laced with a bit of satisfaction, because he had caused so much worse suffering for so many others. Relief that he was gone, and wouldn't ever hurt anyone else. And maybe a little dread, as I waited to see if his Voice would join the chorus in my head. It would be his final, creepy victory to be able to haunt my mind from beyond his watery grave.

Eric's voice interrupted my thoughts, and I was glad to have an excuse not to dwell on Kevin anymore.

'Come on,' he said loudly, 'we should get everyone inside, and get warmed up.' He turned and started to lead the group back through the trees.

I followed him, feeling the urge to look back at the middle of the lake, but ignoring it. The last thing I wanted to see was an apparition of Kevin out on the ice, staring at me with white glaring eyes...

We reached the cabin quickly and as soon as everyone was inside, Eric stoked the fire in the wood stoves and started making tea and hot chocolate.

'I don't really know what we would have done with Kevin, if we had caught up with him,' he was saying to Josh's parents as they set out mugs for everyone. 'It's not like we could lock him up or something, and I'm guessing no one here would have wanted to become an executioner – maybe it's best that it happened this way; his death was no one's fault but his own.'

Gary was being tended to by Joe in one of the back bedrooms, and Emily seemed to have disappeared, but the rest of the group was cheerful and chatty and grateful to be out of the blizzard.

'I think she's afraid to face you,' said Andy in a whisper, when he saw me looking around for Emily. 'At least she should be, after everything she did to you.'

I shrugged, not really feeling any particular way about Emily anymore. 'She's the one who has to live with her decisions,' I said to Andy, 'her actions can't affect me unless I allow them to. I'm done being bullied. And I'm finished with letting others dictate the way I feel about myself. It's my life, I'm going to live it on my terms. No one else's... So there.'

He smiled up at me, and his eyes widened in surprise. 'Your colors, Gracie... Like light shining through a thousand prisms...'

He gazed at me in wonder, until I had to tickle his ribs to get him to stop. 'Cut it out,' I said, feeling myself blush, 'go get some marshmallows or something.'

He giggled and then stood up and walked away, leaving me and Josh alone together. Josh just squeezed my hand and winked, but I could see the admiration in his eyes. I felt my heart swell with love and relief.

I looked around the room and felt a pride and peace that I had never felt before. All of these people... We would now survive together. We would create new friendships and I would connect them with their lost loved ones... My gift, which had felt like such a burden for so long, had saved all of us.

Loved ones had reached past the obscurity of death to help the living. Death had not destroyed the bonds of love. Love had survived. Love would always survive. Love is stronger than hate, and it is stronger than grief. Grief is powerful, cruel, and never truly goes away, but, as time passes, it changes, diminishes, and finds its space in your heart. It will no longer consume you. The thing that is steadfast, everlasting, and larger than life and death, is love.

A misty sparkle in the far corner of the room caught my eye. She had finally appeared to me. My mother, looking as beautiful as ever. I soaked up the sight of her, worried that she would disappear again. But then I realized that she had always been with me, and would always be with me whenever I needed her, just as she had been in life. Whenever I felt down, or lonely, or afraid, I would just have to remember my mother, her laugh, her love, and I would be okay.

She would forever be my light in the dark.